ROMANI REDD: STRIPPED

www.mascotbooks.com

Romani Redd: Stripped

©2022 Cindy Summer. All Rights Reserved. No part of this publication may be reproduced, stored in a retrieval system or transmitted in any form by any means electronic, mechanical, or photocopying, recording or otherwise without the permission of the author.

For more information, please contact:
Mascot Books, an imprint of Amplify Publishing Group
620 Herndon Parkway, Suite 320
Herndon, VA 20170
info@mascotbooks.com

Cover illustration by Stephanie Fliss Dumas

Library of Congress Control Number: 2022900963

CPSIA Code: PRV0622A

ISBN-13: 978-1-63755-282-7

Printed in the United States

To my dad, the most supportive, generous, and loving father a girl could have.

ROMANI REDD:

STRIPPED

CINDY SUMMER

 MASCOT® BOOKS

PREFACE

I walked across the warm granite floor, scattering pieces of clothing as I peeled them off my body, one by one. *The floor must be heated,* I thought. *Why does that not surprise me?* An onyx-silver swirled pattern covered the lavish floors and shower. It was so masculine that I hoped I was bordering on paranoid—just the energy of the room, right? I supposed it was my steward's taste in décor. I opened up the glass swivel door with my good hand, releasing an echo in the spacious bathroom. Once I pulled the lever, copious amounts of hot water poured out of the waterfall faucet onto my head, soaking my long auburn hair, streaming down my back. Never was a shower so comforting. My eyes were closed as the water ran down my face, steam curling into my lungs, with my hand pressed against the hard granite wall for support. It was the first private moment I'd had alone in weeks.

I expected to savor the momentary solitude, but instead, I found hot tears welling up in my eyes. I hadn't allowed myself time to grieve since that pivotal evening when lives changed forever—all because of me. Regret flooded my heart and left me gasping for an opportunity to reverse what I had done. But now, there was no going back.

Then—I smelled something—something familiar. No—it couldn't be. I waited for the odor to fill my nostrils again; I had to be sure. And then—there it was again—cigar smoke. At that moment of recognition, the hair on the back of my neck stood up and chills ran down my spine. The voice said, "It wasn't your fault." My head swiveled nearly off my neck toward the source of the voice—but there was no one there. I inhaled deeply, but the cigar smoke was gone. *Pull it together. You can't afford to lose it now!*

Could I help it? I'd rehashed the scene in my head a million times. I didn't know what I was doing—I couldn't control myself.

I now had no choice but to pick up the pieces of my broken life and start anew, for I was stripped.

CHAPTER 1

THE READING

*I*t. You know, *it* was hereditary, passed down from generation to generation. I guess it was debatable whether *it* was a blessing or a curse. As far as my life was concerned, I'm going with blessing. I had no reason to hate *it* since *it* made us who we are—both light and shadow. We all didn't have *it*, but *it* was strong in the house of Gáspár; *it* ran on Mom's side of the family.

My long olive fingers clutched my phone as the snow melted on my face upon contact. No—I wasn't a kid anymore—at fourteen, I was practically an adult. I exhaled and watched my breath exit my mouth, translucent and ghostlike, disappearing in a matter of moments. They say the winters in Uniontown, Pennsylvania are crisp—that the cold, dry air stings when you breathe. I say that's only for the weak.

"Slow down, Sloane!" Yvette Appleton whined from several yards behind me. "Not everyone has legs up to their neck," complained my waddling friend. If we were birds, I'd be an all-legged crane while Yvette would be a penguin. Poor Yvette struggled to find herself. She still hadn't found her niche in life—still searching for what might make her passionate. Problem was—her parents were into conformity and dictated everything in her life, from eating habits to fashion trends, or lack thereof. They wanted Yvette to be a mini version of themselves—it wasn't working.

I had to admit, Yvette was right. Once I was on a mission, I saw nothing but the goal, always living in the moment, so I literally forged ahead. Sometimes, it was at the cost of others. I'm still working on that.

As the wind cut through my Gap jeans, I quickened my pace, forcing both of my friends to keep up. Main Street, Uniontown, housed a historic district that included theaters, shopping, and restaurants with a wide variety of architecture. I was proud that my hometown was a stop along the Underground Railroad that helped slaves escape. The idea of the lack of human rights pushed me over the edge.

I saw our three reflections in the glass storefronts as we headed toward our destination. Zariah Baker, who was right behind me, was my other best friend. She was more like a swan, gracious and elegant. "Girl! I've never done anything like this before—I'm kinda ek-sie-ted!" rapped Zariah like it was second nature. She was the talented one—the triple threat who could dance, sing, and act—and I mean, really well. On top of her talent, Zariah's face may have broken the mold for stunning bone structure, especially her high cheekbones. I always wondered if it was fair that she had talent, looks, and money, being the daughter of two doctors. The girls finally caught up to me.

Smiling from ear to ear, I flipped my auburn ponytail from one side of my neck to the other so I could see Zariah pull off a *pas de bourrée*—she was born dancing. Yvette clapped vigorously with her flippers and belted out, "Whoot! Whoot!" Yvette's cheeks had a pinkish hue where the cold stung her face, but her lips were like rosebuds and her eyelashes long and opulent. "I've never had this done, either!" chirped Yvette. "I'm nervous." Yvette and Zariah were the opposite of one another, but I still think Yvette had enormous potential. She was like raw sugar, a little went a long way, but too much was grainy. She needed to strike a balance. How do I know? *It.*

I glanced again at the shiny storefronts, staring at my reflection. My almond-colored eyes were framed by dark manicured eyebrows women would kill for—at least, that's what Mom said. Personally, I found brows to be high maintenance. The warm olive glow of my skin was likely due to the hybridization of my Italian father and my Romani mother. I was conspicuous—well, most of the time—commanding a presence, just like the endangered crane.

The waddling Yvette, a bit winded from her efforts to keep up, said, "I can't believe I'm getting a reading from a real Gypsy!"

I stopped dead in my tracks, pivoted on my heels, and said flatly, "Yvette—we don't use that word! It's highly offensive."

"What? Sloane—what do you mean?" my naive friend retorted. "I-I don't know what's offensive." She looked like she was about to cry. "It *is* a reading, right? I thought that was what you said."

Zariah shook her head. "Nuh-uh, girl! I don't think *that's* what she meant," correcting Yvette on the downbeat. She crossed her arms and looked away; she must've been afraid I'd rip Yvette a new one.

I didn't want to ruin our day out—she didn't know better. Unfortunately, it was a commonly used word. "Okay," I said in a motherly tone, taking a second to take it down a notch. "Here's the deal—we say 'Romani,' which rhymes with hominy, not 'Gypsy.' It doesn't set me off too much, but if you say that in front of my family, they'll be insulted. Not a good idea!"

Yvette nodded, looking more like a baby penguin, big-eyed and genuinely fearful. "Okay, Sloane. I'm sorry! I didn't know."

Zariah mumbled something about it, "not setting me off too much," with a roll of her eyes.

Fine—I wasn't particularly tolerant of shortcomings, but I had to set her straight. My family had lost so much from racial persecution and hatred. I felt protective of them. I was lucky to have been raised in the U.S., where the tolerance level is higher than in Europe, where my Hungarian-Romani family originated. But, in all fairness, I recently revealed the well-kept secret of my race to my friends. They actually thought it was cool! Not the reaction I expected. Had we revealed such a secret in Europe, we'd be shunned. Maybe I needed to cut Yvette some slack; it wasn't like we learned about the Romani people in history class or anything.

I paused, realizing I could have gone a little easier on her. "It's fine—you didn't know."

Yvette acknowledged and wrapped her arms around me with a hug.

Zariah and I made eye contact. I could tell the caravan wheels were turning. She said, "So—what do we say?"

I rubbed my hands together, having forgotten for a moment we were still standing outside in the freezing cold—the sun was setting. "What do you say about what?"

"How do we treat your family?" she asked as if we were Martians. This time, she wasn't dancing, having tripped rather than glided on the swan's lake.

I wasn't sure where Zariah was going with that. "How about like anybody else?" I could be both territorial and vocal.

Zariah put her hands on her chiseled face to warm herself. The sky resembled pink and blue layered frosting as the sun dropped further. "I mean—I don't know what to expect," she said carefully, trying not to reveal her fear. At that moment, she was the swan with her neck submerged under the waterline.

Maybe I should have educated my friends *before* our outing. There were too many rumors and mistruths about my people. "Look," I said to them as I mustered my best people skills without coming across as demeaning, "my great-grandfather and great-aunt own the store. Treat them like you'd want me to treat your grandparents; just be respectful, okay?"

Yvette nodded. "Yeah—right—so are there dolls with needles sticking out of them?"

"No! You're thinking of voodoo; that's totally a different culture," I said, wondering who the Martian was now. *"Pápa* and *Bibíyo* Jeta sell handcrafted jewelry, gems, and incense, like a metaphysical store. They have Romani store readers from the area to help support one another; *Bibíyo* reads too, but that isn't a good idea to have her read for us because you're my friends. It's better to have a stranger with no biases—it's more accurate that way."

Yvette's eyes grew large again. "Oh, my God! Will she tell my mom? I'd be in trouble," she said, flapping her wings to keep warm.

I rubbed my arms vigorously since it was ridiculously cold. I forgot Yvette's mom was originally from the deep South—Bible Belt territory—fortune tellers were considered evil by default. "No—no way. Readings are confidential. They're meant to help you navigate your path in life. Don't worry about it." *Pápa* and *Bibíyo* wouldn't associate with the *gazhe* anyway, outside of the store. There was always underlying suspicion.

Yvette breathed a sigh of relief, and Zariah was back to herself with a big smile plastered on her perfect face. Excitement was back in the air as we continued to head toward my family shop, The Crow's Nest, with the red, blaring neon sign in the window: **PSYCHIC READER.** The three of us walked in unison as our excitement rebuilt. I never tired of a good reading—*Bibíyo* and *Pápa* were well connected, like most Romani, when it came to Who's Who in the world of divination. We were a tight group, the Romanies—kinda had to be after all we'd been through.

I pulled open the frosty front glass door, which triggered the sound of the chimes announcing our arrival. My friends scooted in quickly behind me, to warm themselves and to follow my lead. We were greeted with the aroma of lingering cinnamon incense and soft Hungarian violin music in the background. The store was a cozy size, and it was adorned with bold-colored trinkets for sale in every inch of space. Sheer fabrics in warm hues were draped from the ceiling down to the floor, sometimes wrapped around a metal frame for effect. It was *Pápa's* way of separating the retail portion of the store from the reading and healing section. I guess it was for privacy.

Display cases lined the store with beautiful jewelry made by *Pápa*—he crafted metals like no other. The cheaper stuff hung on displays on top of the cases, with mirrors scattered throughout the store for viewing. Traditional Romani clothing was available for sale too. I wasn't sure if *Bibíyo* did the sewing or not; I wasn't into wearing the traditional clothing. Mom kept us Americanized; besides, I preferred Forever 21. It was hard to know where to look first. My friends, being psychic virgins, stood right in front of the doorway, taking in the view.

It didn't take much effort for my lovable ethnic family to draw attention. *Bibíyo* Jeta Gáspár was the matriarch of our family. She, who perpetually had a smile on her heart-shaped face, glided toward me and my friends with her long jade skirt, swooshing as she walked. Her legs were covered to avoid shame.

Bibíyo, who was always in traditional Romani dress, wore a scarf on her head with her long hair braided. I'm told her hair, in her younger days, was dark brown with hints of red streaked in. That's probably where my red undertones originated.

She covered herself in jewelry, and there was no such thing as too much. Bracelets, rings, and a variety of necklaces were always at her disposal. She said it was good for business. Truthfully, the Romani had to pick up and move on a moment's notice, not too far in the distant past, so it made sense to keep jewelry on their person, just in case. *Bibíyo's* arms were my favorite. She wasn't chubby, but her arms were doughy, with slight wrinkles. When I was little, I'd squeeze her. She was as close to a grandma as I'd ever get.

Bibíyo grasped each side of my face. "Sloane—my sweet! Let me look at you," she said. Then she reached up on her toes to kiss my forehead. I had to bend down to meet my tiny aunt halfway. "Django—come! Our Sloane is here with friends!" Both Yvette and Zariah stood there mesmerized by my colorful secret of a family.

Pápa Django Gáspár was my maternal great-grandfather with whom I was close. He used to babysit me while Mom worked, but they had a minor falling-out. Neither one of them would tell me the story, but I figured it had something to do with Mom's insistence on assimilating to our watered-down Romani-Americanized status while *Pápa,* patriarch and head of the family, insisted on teaching us the old ways. Guess what? The old ways included *fármichi*—I was all for it! In my eyes, *Pápa* could do no wrong.

Tucked in the back of the store by his workbench, *Pápa* preferred to let his younger sister run the store since he considered that "women's work." What could I say? They're from a different generation. I wouldn't have tolerated that from any man except *Pápa*. He was a master metalworker and had eventually learned to make jewelry. *Thud—Pápa* must have put his pliers down because then I heard his trousers rubbing together as he headed toward us. He shuffled to start—he couldn't help getting a stiff back from having worked so hard over his workbench.

He, too, dressed in traditional Romani clothing; his ensemble consisted of baggy pants, a blousy shirt, a vest, and a bright-colored neck scarf. *Pápa* was handsome as far as grandpas were concerned. His dark eyes always twinkled, and he always had his beard trimmed carefully. I don't think I've ever seen him without facial hair.

"*Nepáta!* How I miss you!" he said as he *chinged* with each step. *Pápa,* like his sister Jeta, was superstitious. They did everything they could to keep bad luck away; he wore bells on his clothing more often than not. They swore by any amulet or charm that was considered good luck, including the gold coins *Bibíyo* wore around her neck.

We hugged as if we hadn't seen each other in weeks, but it had only been days. I sniffed my most favorite scent in the entire world—his cherry pipe; it must have lingered on his clothes. I adored him and tucked memories away every time I saw him. I wasn't sure why.

In the corner of my eye, I could see Zariah and Yvette grinning from ear to ear. I guess I got a little sappy, and they thought it was funny.

"*Pápa* and *Bibíyo,* I'd like you to meet my two best friends, Zariah Baker and Yvette Appleton." They just stood there. It was like my friends forgot ordinary manners. Seriously?

"Welcome!" they said with their heavy accents. Their language was a Romani dialect laced heavily with Hungarian when they were alone, but they did their best to speak English when the *gazhe* came to visit. There were lots of Romani dialects, in part because of the native country from which they hailed, but also because horrific events dictated the Romani language banned in some cases. Crazy.

Once my friends saw how cool they were, they nodded politely, and each headed toward the various displays that interested each girl; Zariah headed toward the jewelry and Yvette to the geodes and minerals. I was just happy to be there.

"We have a special reader for you," *Pápa* said with a mischievous twinkle in his eye. "Come, *Nepáta*, I'll introduce you." He held my hand like he always did, as if I were a little girl, and pulled me behind one of the sheer fabrics where the reader was waiting. "Sloane Gáspár, this is Madame Sinfi." *Pápa* liked to leave out my last name, Barzetti, because he didn't like my biological father, Tony, but neither did I, so I was okay with it.

Madame Sinfi gestured for me to sit as she shuffled the Tarot cards. She couldn't have been much more than Mom's age, thirty-five at most. Her dark hair was gently curled and tied on one side of her head. Her embroidered vest and skirt were a bronze color that brought out the hue of her amber eyes. She said with an accent, "It is my pleasure, Mademoiselle Gáspár, to make your acquaintance."

Pápa lowered his head slightly in a bow. "I leave you now, *Nepáta*, to return to my bench." He shuffled away with a grin on his face.

It was hard to take my eyes off Madame Sinfi, but I checked briefly on my friends who were in eyeshot. *Bibíyo* offered them some tea, but I knew she'd use paper cups. The Romani were careful to keep eating and drinking implements separate for non-Romani visitors, as they considered it unclean to do otherwise. My *gazhya* friends wouldn't be using my families' dishes—at least, not at The Crow's Nest.

Madame Sinfi stared into my eyes for what seemed an eternity. I couldn't help but notice her eyeliner around her amber eyes—it was meticulous, like a piece of art, so I stared back. I would have been uncomfortable had I not known what to expect. She was gathering information—like a psychic download—it took time and patience. She shook her head slightly. "My God—vat a life!" She continued to stare at me— only—she looked right through me, not at me.

Was that good or bad? Did she mean my life up until now? That didn't make sense—I was fairly ordinary.

"Vere to start? Ah—*oui*—vit your papa." She continued to shuffle the Tarot cards. "Is 'e in spirit?"

Hmmm—that was complicated. "No—they're both alive." She stopped shuffling and put the cards down in a stack. "Uhmm—there's my birth dad and my stepdad."

She bit down on her lip. "Zair vill be death vit Papa;" she pulled the top card over. Had I not been sitting there, I never would have believed it. It was the Death card.

"No—you mean a symbolic death—right? I've had enough readings to know it's all in the interpretation. They're both too young to die." I was unsettled—even squeamish. "Wait—which one do you mean, anyway?"

She tapped her ringed index finger on the Death card. "I see ze body. Zis is—vat you call—literal. And—ze cards—zey never lie!"

Maybe Madame Sinfi wasn't good—or maybe she was having an "off" day. "Which father? Can you tell?" I still felt sick. I may not have had a good relationship with Tony, but I sure didn't wish him dead.

She continued to tap the Death card. "It is ze one you love ze most!"

Oh, God—my stepdad! He had been ill for months. It must

be him. What if she was wrong? Worse, what if she was right? I had to process, so I sat there, unable to move for what seemed an eternity.

"When—when will this happen? Is there something I can do about it?" I felt panicked—as if his life were in my hands. It seemed the violin reached its crescendo at that very moment at The Crow's Nest.

Madame Sinfi pulled the next card, turning it over. It was the Eight of Swords. It showed a woman tied up, blindfolded, walking through eight swords sticking out of the ground like a prison. "Zair is na'zing you can do, Mademoiselle. You are, as ze cards show, restricted, entangled, and bound to your destiny. You are ze dark 'aired voman in ze card."

Do I say anything to Mom? No—no sense in creating stress when Madame Sinfi could be mistaken—it's happened before in divination. It wasn't a perfect art.

She looked right through to my soul as I stared at her eyeliner. Maybe she used a stencil? Maybe I'd better pay attention . . .

She paused, adjusting one of her bangles. "You do not know 'ow important you are, Mademoiselle. You 'ave ze marks of a leader, but I do not know if zis will 'appen."

Hell—I wasn't sure how that could be true. My interests were STEM related (Science, Technology, Engineering, and Math). My people skills weren't the best, either. "Go on," I said. I did like the idea of leadership, though.

"You will be force to be—vat zey say—reckoned vit. You are wise. Zey tell me, aggressive. Zis is vat zey need from you. Let's see what ze cards say." She flipped the Emperor card. I never liked that card. It reminded me of Napoleon Bonaparte.

Madame Sinfi nodded. *"Oui—c'est vrai.* You see?"

I couldn't believe how her reading mirrored the cards so

easily. Was there a chance she rigged the reading? I reached over, took the deck of cards, and shuffled them myself. I wasn't taking *any* chances.

"Ahhh—you question! Zat is good—you *are* ze Emperor—do you not see? Ze Emperor leaves no'zing to chance. 'e is too vise for zat." She looked smug.

I glanced in my peripheral vision at the store and saw Yvette and Zariah talking with *Bibíyo*. I was glad the girls seemed to warm up to her. I wondered if they were worried that we were going to sacrifice chickens or something.

Madame Sinfi stared into space, waiting to get clarity on the reading. Like a radio on the perfect frequency, she said, "Now—zair is more." She tapped her ringed index finger on the brilliant purple tablecloth as she paused to get more information. "Zey tell me zat you vill 'ave ze sudden change in your young life. Zis is important for ze growth, but it is *tragique*."

"Are you saying my life is going to be tragic?" *I really hope she's completely off. Like I need that kind of future!*

She tapped, paused some, and tapped more. She looked at me with her artwork for eyes and said, "Not ze whole life—no. Ze sudden change vill be *tragique*." She pulled the next card. Unbelievably, it was the Tower. The card, sadly, reminded me of the footage that's played each year on TV of the planes that crashed into the Twin Towers on 9/11. It was pretty impossible to find anything positive about this card. "Ze tell me zis is necessary." She licked her lips, pausing and staring again. "Vait—zair is more. Zair is still hope."

"I don't get it. My sudden life change, like falling out of the Tower, will somehow end well?" I had to make sure I understood; this was too big to leave muddy.

"Hmmm—not ze fall itself, but ze time after ze fall. You vill inspire, Mademoiselle, only I do not know 'ow."

Just then, *Pápa* peeked his head around the sheer fabric and said, "You done, yes?"

Madame Sinfi said, "Ah, dear Django—in a minute. She 'as question for me, I zink."

Pápa shuffled away. He'd likely tell *Bibíyo* that we were nearly finished; Yvette and Zariah could then fight over who got to go next.

I hated that reading—it was out there—not at all what I had expected. Maybe she had the wrong person—maybe she confused Zariah with me? "Yeah—I do have a question—how accurate are you?"

She inhaled and fixated her calligraphy-framed eyes on me again. "But of course! You doubt—it is important, *oui*—to question that vich scares us?"

"*Oui.*" Tell me you misinterpreted. Tell me Dad won't die.

I saw my friends pacing—they were ready for their turn with Madame.

"Mademoiselle Gáspár—I am accurate. You vill need to be strong."

Not what I wanted to hear. I wondered aloud, "Advice—I need advice. You're telling me my life is about to suck. What do I do about it? There must be something!"

She tapped her finger. This time Madame Sinfi tapped in a pattern—one, two, three, pause—one, two, three, pause. "Zay tell me you should focus on ze war, not ze battles."

I wondered what she meant—she probably wasn't sure herself. I needed to hear something more, but I could tell the connection was lost when she stopped staring through to my soul with her amber eyes. The remark about leadership was intriguing. Did she mean a role model like Maya Angelou or Rosa Parks? Leaders who quietly yet strongly made a statement that provided a basis to pave the way for future generations. Or did she mean leadership like the Dalai Lama or Moses, who literally led with resolution against all odds. It also wasn't the first time I heard that I was a force to be reckoned with. Another reader, some time back, told me I was like a pit bull. It was true—I had teeth and wasn't afraid to use them.

I saw Yvette approaching while I stood up. It was likely the swan graciously gave in to the penguin. I'd keep my cawing quiet for now—it was a disturbing reading, and I didn't know what to do with it.

While I walked out, Yvette swooped in as fast as she could waddle. Once my crane leg was out of the curtain, Zariah linked arms with me, tilted her head toward my ear, and asked, "So? What'd she say?"

I tried to peer around the curtain, not to see Yvette, but to catch a glimpse of those amber eyes inside that fascinating liner. No luck.

"Uhh, nothing really. Hopefully, she'll be better with you guys."

I couldn't concentrate for the rest of the day, *or* the day after . . .

CHAPTER 2

DOPPELGÄNGER

I live a double life. One foot is in the world of the healer, extraordinary, and the other is in the world of the actuary, ordinary. It takes my waking each morning to realize which world I will inhabit. Today, I am in the world of the extraordinary.

I tried my best to deny my gifts and even my culture, wanting nothing more than to fit in like a quart of homogenized milk—plain and inconspicuous. I did whatever I could to support that desire, including finding a profession that was considered "safe," more like bland, involving math and computer calculations. Actuarial science is a respectable profession, a key ingredient, since it added no mystique and would only contribute to my success at blending in. Insurance companies would always have a need for actuaries to predict life expectancy. In the back of my mind, I am tempted to run the algorithm on the length of my expected life span, but I decide against it for two reasons. First, do I really want to know when I am expected to die, especially when the odds are stacked against me? Second, no forecast is ever foolproof.

The odds have not been good in the past for the Romani people. Images such as caravans, bangle bracelets, and crystal balls emerge. We are both romanticized and feared; we are considered to be nomads, but by no fault of our own. Some even say we are thieves and steal children in the middle of the night. Many think of the Romani as a lifestyle choice, but our DNA is specific, and therefore, genetic, like any other race. I'm opposed to the racial slur my culture has endured; therefore, I never use the "G" word. Few recognize the persecution my race has suffered for nearly a thousand years. I am not the modern stereotype. However, I am better than I was years ago at accepting my heritage and the "fortune teller" abilities that we are often known for, but I make a point to avoid predictions unless the prediction is repetitive. Ironically, I have traded one predicting type of career for another.

I tucked a piece of chocolate brown hair that slipped out of my French twist behind my ear. It's likely Jeta would've disapproved of my manicured hands donned with only one ring per hand—and no bangle bracelets. All that was left to do was put my phone on silent. During my healing sessions, I did not allow any interruptions.

Lavender essential oil infused the molecules of the healing room that I sprayed earlier to help calm my young client. Vibrant, lush plants, mainly pothos and philodendron, graced my studio wherever I could find space. Some sat on tables and others were housed in their own unique plant stands. Vines crept along the floor, inching their way wherever they pleased, as if they had a mind of their own. Looks like several of them were due for a haircut.

My thirteen-year-old client, Lane, awkwardly sat across from me, looking at the floor over a nose speckled in freckles. He was conflicted because he was deeply intrigued but equally terrified at what I might say. He wasn't accustomed to being the center of attention; it was awkward for him. While Lane hoped to transform into a chameleon and blend in with the chair, his mom shifted her legs, crossing them every which way since she wasn't sure what to do with them. After all, it isn't every day you take your child to a healer. At least she knew what to expect from a counselor or pediatrician, since she had tried it all for her son. Nothing seemed to help.

How do I know these things? *It.*

"Hello Lane. It's nice to meet you," I said, shifting into the Fairy Godmother minus the wand. "I want to tell you a little bit about myself, so you'll have a better idea of what it is I do." I flashed a heartfelt smile at him.

"Okay," uttered Lane, barely audible, as he started nibbling on a nail he had managed to chew down to a stub prior to his arrival.

"I'm Katya Gáspár. Your mom told me you haven't been feeling well," I said as I looked at Beth, Lane's mom, to get a fast read on how much she actually told Lane. I got the sense there had been communication, but I wanted to use my own language, just in case Beth wasn't clear. This poor kid was uncomfortable enough. His eyes grew larger with anticipation. "I'm an intuitive. Some people might use the word 'psychic,' but that may sound more like a fortune teller," I said with a grin. They had no idea of the naked truth behind what I just stated, and I planned to keep it that way. These gifts were dominant in the Gáspár family line, and I was the granddaughter of Django Gáspár. "I have a strong sixth-sense that makes it easy for me to feel what other people feel or see what most people cannot see. For instance, I could feel how nervous you were before you arrived."

"Really?" he said as he gazed up from under his wild hair.

"Yes. I feel nervousness wherever you feel it, but I know it's not mine. It belongs to you."

Lane leaned forward in his seat, wringing his hands.

"Can I ask a question?" said Beth meekly. "How do you know it isn't you?"

"Initially, it wasn't an easy task, but I've had lots of practice. It has only been the last few years I've learned to manage it. As a teen, I found it overwhelming to be at school. It was exhausting."

"Me too," chimed in Lane, only this time with more gusto. He started to make eye contact. Good—he's more comfortable.

"Can you read minds?" Beth asked.

"No. I can only read energy. I know if someone is distressed or delighted. I know if their intent is pure or if they have an agenda. It's a mixed bag of tricks."

"Cool," Lane said as he bobbed his head up and down.

"I'm also a healing repository. If the Universe destines that someone is to receive a healing, it will happen. Healings come in many forms; so, for example, pain may be removed, or bodily organs may be repaired."

"What do you mean by, 'destined'?" inquired Beth.

"Because I am not omnipotent, I do not know each person's blueprint for that particular life. Only the Universe can determine whether someone receives a healing." Lane and Beth soaked each word in. I cleared my throat. "I should also clarify that I'm not the source of the healing."

"Can you see dead people?" Lane asked robustly.

"Yes, but only when it's warranted. First, and foremost, I am a healer."

Grinning, my client mutters, "That's dope."

"Since this topic is so vast, I'm going to suggest we save it for another time," I said brightly. "Let's swing back to what brings you in. Lane, does your right big toe hurt?"

While Lane acknowledged, Beth said, "His toe hurts almost every day; and sometimes, it hurts so badly he has to come home from school."

"Uh-huh, I get that. It looks inflamed—even raw. What happened?"

Beth responded slowly, processing my abnormal statement. Luckily, I was used to my clients' initial denial. "How do you know that? His shoe is still on his foot; I *never* told you the problem." She sat with her jaw agape. Little did Beth know that their lives were about to change from this session. No science could explain it.

Lane pulled at his shoelace; then he took off his shoe and sock to show me what I already knew. His toe was puffy, red, and oozing with pus. I wondered how long he had suffered from such an ailment.

"That looks tender, Lane," I said, knowing first-hand how ingrown toenails could put even someone with a high pain tolerance through the roof. I refocused on Beth and said, "I'm a clairvoyant—that means I have the ability to see beyond the five senses. My clairvoyance is especially sharp at seeing inside of a body, or in this case, inside a shoe. I'm like my own X-ray machine."

Lane exhaled loudly. "Seriously?"

Beth reprimanded him, "Lane! You need to be respectful of Miss Katya."

I was humored—definitely not insulted. I had daughters and was used to the lingo.

I smiled. "It's okay. Are you weirded out?"

His head bobbed some more. "Yeah."

At least I got Lane to speak a little bit. "So—is it an ingrown toenail?" I didn't want to assume, although I was pretty sure.

She threw her arms up in the air out of pure frustration and added, "Yes, and we've taken Lane to the doctor more times than we can count. He has juvenile diabetes; that's why it isn't healing right. We're at our wits' end!"

I'm sure they must be—diabetes is a problematic disease. "Have you had that portion of the nail removed?"

"Yep," said Lane.

"Now, let's get to work on your toe." I leaned back in my chair so I could feel Lane's healing. There was nothing quite like experiencing the phenomena of another being healed. It was a privilege. "Alright—the Light is starting to flow."

Beth asked, somewhat alarmed, "How do you know?"

"I know because the Light beams into my head, out of my heart, and into Lane. My body is made different—I screen what otherwise would be too strong for Lane's body to handle. Now, just sit back, sink into your chair, and close your eyes."

It didn't take long for a reaction.

"I just saw a flash of white light!" Lane said, barely able to contain himself. "It was bright—almost too bright!"

Good. The session was coming along nicely. "Can you tell me what you're feeling in your toe?"

He sighed, trying to figure out what he felt. "Uhhh—it feels colder, but just the toe. I don't feel the little heartbeat in my toe like I did earlier."

"Yes—the coolness is reducing the inflammation—like an ice pack." Funny—I never tired of the unique ways clients described their healings; each experience was special.

Time ticked. Healings were usually not instantaneous. After ten minutes elapsed, I felt the intensity of the Light wane and then slow to a halt.

"Take your time as you open your eyes, shift your body, and come back into the density of the third dimensional body," I softly suggested. This was my clients first time experiencing a high vibration. It was likely they were spaced-out after having entered a realm that was foreign to them.

Once Beth unplanted and moved her body, she looked

down at Lane's toe and furrowed up her brows, as if she couldn't believe what she was seeing. She blinked, stared, and blinked again.

Lane beamed, "I have no pain! And look—it isn't puffy anymore!"

Beth got out of her chair and kneeled down to take a closer look at Lane's toe. "I would never have believed it without seeing it with my own eyes," Beth stated as she looked up at me, reflecting.

After the appointment, I plopped down into the over-stuffed recliner, reached over, and poured *eau de cologne* on my hands and rubbed them together. I inhaled the sweet orange scent subtly infused with lavender and clove. It was invigorating. As I gazed at one of my many lush green plants, I reflected on Lane's success. Yes, this work was fulfilling. I enjoyed it—immensely.

My health was essential for this work, and one of the best ways to nurture myself was through meditation. Warmth filled my limbs as I altered my state of consciousness while I leaned back in the recliner with my eyes closed. The deeper I went into the state where my body, mind, and spirit melted together, the more it reminded me of a golden sunset dipping into a calm ocean.

Thoughts melted away as I became one with all there was. That was the state of being that's beyond astounding—it was where my sixth sense was at a pinnacle—sharp. Once I cleared my aura and raised my vibration, which came with practice and patience, I was brilliant, like a star piercing the night sky.

Time gently trickled away, just like my water fountain sitting next to me, only I'm not sure how much time had expired. For as perfect as life felt at one moment, the next moment caused me to shudder; I felt disturbed—awry. My eyes opened wide, and my eyelashes stuck to my eyelids like glue while my nails dug into the armrest of the chair. As I held my breath, I got a vision of a statuesque, slender young woman with wavy auburn hair halfway down her back.

Sloane!

Was it a vision presenting itself in real-time, or was it a future vision of my firstborn daughter, despairing?

Something was wrong—*very* wrong.

CHAPTER 3

DONE

'mon, Jessica! I played with my phone out of pure boredom while I waited for her to finish the math problem I just assigned. The public library was our tutoring spot—we picked Saturday mornings as our time to work on math. Jessica just didn't get that subject. Our study room was sandwiched between the Teen Section and the Audiovisual Section. Some kid with fluorescent ear buds combed through the CD collection, probably in hopes of pirating music.

Tutoring was as good as anything to do in the freezing winter in Uniontown. I gave up on athletics; I had tried everything known, but nothing worked. When I say nothing worked, I'm referring to my body—my brain never seemed to get the signals to my body fast enough. I think it was because, at fourteen, I was already six feet tall. And no—to everyone's disappointment—I did *not* play basketball. Instead, I focused on my mad math and science skills.

Alright—I'll admit—I was a nerd. So what? I was tall and smart—I intimidated the hell out of the boys, but I didn't care. I was going places—I wasn't exactly sure where—but somewhere. Just try to keep up with me.

Jessica was a sixth grader at my school, Mountain Ridge Academy, where she struggled with math. When she and I started working together, she had somewhere around a "D" in the class. Since I was already in eighth grade, I knew the material. We connected—which was cool. Anyway, she's now getting an "A" in the class, and I'm feeling good about it. Mom won't let me charge for it, but she said I should put the experience down on my college applications. Sometimes, Jessica's mom slips me a gift card—pretty sweet! It's basically a win-win.

"Sloane," said Jessica sheepishly, "I think I got it." She pushed the paper toward me so I could check her work. I recalculated to find the least common multiple to arrive at the common denominator of the two fractions I just made up.

I smiled. "It's right, Jessica. Good job, but let's do another one. You're not looking too confident." So, I made up another problem—I needed to make sure she was good until I saw her again. I didn't want her to slip—I was proud of her. I pushed the paper back to Jessica, feeling the friction of it against the table.

I checked my phone—just a couple of minutes left, and my ride should be here. I preferred Tony over Ivy—he was slick, but she was abrasive, like bathroom scouring powder. If I were made of marble—I'd have scratches and pits thanks to her. It was their weekend—lucky me. I was saddled until I could go back home on Sunday evening. Tony was my biological father—although I see him more like a sperm donor. Out of survival, I called him "Dad" in front of him and Ivy, but anywhere else, he was just Tony. He didn't deserve my respect.

She slid the paper back again, interrupting my thoughts. "Let's see how you did." I touched the tip of the lead pencil to each portion of Jessica's work, like a teacher, wanting to give partial credit in case the answer was wrong. I didn't want to destroy any confidence I had helped build. She had relied on me—trusted me—and I wasn't about to let her down.

I grinned. "You got it! How are you feeling?"

"Kinda better, thanks, Sloane." She let the idea of success sink in for a moment. "Hey—can I text you if I get stuck on my homework?" she added.

"Totally," I said. "I prefer you ask right away—don't spin your wheels, okay?"

She stacked her made-up problems and stuffed them into her pocket folder, then stowed away her pencil in her fuzzy Hello Kitty pencil pouch. While looking at me, she said, "'Kay—no spinning, I promise." Jessica unzipped her matching backpack and pulled out a holiday gift bag etched with silver glitter bears dressed in Santa hats. "This is an early Christmas present from my family."

I gleamed. "Jessica, you didn't have to do that."

"Aw—Sloane—thanks for everything," said the shy girl. "My mom insisted."

The gesture viscerally warmed my face. "You're welcome," I said, but I couldn't wait. The anticipation was killing me. Inside the bag, I found a movie theater gift card and Sour Patch Kids—the super sour kind that I loved. "I know what I'm doing over winter break."

Just then, her phone buzzed. Jessica picked it up, read the text, and said, "My dad's here—gotta go." She scrambled to fill her backpack with the folder.

"Thanks for the gift—it was really nice," I said as I gave her a hug. "See you next Saturday?"

"I'll text you," Jessica said as she slung her backpack over her shoulder and scampered to the front door of the library.

Glancing up at the glass wall of the library's study room I

reserved for tutoring, I stared at my own reflection. *Bibíyo* always said that I got my mannerisms from Mom, but that my height and thinness were from Tony. There was really no getting away from him. I shook the thought away and rubbed my hands on my jeans. I was never a girly-girl like my sister, Noelle. I preferred T-shirts and hoodies, probably to Mom's dismay. As a small child, she dressed me in frilly dresses, little white socks with lace, and styled my thick auburn hair with gentle curls that reached halfway down my back. Nowadays, it's pretty much a ponytail. Noelle's now the fashion diva, and she's good at it.

She's technically my half-sister. The first time I heard someone say that word, I was offended. Some kid at school picked up on the different last name—I'm Barzetti and Noelle is Mackenzie; my mom married my stepdad, John Mackenzie, and they had Noelle when I was little. He's been my dad ever since.

I slumped back into the hard, sturdy wooden chair—the warmth of my volunteer work evaporated and was replaced with the frigidness of my dismal reality. Which one would pick me up—Tony or Poison Ivy? I hit the button on my cell to see the time. Crap! I estimated the hours remaining until my weekend's prison sentence was up. Anytime was too long. I touched the timer app on my iPhone and punched in the hours. I'd rather overestimate—that way, I wouldn't be disappointed if the timer went off prematurely and I found myself in inmate status. I watched the time erode second by second. Time was fickle.

Today, Time was my jailer—sadistically attracted to tight bonds around my arms and legs, cutting into the flesh, restricting hope of movement. I could hear Time laugh—it was a guttural sound that made the hair on my arms stand up as I allowed the hope of freedom to sink into my mind. Time didn't like freedom—he was his bane. He told me I was a fool—told me freedom would elude me at all costs. Time said he may be my jailer, but Tony was the warden. Like men who abuse power, Time said the warden basked in the idea that my ass was his for the next four years. He laughed. No chance of parole until I was eighteen. I told Time I didn't belong here! He rolled his eyes—right—that's what they all say. Get used to it, Sweetheart. It's supposed to suck!

I hate you, Time.

Stupid idea—I cleared the timer and slid my phone closer to my metallic turquoise backpack. I'm not giving him any power over me. Go screw yourself!

My cell whined like a wailing banshee almost off the table. I picked it up and said flatly, "Hello." What choice did I have?

"Where are you?" Ivy honked like a goose. "I've been waiting in the parking lot for like, two minutes—get out here! I've got shit to do."

Looked like the scouring was starting early today—lucky me. "If you had texted me, you wouldn't have had to wait, Ivy. I've *been* ready," I spelled it out for the village idiot.

"Whatever," she mumbled. She hated when I was right, and I was always right.

I put my coat on and slung my backpack over my shoulder, wishing I had another student to tutor. That was actually a good idea—a way to burn Time. Only problem was, the warden wouldn't like it. It was like allowing the inmates too much outside time—a little too good for morale. If morale was good, that meant Time was not oppressive enough, and oppression was the ultimate goal. How else would the warden get his point across?

I pulled the lever up to spring the front passenger seat, pushed the seat forward, and tossed my backpack onto the rear seat, which seemed to agitate her further. It hadn't occurred to Einstein to buy a four-door instead of a two-door—the norm, I would have thought, for anyone with kids. It was especially a pain when the three of us went somewhere. It was near impossible to get my long frame into the back seat without scraping my back or hanging myself on the seatbelt. Hmmm—actually, that made sense once I thought about it further. How important could I be? Sometimes it's the little details that grate the most.

After pushing the seat back, I squeezed into the front passenger seat and adjusted the lever under my seat while pushing my feet so that it would go back as far as it could. Ivy's new car was already infused with her perfume. I don't know what scent it was supposed to be, but I can say it smelled like a brew of sweat and musky old lady. Making matters worse, she had a lemon air freshener hanging from the rearview mirror, but it actually made the car smell like a funky layered stench which assaulted my senses. It didn't help, either, that the car heater was blasting.

Ivy was big; there was no getting around it (or her, for that matter)! She was of average height, but she loved to put her boobs on display. They were shelved on a thick waist, or at least, what used to be a waist. Her arms and legs were round, but she didn't let that stop her. As far as Ivy was concerned, her skirts couldn't be short enough. Her favorite was black and white leopard print. I don't know—maybe she thought she was a tigress or something. Years of smoking had turned her complexion sallow and aged her prematurely. Since she wasn't allowed to smoke in the car with me, she smacked her gum. It was annoying. Her thin lips were usually covered in gaudy red lipstick, which did nothing for her. Cheap. Cheap was the best way I could describe Tony's girlfriend.

I could tell from the direction we were headed that we weren't going back to their house. "Where're we going?" I asked.

She snorted, like a pig, and said, "Runnin' errands—what do ya think?" She looked at me like I was a moron while her sausage fingers sunk into the steering wheel covered in faux cashmere. It was supposed to look luxurious. Great! I've got a load of homework to do, and I'm out with a Kim Kardashian wannabe. Gross.

Ivy was a connoisseur of drugstore hair dye. She made her rounds with not only different brands, some better than others, but she also sampled colors like a hoarder with money at a flea market. This week's featured color was a skunk look—stark black hair, which didn't work with her complexion, and a platinum blonde streak down the middle. I don't think I've ever seen her natural color, which was probably attractive at one time. Okay—now I'm being generous.

I held onto the grip on the car door as she took the last corner fast. Her eyes darted at me—she didn't like the fact that I had a death grip, so I waited for a comment. Instead, she said, "When are you gonna get a job? You need to start thinkin' about how you plan on payin' for college."

I waited a moment to absorb her snub. I'm pretty sure I heard correctly, so I said while trying not to laugh, "You do know I'm going to a hard-core college-prep school—right?"

She chomped on her gum like a goat eating hay, and said, "So what? Get a babysittin' job or somethin'. You're wastin' time when you could be makin' money—what do ya call it—volunteerin'. That's just stupid. Who does that?"

"I do—I do it—I'm helping someone out. And it'll look good on my college applications," I said to her as I shook my head. Seriously, one plus one equaled two.

She swerved around the next corner because she knew I didn't like it, only this time it had more force behind it. It didn't occur to her that her tires could slip on the snow.

Ivy belched. "Your father and I are gettin' sick of driving you to that damn library."

I furrowed my brows and said, "What—sick of driving me once every two weeks? That's nothing!" I can't wait to drive myself!

"Why doesn't that mother of yours drive you?"

"Yeah," I stated with lots of attitude. "She does—all the time." Imbecile!

In between chomps, she said, "I'm gonna talk to your father about it."

"About what?"

"About you gettin' responsible and quittin' that volunteerin' shit—makes no sense to call it a job—you don't get paid."

By this point, my anger was mounting. "Getting responsible? It's not enough that I do well in school? Isn't *that* my job? Getting a good education?" I knew the answer to that—she and Tony didn't value education.

She snorted again. "You know, like your father says, 'the world needs grunts too.'" Just then, she pushed down the window lever, and spat her gum out the window like a dim-witted hick. I smoldered!

I wanted to dig my nails into her fat arm. Instead, I gritted my teeth. "Just because you didn't go to college doesn't mean I can't!" Ivy had made her rounds at several jobs—she worked at Walmart for a while, and recently earned her license as a nail technician. I didn't care what she did, or for that matter, what she didn't do, but she had *no* business telling me what to do. I bet Tony put her up to it.

"We'll see about that, you spoiled little brat. Your father and I aren't payin' for college."

I huffed. "Like I was expecting you to—yeah—right," I said with sarcasm drizzled all over it. I had learned the hard way that I was way better off if my expectation level was bottomed out when it came to them. That way, I couldn't be disappointed. If they did anything decent, it was a happy surprise.

Ivy made another hard right. This time, the driver behind us honked his horn for an extended period. She responded by giving him the finger up by her rearview mirror while muttering a four-letter word underneath her breath. It's not like I was offended by her language. It was her raw ignorance that I found offensive—like a piece of meat left in the sun.

She dug her sausage fingers into the faux fur a little deeper. "What's that supposta mean? We buy you things—you're ungrateful," she snarled. "It's your mother's fault—we blame her for the way you turned out."

There was *so* much wrong with that statement. What does she mean "we?" First, Ivy placed a lot of importance on herself, as if she were integral. Second, Tony deserved no credit for how I turned out. And third, as far as I knew, they were the only two people who had a problem with me.

My face stung with anger—and hurt.

Just then, Ivy took one of her sausage hands off the faux fur-covered steering wheel and held it to her mouth. Then she hacked—sort of. She gestured to her throat and managed a *kaff, kaff,* but her eyes started tearing up—with the car moving at 47 mph in a 35-mph zone.

"Are you okay?" I asked, concerned. She wasn't able to answer; so I was a step closer to freaking out because the tears were running down her face, no sound was emerging from her throat, and she wasn't slowing down. "Ivy! Pull over!" It resembled choking—but on what—her spit?

She whipped into the parking lot of a bank—our bodies pushed hard to the left as inertia forced our upper halves to compensate. Ivy slammed on the brakes, and we screeched to a halt, leaving skid marks in the parking lot and onlookers with mouths open.

Ivy's face flushed pink—a good sign. She was getting oxygen—enough that she could cough again. I breathed a sigh of relief. She took in deep breaths and slowly returned to some form of equilibrium—at least for Ivy. We had averted a car accident. It was then that I realized how tense my body had become during the close call.

"I don't know what happened," she said, as if talking to herself. "All of a sudden, I felt my windpipe tighten, and then I couldn't get air in."

Scanning my vault of a memory bank for reasons why a throat might close up, the only idea I could come up with was, "Did you accidentally eat an allergen for breakfast?" There certainly weren't any bees in the car during our Union-town winter.

"What," she said, "you mean like peanuts?"

I shrugged, "Yeah—I guess—what else could it be?"

Ivy wiped the tears from her face while composing herself. "No—I don't have food allergies—that came from nowhere." After a brief pause, she pulled out of the bank parking lot and got back on the road.

"You should probably get it checked out anyway."

For a split second, she knew I was right. Throats don't close up at random. Curious, I took out my phone and Googled asphyxiation. No—wait—that assumes death. What about choking?

"What are you doin'?" she asked.

"Looking up reasons why that might happen," I said, scrolling down an article.

She scrunched up her face. "What—are you gonna tell your mother I had to pull over or somethin'?"

God—what's with her? "Uhm—I wasn't planning on it."

She huffed and said, "You better not! It's none of her business what I do."

I had to gather my thoughts. I'm not sure what Mom has to do with it, and more importantly, why does Ivy care? What really agitates me is the fact that I was trying to help her. Why do I bother? "Just forget it," I said sharply.

She snorted. "I'm *not* going to forget it. What *we* do *isn't* her business," she said, as if she had a mouthful of sour milk.

Not far down the street from the bank, Ivy pulled into the mall parking lot. Great! I get to go shopping with her. This should be interesting.

"That's not what I meant," I said as I slammed the car door shut, setting foot on freshly laid, crunchy snow, shoving my phone into my jeans pocket. "Look it up yourself." Even though I didn't want to shop with her, at least I breathed the fresh frigid air. I needed a break from her cheap perfume. I had to look for the small freedoms—even if it was purely olfactory. Sad, really . . .

I didn't know which stores we were hitting, but I knew which mall entrance was closest, so I took my normal long strides, which left anyone in my wake, but I didn't care today. I just wanted to see her struggle to keep up. Internally, I laughed. Once she caught up to me inside the mall, I waited for her verbal thrashing. But first, she had to catch her breath.

"You could have waited for me, ya know," she said as she crinkled up her nose. "Let's go."

What treat was I in for today? "Where are we going?"

"To Naughty Natalie's—were gonna find some lingerie for your father," she stated.

What? My eyes popped out of my head. Did I hear right? Ivy can't be that stupid! I stopped dead in my tracks, looked at her like she was a moron, and said, "You *are* kidding?"

"No, I'm not. It's perfectly natural, but you better not tell your mother I took you here," she threatened. "Our anniversary is coming up."

So—she knows it's inappropriate. Here's the other thing— what makes Ivy think I'm loyal to her? I'm not responding to her threat. I'll do what I want anyway. I'll just walk around the store—the opposite side from where Ivy is looking.

Finally, after what seems to be forever, Ivy emerges from the checkout line with lingerie for herself, and says, "It's your turn."

I'm stunned. After a long hesitation, I say, "My turn for *what?*" *I hope this isn't going where I think it's going.*

"We're gonna buy you some lacey bras and underwear." She said it so casually, like it was—a thing.

My brain churned out flow charts and their potential outcomes from every angle. Ivy had only one motivation—to buy me something over the top in order to stir the pot. I'm not playing.

I scrunched up my forehead, crossed my arms, and said, "That's not gonna happen."

She reached over to pull me by the elbow, but I recoiled. "What did you say? Don't you argue with me! We're gonna get you measured."

"Get away from me!" I scowled while leaving the store, digging into my jean's pocket and pulling out my phone. I'd had enough.

I glanced up at Naughty Natalie's, where Ivy seemed to be bad-mouthing me to the salesgirl, who was probably college aged. Mom's phone rang and rang. She always picks up—where is she? Did she say she was in session today? If she is, that means her phone is off. I'm not going back in there—hell no!

The poor salesgirl looked like she wanted to crawl under the countertop. No—it's not you—it's her. Eventually, a woman, who seemed to manage the store according to her handful of keys jingling on her upper arm on an accordion band, rescued the girl by acting as a buffer. The manager nodded her head intermittently as Ivy's flailing copious arms told the story of her frustration with me. Pacified that someone listened, Ivy walked out to the main mall area where I sat and waited. She waddled toward me, her eyes dark as coal.

"What were you doin' on your phone? What did I tell you 'bout that?" she complained.

I gave her my "I don't care" look and said, "None of your business." Two can play at that game. She didn't like it when I was in contact with my family or friends, probably because it made my sentence more tolerable—human contact. With no option, I had to follow her out of the mall, but I was sure to leave plenty of space between us as a cushion. Ivy was fuming—and considering her skunk-do—I ran the risk of getting sprayed with witlessness.

It had snowed more while we were indoors, so her car was covered. Abruptly, she flung the car door open and threw the snow brush in my general direction, but it landed near my feet. Had I been standing any closer, it would have wacked me in the head. "Brush the car off," she said as she got in and started it, cranking the heat to full blast. What if she left me? I liked the sound of it! I'd go back into the mall, redial Mom, and eventually we'd connect. She'd pick me up, make me some comfort food, and sympathize with me. Okay—stop dreaming. I'm stuck with Tony and Ivy for another twenty-eight hours. The conversation in my head was sometimes very real. I shook off the cold and started brushing, but I was sure to take my time.

Back in the car, the stench invaded my nose, and Ivy wouldn't shut up. I tuned her out—it was a survival technique I learned from doing time. She drove like a maniac all the way home because she was livid at my blatant "disrespect."

I didn't see Tony's truck when we got back to their house. It wasn't like I was expecting him to rescue me but, on occasion, the warden put the brakes on when she took the agenda too far. I headed to the kitchen, which consisted of a vast array of stainless steel appliances surrounded by black cupboards accented by black dishtowels. Ivy's kitchen décor had a mime theme, and mimes had those creepy black and white faces, which reminded me of clowns—disconcerting. It was a newly refurbished kitchen, but dirty. The floor typically had crumbs on it, with dust bunnies that floated across the floor when someone moved too quickly.

Actually, every room in the house was dirty. Never once did I see either of them run the vacuum. I dropped my turquoise backpack onto the kitchen chair and opened the fridge, only to find cat hair sticking to the inside. My skin crawled. While at their house, as a rule, I was on my own for meals except for dinner. I grabbed the spongy bread and slathered on peanut butter and jelly, sprinkled some chips on the side, and garnished with pickles. Not dill, but the sweet, crispy kind. I contemplated where to eat. No—the kitchen was a cold place. I'll head down the hall to my room—my sanctuary when all else failed. This way, I could eat and make a solid dent in my homework and call Mom in private.

While I carried my lunch out of the kitchen, Ivy said, "Where you goin'?" Apparently, she had been watching my every move, but I had been too lost in my thoughts to notice.

This can't be good. I hesitated, and then said, "To my room." I wondered what the problem could be now.

"You can eat in here," she said as she headed toward the living room, which resembled the faux fur on her steering wheel—gaudy. "We're goin' to watch a movie together."

"Yeah—I'm good—I've got homework to do." I shrugged as

I walked to my room. Even if I didn't, I would have made up any excuse to get away from her. My sanctuary also served as solitary confinement, but it was better than hanging out with the prison guard.

She folded her arms over her heavy chest. "No—you need to watch this with me. It's supposed to be good—just sit down."

Now she piqued my interest. "What is it?"

Ivy took the bag of pretzel rods, which had been sitting on the living room table from the night before, took a bite, and said, "You'll see. I don't want to spoil the surprise."

I guess I could spare a couple of hours, especially if it got her off my back for the rest of the day. I sighed and said, "Alright, fine," but I made sure I sat away from her. Compromise was the key to survival in this house.

Just then, I heard Tony set his keys down in the foyer. He's back from wherever he went. Ivy hit the play button and the opening credits rolled. Curious—I had heard of these actors' names before, but I wasn't sure from what film. Soft piano music played in the background with a black and white backdrop. Then I saw it, but I couldn't believe that Ivy could be so brazen. That she would insist that I watch a film that was controversial, even for an adult, let alone a teenage girl. So—I got up and walked out of the living room—more shocked than anything.

"Get back in here!" Ivy bellowed with a mouthful of pretzel. "This movie will teach you a few things you're old enough to know about." She must have pressed pause because the piano stopped playing.

"What's goin' on?" Tony asked, having caught Ivy's comment. Tony lived mostly off of nicotine and coffee. I wasn't supposed to know he smoked, but you didn't have to be Sherlock to figure it out. He had a full head of dark brown hair that he wore slicked back in a ponytail, often in a frizzy little nub at the base of his neck. "Sloane, where're ya goin'?" His Italian traits surfaced as he spoke more with his hands than his voice.

"Huh?" I snorted. "I'm going to my room—to be alone," I said, dropping the hint loud and clear. This situation oozed toxic, so it made the most sense to get some distance. With any luck, she'd drop it, but I could hear murmurings in the mime kitchen. Ivy would campaign to get Tony on her side, and I would be outnumbered as usual. In no time, I heard them make their way down the hallway toward my cell. Without regard for my privacy, I saw the doorknob turn, without so much as a knock, and sausage fingers pushed the door open. I was already sitting on my bed with my back to the headboard, knees pulled up to my chest. I whiffed the air, and within moments, my room smelled like an ashtray as the warden and prison guard entered.

"Don't you ever walk away from me again," Ivy cackled. "We are tryin' to fill in the blanks where your Mary Poppins mother has miserably failed you. It's high time you learned about the birds and the bees." Tony just stood there and fumbled with the pack of smokes in his pocket that I wasn't supposed to know about.

I'm not sure what part of this conversation I hated the most! First, do they even know how old I am? Second, what the hell? I had a couple of choices—none of which were good. I could tune her out, but that would be tough considering they ganged up on me. I could counter every point she made, including the insults, but Ivy was looking for a fight ever since I got into that car. Or I could yield to her ridiculous wishes. That was not going to happen under any circumstance. Looks like I'm countering because I'm pissed off! My pit bull bared her teeth; the elegance of the crane was a memory.

"You think that movie is about the birds and the bees?" I said, bordering on manic anger. Isn't that a term a parent would use for an eleven-year-old?

She crossed her arms. "How would you know?"

I leaned forward. I just decided I'm in the mood to give her a verbal ass kicking. "Anybody who's even semi-informed has some idea of the content of that film."

"So, you've seen it?"

I wrinkled up my brows. "Seriously? No, I haven't seen it." I had to take a breath to regain some composure. I didn't like how she easily influenced my moods. "But I don't need to in order to be informed about the content." I rolled my eyes because she had a stupid blank look on her face.

"Are you tellin' me your friends saw it? That's what we were hopin' to avoid. We'd rather you talk to us about it," she said, slapping the bed as if it were my face.

"Talk to you—Talk to you!" I said, getting louder. "I don't want to talk to you about that! And no, my friends didn't see it. We're fourteen, Ivy! Why do I have to tell you it isn't appropriate? Who's the adult, here?"

Ivy started doing that coughing thing again, and Tony looked worried. Oddly, his gaze was not on her, but on me. He didn't like the fact that I grew incensed by the minute. Could it be possible he knew I was right?

Unfortunately for me, the coughing didn't last long. She croaked, "Back me up, Tony!"

It was a strange sight, but he acted as if he wore two different shoes. He shifted his weight but couldn't seem to find a balance. "We just want you to be informed," he said quietly.

Ivy was red and sweaty. "You can do better than that," she scoffed. "She's your daughter—get her in line!"

Tony added, "She doesn't have to watch that movie, Ivy."

"What? We talked about this."

Hmmm—looks like it was premeditated. Sometimes they played good cop, bad cop, only Ivy wasn't bright enough to get that Tony was okay with letting her touch some grass. *I'm sick of their damn games!*

"Let it go, Ivy."

"Do something!"

He shook his head. They had gone overboard in their zeal, but he was smart. He knew when to call it quits. This had the potential to blow up in his face. He was between the bite of brambles and the blistering burn of Poison Ivy.

I've had enough of her insulting my mom and my intelligence. She's nobody; she holds no weight with me. She's managed to ruin my day, no, my weekend, again. I'm no fan of Tony's, but where did he find her? I'm not keeping quiet to keep the peace—that was ruined long ago.

I stood up from my bed, glared at Ivy, and said, "No adult in their right mind is going to insist that a kid watch *Fifty Shades of Grey* to learn something."

"Are you callin' me stupid?" she said, fuming.

"You said it, not me!" I said hotly.

"She's outta control!" she screamed, eyes piercing Tony.

He just stood there with his thumbs in his front jean pockets and shook his head.

"That's it! I'm outta here!" Ivy yelled as she marched out of my room, barreling toward their bedroom, but not before she started hacking. *Kaff, kaff, kaff.* I could tell she was having problems getting air, but I didn't care—what was wrong with her, anyway?

He went after her. I could hear Tony say, "Where are you goin'?" He didn't seem too worried about her gasping. It took a while for her to have a clear enough airway to return to speaking. Dumb Ass should probably get that looked at.

"I don't know—anywhere but here," she said while she slammed her closet door open. I guess she was packing.

For once, Ivy had a good idea. I pulled my overnight bag out of the closet while I dialed Mom. Again, it rang and rang. Of all days! I stuffed my remaining books into my backpack, along with two trinkets of sentimental value. I had no intention of coming back to that place. *Nobody treats me like leftover scrambled eggs—the crappy powdered kind.* That was the first time I had ever insisted on going home. *Anything's better than this.*

Tony stepped into my bedroom with a look of shock on his face. "Where are you goin'?" he said, fearfully.

Out of the corner of my eye, I could see a woman with long dark hair wrapped in a *diklo*. She was staring at me, trying to get my attention, and then I smelled it—a cigar. She nodded her head as if to say "yes," only I didn't know if she was talking to me or to Tony. The next second, I turned my head to make eye contact; only she was gone. *Maybe I'm seeing things*, I thought, so I snapped out of it.

"I'm done! I'm not doing this anymore!" I screamed as I bulldozed past him. "It's either Ivy or me! Take me home or I walk!"

I didn't wait for an answer. I began walking toward the front door, not caring that the stuff I packed and slung over my shoulder hit walls, chairs, and even a framed picture of me on my way out. Glass, which previously protected my second-grade school picture, shattered when it hit the ceramic floor. Did Tony follow me? I didn't turn my head to see. I didn't frickin' care.

CHAPTER 4

ABANDONED

As I watched *my* daughter walk into their stone-faced Cape Cod house, which really should be part mine, considering I paid child support to that ex-wife of mine, I should've put my truck into drive, barreled up the hill, and ran him over. I don't know what got my goat more, their sickeningly sweet landscaping with holly growing across the hill or their stone staircase that led up to the front door. *This should've been my life, dammit. That jerk, John, stole everything from me—my wife and now my daughter. That would've been the end of it—it's only fair—an eye for an eye. I could've called it an accident—my foot slipped and hit the gas. Yeah, that's it; my foot slipped.*

I could say my truck hit a patch of ice on their steep drive-way, and I lost control of my truck. Hmmm . . . would that be considered manslaughter? Wait . . . I remember hearing on the news once—an "accident" once landed some poor guy in the pen. Or was it first-degree murder? Does Pennsylvania have the death penalty? My mind raced while my heart rate beat dangerously fast in my chest. I stared John down as he walked back into my house. *Why is he wearing such baggy pants?* His face even looked different; or was that just my imagination? I snapped out of it and realized I lost my chance. My windshield fogged up from my breath; I turned the dial on the dash to get the defroster to work, but it didn't work fast enough for my liking.

I was fed up! I pounded the steering wheel so hard, out of pure frustration, that the palm of my hand started throbbing. As I checked my rearview mirror to reverse out of their driveway and make it down the hill, I saw myself. *Get a grip, man—this emotional shit isn't you at all.* I quickly pushed in my truck's lighter knob to activate it, knowing it would take a while for it to heat up. Those thirty seconds took forever. Once it popped back out, I took that red circle of heat and pressed it gently to the end of my cigarette as I inhaled those needed fumes of nicotine. Once the end of my cigarette turned red and began to emit a beautiful haze, I placed the knob back in its hole. I took a few deep drags, allowing the smoke to curl inside my lungs; I needed to cool down.

I've got time—nothing but time. *How does that Stones tune go? Ti-i-i-ime is on my side, yes it is.* Nothing like the classics . . . they don't make music like that anymore—just a bunch of trash by some wannabes.

I had to come up with something good, but what? It needed to hurt. Get Katya where it counted. I couldn't let this chance pass me by, not after over a decade of waiting for the right moment; not after she left me with nothing and hooked up with that pretty boy. She always thought she was better than me anyway. I had to have freedom—come and go as I please. That's what the old man used to do, and it worked just fine for him. Miss Big Time Actuary with her big-time degree—let her make the big bucks and deal with all the crap that comes with it. She was too busy to notice I had spare time on my hands. It wasn't until Sloane was born that the cat got out of the bag—that whack job Gypsy grandfather of hers spilled the beans that I was fooling around—some nark must've told him. If he would've kept his big mouth shut, I'd still be married to Katya and living large. Now, I had to work! What was Katya's problem anyway? It's not my fault I'm popular with the ladies.

First thing—I've got to find out where Ivy went. That can't happen—both of them gone—I should get Ivy back first since she'll be easier to convince. I rubbed my dark goatee; it helped me think. *Before I look for her, I better figure out how far I'm willing to go, and what I'm willing to give up, because my back is up against the wall. I reached into my secret stash for another smoke before I headed out to Sal's Coffee Shop to get my head together. It'll do me good to relax and talk stuff out. Sal's been like an uncle to me since I was a kid—he's from the old neighborhood and knew my parents, mostly my pops, back in the day when we lived in Bloomfield—Pittsburgh's version of Little Italy. It seems like life was much simpler back then. Since then, Uncle Sal has a new coffee shop in Uniontown, the same city where Sloane lives—convenient—since I like to shoot the breeze with Salvador Russo and his wife, Liliana.*

I drove the rolling hills and took up two spots to park at Uncle Sal's. My thunderous engine was cut off with a twist of my keys. I had no regrets having bought the truck in jet black with the smokestack extending out of the roof—it made a statement and commanded respect—something I learned from Pops. I smelled freshly roasted coffee along with the scent of deep fried struffoli with orange—Aunt Lil must be hard at work on the Christmas bakery. The Russos had put everything into this business, spending every last ounce of energy and all their money on improving it, living the American dream, man. Uncle Sal, a woodworker in his earlier days, crafted the showcase that displayed their coffee products and the baked goods Aunt Lil made.

"Morning Auntie," I said as I bent down to kiss Aunt Lil on each side of her face. I wiped off some flour that found its way to that plump cheek of hers.

"Tony! Let me-a pour you some espresso." Aunt Lil smiled from ear to ear as she rubbed her hands on her floral apron and grabbed the strong brew, knowing my preference. She was Ma's best friend, so out of respect, I always referred to her as 'aunt.'

"Where's Uncle Sal?" I asked.

"He's in the back working on the thing again—what do you call it? The stove, that's it. I'll get him." She shuffled away quickly and broke into Italian to get Uncle Sal's attention as she entered the kitchen. Having no money as immigrants, she and Uncle Sal had to learn English the hard way. As she scooted away, I took in the view of the coffee house; he always kept a fire roaring in the fireplace during the winter months. The dried wood crackled as the blue flames licked it even drier, but the cracking soon became muffled by Uncle Sal's clanking of the industrial-sized aluminum stove they relied on for baking.

Saturday mornings were typically busy in the store, but I must have timed it during a lull, since only two sets of customers were patronizing the place. Two men, one younger than the other, sat at a small table in the corner near the large glass window, conducting a business meeting. Pulling out a card, the older bearded guy seemed to be trying to sell the younger guy products. Noticing the measuring tape he had attached to his work pants, I guessed it had something to do with home improvement. The younger one kept scratching his head and looked out the window every few moments, letting out a big yawn.

On the other side of the store, but within earshot, were two middle-aged chicks yacking with each other about their lives. They were probably high school friends, since there was babble about who was doing what since their last gossip fest. I was holding back a laugh, as it was comical that each one tried to outdo the other when it came to who knew what. I guessed that was how they kept score—what a stupid game. Women!

"What a nice-a surprise to see you, Tony," said Uncle Sal as he emerged from the kitchen with his arms held up, expressive as always. His comb-over reminded me of Pops.

"It's been a while, Uncle Sal," I said, followed by a slumping of my shoulders.

"Let me clean up, Tony, and we-a talk," he said, and he turned his dirty hands toward me to show the dirt from his labor.

"I knew something was-a wrong the minute you walked in," said Aunt Lil. "Sit down and I get you a nice cannoli. You look-a too skinny." I wasn't a big dessert guy, but it was hard to pass up anything that reminded me of Ma.

When Sal returned, he waved me down to the end of the rose granite counter where we could talk with some privacy; a couple that just arrived had ordered cappuccinos and were involved in a discussion at the other end. "So—you got-a trouble?" Uncle Sal had a concerned look on his face as he spoke, plopping down in a chair to rest his bones and his bum knee. Aunt Lil listened as she wiped the counter, even though it looked spotless, but every so often, she gazed up at her customers to make sure they were content.

I gave them the details of my nightmare; only Uncle Sal and Aunt Lil could possibly understand my problem. It was as if I hit the "pause" button on my device and then "rewind" to many years ago when I was only in my twenties living at home with my parents, Mario and Aurelia Barzetti. We lived in a row house on a narrow street connected by the same wall to the Russos in Bloomfield. The homes were all tall and tight. My time to marry had arrived. I had packed and loaded my car since my fiancé, Katya Gáspár, and I had rented the second floor of a house in another part of Pittsburgh. It should've been a milestone in my life, but instead, it became a watershed moment due to unforeseen circumstances.

My parents had a long history of a volatile marriage, stemming from the Old Man's constant cheating and his outbursts of physical violence, whether his target was me or Ma. He paraded his affairs like a proud peacock, and with each incident Ma withered away a little more each time, looking like a neglected sign that had seen too much sun—faded and chipped. She never found the strength to leave him, but she didn't have to. The very day I moved out to get married was the day the Old Man decided he was going to leave Ma for another woman. It all but destroyed her. I offered to stay, but Ma insisted I was a man and needed to be out on my own—she didn't raise me to be a wimp. I haven't spoken to Pops since then—not after what happened to Ma since he up and left.

Fast forward—it was a couple of years later, right after Sloane was born. We lived a distance away from the old neighborhood; Ma still lived in the same row house next to the Russos, only they were away visiting family in Italy. I was busy and normally didn't keep tabs on Ma—only I didn't know at the time that the Russos were in Italy, or I would've at least called. Aunt Lil always checked up on Ma.

I was at the shop working when the desk phone rang—normally I don't handle that, but the guy that worked the desk had stepped away, so I grabbed it. There was a woman on the other end of the line; she was hysterical—worse—she wanted to talk to me.

"Tony—that you?" she pleaded.

"Ah, yeah. Who's this?" *This better not be a joke.*

"It's me, Tony—Aunt Lil," she shrieked. I looked behind the customer service counter for the stool to sit on because it could only be bad news, but there was a big binder for car parts on top of it, so I had to stand.

"You . . . come home . . . something happen." She was sobbing between her words. "It's your Ma."

"Tell me, Auntie! What happened?" I suddenly felt sick.

"No, Tony—you come home right away," she cried.

"Okay, okay—I'll leave right now—wait! Did you . . . Did you call an ambulance?"

"*Sì*—they here now."

"On my way," I replied, but I was worried I might've been too late. The drive to my childhood home seemed like it took forever. The worst thoughts popped into my head, and I worked hard to shake them away. Maybe I overreacted—I lit a cigarette to calm my nerves and took a deep drag, but it did nothing.

Once I reached my old neighborhood, I saw the Victorian style homes with the three floors stacked, one on top of another; some were brick, while others had aluminum siding, red being the most common color. The lots were the size of postage stamps, and many had no lawns at all. Some homes had striped awnings over the doorways, some had flags flying, usually the Italian flag since most residents in our neighborhood were immigrants. It was like stepping into another world from the rest of Pittsburgh.

An ambulance and two police cars were parked right outside the house; their bright blue beams flashed across my retinas. Within seconds, I felt as if I couldn't breathe right—like I was having a panic attack or something. I gripped my steering wheel tight and double-parked since there was no time to find an open spot on the narrow street. I was close enough to see that Uncle Sal was waiting on the front door's threshold, and I wondered why he wasn't staying warm inside. As I stepped inside, something seeped into my nostrils. An odor permeated from my home—Ma's home. Before I could ask what happened, I was overwhelmed by the most putrid odor I'd ever smelled. In that moment, I knew why he was standing out in that cold.

The bile had built inside my mouth, and I gagged. I wretched in front of my own home—in front of Uncle Sal. He patted me on the back and waited for me to stop. Once there was nothing left, I looked at Uncle Sal and wiped my mouth with my sleeve. We stayed silent—no words could take away this blow; instead, I looked at him with an ounce of hope that maybe there was some mistake—but he shook his head to say, "no."

"Tony, you come to our house and let-a the police take care of this. I had to pour your Aunt Liliana a double shot of Strega for the nerves—you know, medicinal purposes. She's resting now. Come . . . I pour you some too. You feel-a better," Uncle Sal said as he pulled his hands out of his trouser pockets from having tried to stay warm.

"Shouldn't I . . . uh . . . go in?" I asked him as I pointed toward Ma's row house.

"No, Tony—it was enough for Liliana—she identified your ma. I don't-a want you to remember her that-a way—too much! I tell police that you're next door with us if they need you." Uncle Sal knew I was squeamish.

"Yeah—okay," I mumbled.

I somehow found myself sitting on the sofa at the Russo's home, staring at one of their lamp shades, which was carefully covered in plastic to protect it from dust, only I didn't have any recollection of walking into the room.

Aunt Lil, who was still, was curled up on the sofa in a small ball, unable to wipe the scene etched inside her memory bank. She twisted her handmade embroidered handkerchief over and over—it must've been how she felt inside. I don't know who was more shaken-up, Auntie or me.

I leaned forward, my arms propped up on my knees, and whispered, "Auntie—what happened?"

Her eyes were bloodshot and swollen—petite hands continued to work on the handkerchief—she seemed to have aged greatly from the last time I saw her, just three weeks ago. The lines on her face appeared deeper, especially the ones around her mouth, as they pulled her mouth down into a frown. The wisps of hairs that were normally tied neatly behind her head were now frazzled around her face.

"We just got-a home from our trip, and we unpack when I notice too quiet at your ma's house. You know—we live next door for thirty years—thirty! I know your mama's habits—she liked to play-a music in afternoon time—it made the house not so quiet. I hear nothing . . . nothing." She let out a loud sob. "So, I call-a her—but she no answer. I start to worry—think maybe Aurelia with you—but I still worry. Salvatore asked if I smell something when we went upstairs—but we not sure what. We get the key to let ourselves in . . ." She exhaled with a cry attached. "We knew before we go in—we knew." She motioned for Uncle Sal to pour another Strega, and she sipped it as if it would give her the courage to go on. But then I motioned for him to pour me another too. Maybe it would lessen the blow. Auntie cried softly into her handkerchief; it was too hard to relive.

Uncle Sal took over for his wife and said, "I called the police— we knew Aurelia had to-a be upstairs because she wasn't on the main floor. Liliana thought she should-a go upstairs—you know—not right for a man to go upstairs. I told her it didn't matter—but you know your aunt—stubborn."

She covered her eyes as if to blind herself from what was to come.

"Liliana found-a your ma in the bathtub." He choked while he dabbed a tear and hung his head.

Auntie raised her hands as if talking to God, "It's all-a my fault!" she wailed. "I should have insisted she come to Italia with us! I should not have-a taken 'no' for an answer." She agonized over her visit. Uncle Sal moved to sit next to Auntie; he rubbed his heavily calloused hands on her chunky arms to console her.

"Auntie—this isn't your fault. None of this would've happened if it weren't for Pops leaving! Ma shouldn't have died alone. It's *his* fault!" I seethed as I paced the floor, placing blame where it belonged.

"No, Tony," said Uncle Sal while he shook his head. But I gave him a contemptible look that said, "Don't you dare try to defend what Pops did to her."

This was the worst day of my life, so I made a beeline for the liquor. I wanted to numb myself, but my head was spinning before I could tap the stuff. I rubbed my head out of habit, checked the neatness of my ponytail, and said, thoughtfully and slowly, "I'll never forget this day as long as I live."

The three of us shuddered as we thought back to that day that marred each of us differently—when I vowed I wouldn't die alone. No person should be found rotting—I'd do whatever it took to be sure that wouldn't be my fate too.

Auntie cleaned up the coffee station where the sugars, stirrers, and creamers were kept—as if it needed it. It was her way of thinking . . . always throwing herself into work. Uncle Sal rubbed his bum knee and took in every detail of my story. Without my saying a word, they knew I needed their advice.

"I know what you're afraid of—but you—you a young man,

Tony. I try to remember—you-a forty? You have time to find-a someone else," said Auntie gently.

I scoffed. "Are you sayin' I shouldn't go after Ivy?"

"That's exactly what I say." She raised her eyebrows. She wasn't one to mince her words.

Not what I wanted to hear. I looked at Uncle Sal for a reaction; he looked away, and I knew where he stood based on his silence.

"Just give up that easy?"

"Do what you want, Tony," she said as she shuffled away to wait on the happy couple who wanted dessert to go.

"What about Sloane?" I inquired when she finished ringing up the tiramisu.

She sighed. "Tony—there is more to this story—why was Sloane so angry she make-a you drive her home?"

"I don't know," I replied as I shook my head out of pure disbelief. "I didn't do nothin'—I'm not sure why she's actin' that way. Katya probably put her up to it."

"Hmmm—you give it some thought, Tony. Maybe you remember later," she said with disapproval.

I furrowed up my eyebrows with irritation. "Are you sayin' it's *my* fault?"

"You watch the way-a you speak to your aunt, Tony," said Uncle Sal. "You need to be respectful even if you not agree."

"Thanks for the espresso, but I gotta go find Ivy. She probably went to her sister's place," I said. Then I gave them a nod goodbye, too agitated with their lack of support.

As I left the coffeehouse, I noticed that large white puffs of snow had freshly covered the ground in the parking lot, so I reached behind the seat in my truck for the snowbrush. I ran through different ideas in my head, but it seemed best to avoid calling her—*she won't pick up. I'm sure she expects me to go after her.* She'd want an effort. Besides, where would she go? That's why she moved in with me in the first place; she had nowhere to live, and she wasn't able to keep up with the cost of living alone after she shacked up with that bozo ex-boyfriend. She'd have to have a steady customer base to make it as a nail technician, and that obviously hadn't happened yet.

Now, I needed to think long term. Ivy was the easiest to get back. It's simple—give her what she wants, and she won't be going anywhere again.

Looks like I'm settling. . . .

CHAPTER 5

THE FRANCHISE

As I opened my eyes and looked at my bedroom ceiling, light streamed inside, between the cracks in the blinds, and I struggled to determine whether it was real or a dream that finally had me put my foot down with Tony. *God—I don't want to get up!* I was in a twilight state, spaced-out and floating. I blinked a few times to adjust to the brightness of the room, sat up in bed, and stretched while I gave it serious thought. What day was it, anyway? As I stared at my freshly painted aqua walls, I breathed in the mouthwatering aroma of bacon sizzling on the skillet. Yeah—it was real; no more putting up with their crap.

After I gave no thought to which cookie-cutter uniform skirt to wear, I threw on my charcoal-colored sweater and gathered my books to stuff into my backpack. I took school seriously and prided myself on my organizational skills. Mom disagreed and insisted my room was messy, but I knew where everything was located—at least that was my argument. Okay—so maybe it was structured chaos. Some of my friends had rooms that could be considered biohazards, but I never left food lying around; it was one of my own rules, and that's gross anyway. She had more of an issue with having left out belongings that, according to her, needed a home. Most kids got grounded if the parents had issues with them, but Mom never punished us. She repeatedly said that we were self-maintaining; we already knew right from wrong. She was right.

My eight-year-old sister and I were old souls and knew the minute we crossed the line. Anything she considered bad karma was meant with stony silence—a tactic that was effective. Upon experiencing Mom's momentary silence, we felt her disappointment, and nothing could have been worse. She did not have to do or say anything. It wasn't meant to be punitive, but reflective. Mom's tactic was so effective that I cannot remember the last time it happened for me. Now Noelle, she was as close to angelic as humans come, so she was always in the clear. Beyond two incidences as a tot, I cannot recall Noelle ever doing anything wrong. What could I say? We were different.

I caught my reflection in the mirror. *Bibíyo* said that I had what she called that "alluring" look. The debate was coming up with Rayce Rinehart as my opponent—I'd have a better feel for whether he liked me or not once we had more interaction. Yeah—I thought he was into me. And if he wasn't, it was his problem.

"Girls, time to eat!" bellowed my mom from the bottom of the stairs so we could hear. There was a practical need for volume since earbuds were normally stuffed into our ears.

Noelle peered around the corner of my room from the hallway, and asked, "Sloane, could you help me carry my project downstairs?" Noelle's complexion reminded me of the soft petals of a white rose; her hair was the color of copper woven with hints of strawberry-blonde. She had Dad's good looks—resembling the fairer Mackenzies far more than the darker Gáspárs. Sometimes, I called her Little Strawberry.

"Yeah, let me take my stuff down first," I said as I attempted to counterbalance myself with my weighty backpack.

Noelle thanked me with her toothy smile. She had made an Egyptian sarcophagus out of heavy-duty paper and took an entire week to decorate it outside of art class. The palette was rich and deep, and I was sure she did her share of research on the internet for authenticity's sake. "Do you like it?" chirped Noelle.

"I'm impressed!"

We headed downstairs and entered the open kitchen. My favorite part of the ninety-year-old house was each vaulted ceiling. Radiators lined the outside walls of the adjoining great room, giving the house character. Dad was sure the house had been refurbished at least once, but we were stuck with a retro '70s look, at least for now. The kitchen was a mossy green with red brick backsplash and Formica cabinets; the walls had old wallpaper designed with an autumn leaf theme. Dad had a blueprint with a cool looking update, but with Mom's transition into a new career and Dad's lingering illness, the design concept was forgotten.

Breakfast was quiet—I guess it was anticipation that gave it a thickness—like a sultry summer day. I poured myself a mug of steaming hot coffee, leaving plenty of room for a ridiculous amount of cream and sugar. I glanced over at the couch where our red Basset Fauve de Bretagne, whom we named Rouge for her red coat, was nestled in a ball next to my overnight bag. It had been three days since I had left Tony's house, and I had no intention of going back. There was no way he'd pick me over Ivy—I just wanted to see who he'd choose. Now that I've had time to chill, I know he'd never pick me anyway. I may not have liked Tony, but he and I coexisted more like roommates rather than father-daughter prior to Ivy's arrival. At least it was tolerable before Ivy.

As I watched Noelle eat a bowl of cream of rice, I was struck by our oppositeness once again as I noticed she wore one of her many multicolored headbands with her hair flowing down to her waist. She wasn't going to let her school uniform hamper her creative individuality. Each bite of cereal was neat and meticulous as her long alabaster fingers held the spoon with nothing less than grace. We joked Noelle was likely royalty in another life. "Sloane, can you please pass the almond milk?" asked Noelle as she looked at me with her sage-colored eyes.

"Sure," I answered. "Do you have piano tonight?" Then I took a bite of bacon. I didn't want to think about the unpleasant task that was only a school's day away. I forced myself to eat something, but I picked at my food more than anything.

"No, that's on Wednesdays," said Noelle as she dabbed her mouth. "You okay, Sloane?"

"I have butterflies in my stomach," I said as I looked over at Mom, who was uncharacteristically quiet as she slathered almond butter onto bread, making our lunches. Her mouth was slightly drawn, her eyes heavy from lack of sleep.

"Try not to think about it, Sloane. There's always a small chance he won't show up tonight," said Mom, unconvincingly. Mom sucked at lying.

I licked my lips, getting the bagel crumbs off, and said, "I can't do this anymore with him, Mom. I'm not going with him," I said as I crossed my arms like a pretzel. But I could see the worry etched in her face, likely over the games they concocted over the past years.

Mom cocked her head, repositioned her weight from one hip to the other, then said softly, "Tell him how you feel. I'm not sure what else you can do."

Just then, Dad came downstairs in baggy sweatpants,

slightly hunched over as compared to the day before. His face was lackluster, and his wit was all but gone. "Katya, do you need me to drive the girls to school?"

I contemplated Madame Sinfi's insistence that my father would die. The thought ate away at me. On the one hand, I've never seen Dad so deteriorated; however, on the other hand, Madame Sinfi couldn't guarantee that her prophecy would come true. They were subject to change based on decisions. I trusted *Pápa*'s judgment that Madame Sinfi was a gifted seer, but there were always variables. I'd sit on the prophecy for now.

"No, no, I've got it. Why don't you rest? You had such a bad night," Mom said with concern. Her movements were mechanical as she scanned the kitchen for anything left undone. It was as if she didn't want Dad to lift a finger.

"What did the lawyer say about visitation tonight?" asked Dad as he partially leaned on the countertop for support.

Mom slowly closed the dishwasher, took a deep breath, and said, "Well, we went over several scenarios that might take place—it's hard to say how he will react. There's a chance that he'll be relieved on some level—that it's the excuse he's been looking for all these years to forego visitation."

Mom pulled out the chair to sit and motioned for Dad to have a seat, too. "No, thanks—I have less pain standing than sitting."

"John, you're not getting any better. Why don't we go to a doctor and see if we can at least get a diagnosis? That way, you'll know for sure what you're dealing with," suggested Mom. The strain had become more apparent as Mom's face, which was normally cheery, was now somber.

Dad, just then, clenched the top of the chair so hard his knuckles turned white, and he hunched over more than before, unable to speak. He must have had a wave of pain. Mom covered her mouth with her hand as we both watched help-lessly. Once Dad was able, he said, "No, I want to try to heal this on my own; whatever they do, I'm sure it'll be invasive."

I cringed at the thought. I agreed it wasn't much of a solu-tion, but the stress of the recent events was accumulating like the dirty, bulldozed snow at the mall. I looked at Mom. Her abilities had saved Dad's life a few months earlier—but she had rules—and one of them was that the person had to ask for help, so I guess Dad didn't ask this time.

I glanced up at the clock and ran up the stairs to brush my teeth for school, but my mind chatter would not stop. It was *my* life—how could Tony argue? Besides, why would he want to fight it? He wasn't interested in me anyway.

———

After Mom dropped Noelle and me off at Mountain Ridge Academy, Noelle scampered off to lower school, consisting of kindergarteners to fifth graders, while I crossed the adjoin-ing covered tunnel to the junior high school. It was one of those amenities that came with a school made from money; it kept us warmer, especially on a windy day like today. It was hard to believe I was nearly in high school. Most of my time was spent building up my resume for college. Honors courses, STEM club, volunteering as a tutor, and extracur-ricular activities with leadership positions gave me the edge. Mountain Ridge was a coed private school where academics were emphasized, but the importance of having well-rounded students took a close second.

Three years ago, as a little fifth grader, rumors flooded the halls that my all-girls school was to merge with the all-boys school due to rapidly changing tuition costs. Coed schooling was never a consideration for Noelle and me, but there really was no choice. Along with the change in my school came the male gender, and with that, everything changed—including the fact that I now cared what I looked like. My uneasiness turned into enthusiasm when I saw the opportunities before my eyes. Suddenly, boys had become interesting, and even a bit of an enigma. I noticed they thought differently than girls.

They were very physical in that they enjoyed pushing each other around in the hallways when the teachers weren't looking. They seemed to have their own language. It was common for insults to fly from the more aggressive ones and insulting one's mother was the big daddy of all exploits. If the insults emotionally hurt any of the students, it was not as obvious since the survival tactic was to laugh it off. Girls were more unobtrusive but just as vicious if anyone threatened their territories. Not all teens were prone to this kind of behavior. It was as if males and females were two different species, and yet, I found myself intrigued.

I snapped out of observation mode and maneuvered effortlessly into academic mode, where my mind moved swiftly to determine which books I needed as I stopped by my locker.

I found it easy to make pit stops between classes because one of my best friends was two lockers down due to our systematic alphabetized locker assignments.

"Hey, Sloane! What's up, my sista from another mista?" asked Zariah Baker as she rhythmically half sung/half chanted her question. Being so musically inclined, something I was not, Zariah could turn almost anything into song. She handed me my last year's science notes back from yesterday and smiled from ear to ear, where I noticed her magnificently chiseled cheekbones and brilliant teeth. Zariah should do toothpaste commercials.

"You're in a really good mood—care to share?" I asked as I selected my books for the morning and wondered how she managed to maintain such a consistent level of good mood and, on occasion, surpassed it.

"Well," she said melodically, "you are looking at Maria from *West Side Story*!" Then she curtsied in her plaid navy and gray uniform skirt.

"Shut up!" I gasped. "You got the lead role? How is it I'm just finding out now?" I said with raised eyebrows.

"I know—right? I am beyond excited about this. It's going to be so much work, but soooo worth it," she said with flair. "In fact, years will go by, and my fans will still talk about my amazing performance." She sighed, swinging on my open locker door.

"You know they will!" I said as we savored her victory. We walked down the hall together and headed to Mrs. Schultz's algebra class. "The musical is at the Playhouse Theater in Uniontown, right?"

"Yeah—and get this—I'm the youngest to be cast as a lead character at that theater!" said Zariah, jumping up and down.

"No way!" I joined in her celebratory cantor but to a lesser degree because Zariah was so much more animated than I. I was much more reserved. She must have been ridiculously talented to have achieved celebrity status at such a young age. "What did your parents say?" I asked. "I mean, that's a pretty intense role for a fourteen-year-old girl!"

"Fifteen—and they're over the moon about it," said Zariah as I grabbed her wrist to get her to take it down a notch. Zariah was held back a year; a learning disability played a role in her struggle academically, and sometimes I forgot she was a year older. I made a point to avoid the entire subject, even though she spent part of the school day in a classroom with a teacher I never had, so it was pure speculation on my part. Or was it? *It* told me she had a learning disability even though we never once spoke of it. It wasn't important to me, but I knew on some level that it deeply bothered her.

"Sloane—what?" Zariah caught my intentional gesture as I motioned with my eyes to the dark-haired Rayce Rinehart, who strode toward us with enough attitude to stop a plane in mid-air. For starters, he was taller than me, so that meant he automatically made the short list for suitable guys. *But that's stupid—I don't need a guy.* His hair was always tousled in his eyes, his tie was always too loose, and his pants were always too low on his hips, so the principal was continually after him for uniform infractions. I liked the fact that he disregarded the rules. Rayce was his own person, and I admired it.

As our proximity closed in, Rayce flashed his cornflower-blue eyes at me, then his mouth curled up, ever so slightly, to reveal a self-assured smile, and he said, "Are you ready to get your butt kicked in English class after winter break?"

I huffed and said, "They're going to have to scrape you off the floor after I've finished you, Rayce," as we looked at each other, close and comfortable.

"We'll see about that!" he said as he continued to glide along the hall with all eyes on him from the students within range. "Don't forget—you're going up against The Franchise." He smirked. I shook my head in disbelief.

"Rinehart—you're so full of it!" said Jason Pham, giving Rayce a friendly shove, but Rayce returned the favor, only a little harder, and they both laughed. Jason was normally quiet—a guy that said very little—but in Rayce's presence, he seemed to come out of his shell. I thought it possible that part of the reason for Jason's quietness was out of the need to be invisible. Acne seemed to have that effect.

Zariah may as well have been invisible. It wasn't that she was forgettable as much as Rayce was intriguing. "What was *that* all about?" sang Zariah with an air of brashness this time. "I didn't know you knew him?"

We walked until we reached the intersection of the hallway, where we normally parted ways. Zariah and I were never in the same class. "Debate—Rayce and I are going against each other in two weeks."

"You sure you can handle him?"

"It's gonna get heated, and I'm really sure I'm gonna like that—you know me, always up for a challenge. He's like a spicy jalapeno—and no, I don't really know him that well."

"Ha! You coulda fooled me, girl!" She chuckled as she entered her mysterious classroom, the one that we never spoke of, and parted ways until lunch.

I rounded the corner at lightning speed and entered Mrs. Schultz's algebra class, which was one of my favorites. Math and I understood each other—we agreed to always be straight-forward, rational, and balanced. There was never any sec-ond-guessing, interpretation, or subjectivity. Why couldn't Tony be honest like math? Math never lied or played games.

Sitting down at my desk, I leaned over to my backpack, pulled out my pencil pouch, and, as I unzipped it, I could see a palm reach out in my peripheral vision. "You're kidding, right?" I snapped at the boy who sat next to me and had given me nothing but trouble since the first day of class.

"Come on, Barzetti. You know you live to supply me with pencils," said Hutch Markovic, smooth, like a decadent Alfredo sauce, but I couldn't take my focus off his full lips consisting of a prominent divot in his upper lip and a butt crack in the middle of his chin. He ran his fingers through his unkempt dirty-blond mane that I'm sure hadn't seen a comb in some time.

"How many pencils does one person need?" I retorted. "I'm done, Hutch. Don't ask again," I said as I attempted to focus on what Mrs. Schultz was writing on the SMART Board.

"Is there a problem, Miss Barzetti?" asked Mrs. Schultz while tucking a tissue into the bottom of her sweater's sleeve.

"No, I've got it handled," I said as I shot Hutch a look that said, "Lay off." If the class hadn't known of my discontent, they certainly caught wind of it now.

"Fine then—let's continue our discussion of quadratic models," she said as she pushed up her glasses onto her nose and continued with writing the example.

After my momentary attempt to refocus on my favorite subject, I heard the all too familiar crunch of material that was my backpack, and I knew Hutch was up to no good. I gritted my teeth, but this time, I took my foot and mashed his hand against my backpack—not enough to do any damage, but enough to make a point. Our teacher must have been deeply in Mathland as she was unaware of the continued argument behind her back.

"Okay—okay!" mouthed Hutch as he looked up, finally getting that I meant business. I realized my harsher-than-normal reaction had everything to do with my task with Tony, but I was fed up with stupid behavior. He rubbed his knuckles, but I knew I hadn't hurt him—Hutch tended to overreact anyway. Finally, he relented, and reached into his own backpack, where he kept at least a dozen or more sharpened pencils he had nicked from me. He opened the flap and gasped at the sight inside that pouch of his pack. He took the pencils in his fist, and he pulled out a handful of perfectly broken pencils—snapped right in half—as if each pencil had been broken with a tiny saw to make each break so clean! Hutch's jaw dropped, and for the first time in his life, he was astonished.

I stared along with him, and soon half the class was gawking at the strange sight. Anyone who sat within earshot knew Hutch enjoyed his pencil fetish, so it was clear that he had not broken his own collection—not when he looked dumbfounded. He enjoyed attention, but this was not of his own making. Soon there was a low rumble of discussion in the class—enough to capture Mrs. Schultz's attention.

The tiny teacher swiveled her head around, bun and all, and exclaimed, "Mr. Markovic—why did you break all of your perfectly fine pencils? That will not do, will it? Get yourself a new one so we may continue." She hadn't noticed the precision of the breaks, but then again, her eyes were not too good anymore. Mrs. Schultz must have been pushing seventy—at least that's what everyone said. Anyone older than thirty seemed old to me.

Hutch walked slowly over to the garbage can and tossed all but one pencil, since it was salvageable. He mumbled something about there being nothing wrong with the pencils last period, and as he walked back to his seat, he looked pale and disturbed.

I wondered.

He stopped badgering me for the rest of the class, which was quite unusual.

The strange events of the morning were a welcome distraction from the dark cloud that hung over my head, but the pencil incident, and especially Hutch's reaction, was unsettling. After grabbing my lunch bag out of my locker, my stride carried me to the cafeteria in no time, where I sat down at the lunch table and played with my food. The cafeteria ladies had decorated the space with a winter theme. Large white paper snowflakes hung from the ceiling, moving whenever the heat kicked on, and light strings were draped around fake green wreaths in the middle of each table. Yvette Appleton, who had joined the duet of Zariah and me since her arrival in Pittsburgh in fifth grade, dropped her lunch tray next to me.

"Hey Sloane," said Yvette, eyes wide with admiration, which reminded me of a needy baby penguin reliant on its mother. As she leaned in, too close for my comfort, I could easily see the freckles that covered her beak.

"Yvette," I said like a mother, "I'm okay with being friends, but sometimes you get into my personal space, and that doesn't work for me."

"Oh—I didn't—I didn't mean to do that," she replied with a blank look.

Be more tactful, I told myself. "It's nice to hang out with you, but I'm not comfortable with you—or anyone for that matter—sitting so close to me."

She hung her head slightly, as if she'd disappointed me. I could see that she didn't get it. I wasn't about to explain to her that I could feel her neediness because her aura was over-lapping my aura to such a high degree. I don't like neediness.

She nodded her head and awkwardly added, "Okay, Sloane—I'll watch that."

"Thanks, Yvette—so—how is your debate research coming along?" I asked, changing the subject since it was obvious that I had wounded her.

Taking a bite of her overpriced and overprocessed grilled cheese, Yvette said, "It's okay, but I'm not really looking forward to it. I'm not much for conflict," she confessed, ill-at-ease. "What about you, Sloane?" She leaned in again.

"Yvette—space," I reminded her with a gentle caw as she retracted. "And, to answer your question, I love it. There's nothing more satisfying than arguing a valid point, especially one that you firmly believe." Zariah then plopped herself down across from us.

"Hey Yvette—don't you have a basketball game tonight?" chimed Zariah as she dipped her pita chip into hummus. "I thought maybe I'd stay after to watch—you know—support my girl."

"Um—you don't have to do that, Zariah. I'm not very good—I'll probably warm the bench most of the time anyway." Yvette sighed. She had been searching for something she liked, but she had a hard time finding it. Her parents assumed she should be just like them.

Bubbly, Zariah countered, "Don't be silly. I'll be there."

Yvette wrinkled up her nose and said while rubbing her hands up her blonde pixie cut hair, "My parents insist on sports, but I don't know why. I'm not athletic—come to think of it—I'm not sure how I made the basketball team anyway."

"That's because they don't turn anybody away," I added, but Zariah kicked me under the table to shut me up.

"They don't?" questioned Yvette, grimacing. "Are you serious? I thought I had finally accomplished something!"

Zariah, velvety like, added, "Of course, you accomplished something; you made the team. I'm going to be there after school, bench or no bench. Sloane, you *are* coming too, right?"

How would I remedy this situation? My knack for candor, on occasion, was poorly timed. "I can't. I'm going to blow Tony off."

"What?" toiled my friends in unison.

My girlfriends were aware of my continued disparity over my relationship with my biological father, and now his dumb girlfriend, but I had to supply an update regarding this past weekend.

"So—can you do that? I mean, can you actually tell him to go away, and he will?" asked Zariah as she buffed her apple against her blouse.

I sighed. "I don't see why not. It's my life, after all," I said as I rubbed my lips together.

Yvette's eyes popped out of her head. "Dude. You *are* serious, aren't you?" I nodded. "You *have* to let us know what happens."

"Yeah—text us right away. It's not like this kind of thing happens every day," said Zariah, with her apple shining brilliantly. "Aren't you nervous?"

"I would be," added Yvette. "My parents don't let me decide anything—if fact, I don't think they care about what I want."

Zariah sang, "You think?" with sarcastic undertones.

"My parents get it—I mean, they've seen firsthand some of the messed up decisions he's made—like that time he took me on a boat with his friends while they were drinking," I said.

"What?" exclaimed the duo.

"And Ivy—she's just as bad. She hates my mom."

"Seriously?" asked Yvette. "Why?"

"My dad thinks because she's usually happy—some people don't like happy people."

"Sure," said Zariah with a blank look, but I knew Zariah was not one of those kinds of people.

Once Noelle and I got into our used Ford Explorer for the ride home, the butterflies started again. I wanted to bypass this dreaded moment—it would have been easier to just send him a text.

Considering it was December, the temperature neared sixty degrees and, coupled with the sun shining, much of the snow melted. It seemed Earth had refused her cyclical winter death and clung to autumn. Our driveway was clear, which would allow my task to be made simpler, rather than having to battle the snowstorm that was raging just a few days earlier.

After we pulled into the garage, I could hear the gleeful yips of Rouge. Our arrival home, especially Mom's, meant a good scolding from Rouge, as if she barked, "Where have you been? I've been waiting by that window, worried sick!" She was meant to be for Noelle and me, but she's been at Mom's heels since day one. Dad always jokes that Rouge would take a bullet for her, considering she inadvertently rescued her from a breeder that we suspected was abusive.

After the volume decreased to a rhythmic panting, Noelle asked Dad with concern in her tone, "How are you feeling, Dad?" while hanging her coat on the hook opposite the door.

"Not well," said Dad, who was generally a man of few words, especially as of late. He gave each of us a gentle touch on the shoulder since a hug was out of the question. Dad guarded his abdomen with fervor over the last few days, and it was clear to me that he had worsened.

While leaning over the chair, he said, "Katya, could you juice some vegetables for me? I don't think I can do that anymore." He grimaced. "Do you mind adding some turmeric too? I read it's supposed to help inflammation."

She summed up the situation and bit her lip. "Umm, yeah—is that the golden-colored spice?" Mom looked distant. "Do you think he'll have Ivy with him?"

"He better not!" I dropped my science book mid-sentence.

Dad said, "It isn't a smart move to bring her, especially since Ivy was the catalyst for Sloane leaving . . ." But his voice trailed off, as he had to stop speaking in order to rest.

"I ran through every scenario I could conjure up in my head about what might take place today, but I've only succeeded in making myself crazy," said Mom, pulling lettuce out of the refrigerator. "I'm not sure how he will react, nor am I sure what will happen with the vacation he wants to take over Christmas break."

"Mom, we do know what's going to happen with the vacation," said Noelle, bright-eyed. "Remember when we took the walk in the snow, and I saw the pretty lady in a gown? She said Sloane wouldn't have to go."

Mom nodded. "I do remember, sweetie. I just hope it isn't wishful thinking—that's all."

"Mom—you don't believe me." Noelle pouted. I could tell she was hurt, so I snuggled up to her little face and kissed her on the cheek, and she kissed me back. Her hand found mine, and I knew this gentle soul, without doubt, loved me deeply. Noelle, only eight years old, was very gifted, just like all the Gáspárs. Her specialty was communication with beings on the other side.

"Sweetie, it's not that I don't believe you—it's just that I don't want to be disappointed should Sloane have to go with those two." She shuttered at the thought. "It's such a worry."

She wrapped her peaches and cream arms around Mom's waist and said, "It'll be okay, Mom." Noelle brimmed with confidence, and she took her backpack upstairs and started on her homework.

In the distance, I heard the loud diesel engine of Tony's truck—the volume increased as the gap decreased, and my nervousness tripled. A memory flooded back to the time when I was five years old—he showed me how to make grilled cheese over the gas stove—authentic grilled cheese, not the rubbery cheese sandwich Yvette was eating earlier. At the time, he said I was old enough, but he warned me to remember to shut it off when I was finished. From then on, I was responsible for making my own lunch. He had then gone back outside to work on one of his many projects. I had spent yet another Saturday alone, inside his house, where I was expected to not only entertain myself, but cook for myself. I wasn't even in kindergarten then.

"Remember," said Mom as I could feel the warmth of her hands holding mine, "tell him what you want, but keep it short." I nodded.

The volume of the engine was sufficiently loud enough to suggest he was in front of the house, so I made my way to the garage. As the truck revved to climb the incline of the driveway, I heard a deafening *whoosh, whoosh* in my ears that seemed to synchronize with the engine. I then realized it was my pulse that I could hear—I don't think my heart ever pumped so hard.

Light blinded me for an instant. I heard a squeak as the garage door opened fully; then I headed toward him. I no longer felt like a fourteen-year-old girl, but a protective pit bull. I wasn't going to wait to be on the defense; now I was on the offense—I was the attacker.

He stayed in his truck with it running and rolled down his window. I could smell the stale cigarette smoke. Tony made eye contact for a split second and said nonchalantly, "Sloane, what's going on?" as if he didn't have a care in the world.

I approached my prey with a swift, short rush. "I don't want to see you again," I snarled.

His mouth hung open for a moment, but he recovered and said, astonished, "What? You mean, ever?"

Within charging distance, I stepped closer and snapped, "That's exactly what I mean."

What came next was the most troubling of all. My prey should have submitted on some level, but instead, his lip curled up on one side.

Tony let out a stifled laugh, shifted the gear into reverse, and shouted out the window as he pulled out, "I'll see you Friday, Sloane."

I seethed with loathing as the sperm donor left without so much as licking his paws from what should have been an emotional bloodletting.

After I updated my pack on the moment, we all took time to recover from what could only be described as abnormal.

Fervently, I said, "I swear he was almost laughing. He should be devastated." My hair shifted to the other side of my head as I ran my fingers through it.

"He should be—I would have been if I were in his shoes," Mom said, shaking her head, "and all that worry for thirty seconds of nothing."

Coming back to his discomfort, Dad braced himself against the frame of a chair; after the wave passed, he said, "This isn't over—he'll be back. Then what happens?"

Mom and I looked at each other, both expecting the other to answer Dad's question. Neither of us could.

I pulled out my phone and sent a group text conversation to Zariah and Yvette. I hoped they could see a perspective in this situation that I couldn't, but somehow, I doubted it; I was the perceptive one.

CHAPTER 6

PUNCTURED

My fingers rhythmically hit the numeric keypad on my laptop as I mechanically progressed through the motions of the mathematical calculations. *Tap, tap, click, click. . .* The desk in my home office was large and made of cherry, with drawers on each side filled with paperwork from clients. A part of me was enthusiastic about what I understood to be a professional transition—the death of my muggle job, and the birth of the magical job—but a part of me remained apprehensive. I had one muggle client remaining, and that client was clear that my job would end once her company moved to the East coast. This meant I was the sole provider for my family, a provider with a flimsy foundation. I had just started my healing practice; John was deathly ill, and Tony was Tony.

Tomorrow, Tony will arrive to pick Sloane up for "his weekend," but she has no intention of going with him. I couldn't understand his reaction, and in fact, I'm not sure I ever understood him. Tony was crafty, but he was also very lazy. A few weeks of Sloane refusing to visit Tony would likely get old quickly, so I was optimistic that this problem would disappear on its own.

After I hit the print button, I smelled freshly churned out paper, organized them into stacks, and pushed the stapler down every so often.

"Mom!" yelled Sloane from the kitchen. "Where do you keep the red sprinkles? I want to get this baking done before *Grey's Anatomy* starts." Normally, a Thursday evening was just another school night, but tomorrow was the last day of school before winter break, and the girls were making cookies for Noelle's class party. I heard one of them open a cupboard, and then came the sound of several cookie sheets tumbling onto the floor. *Crash!*

"Whoops!" Noelle giggled.

Kerplunk, sounded the stapler. "Let me think—they are in the cupboard over the stove," I shouted to make my voice carry to the other floor. "Maybe," I said to myself. I didn't have time to look since I was on a deadline to get this work wrapped up.

Bang, bang went the sound of the cookie sheets getting restacked. "Mom—I don't see them," Sloane complained loudly.

John slowly inched his way into the kitchen, hunched over, at the same time I had arrived, and he said, "Katya, can you help me get upstairs, I can't—can you keep it quiet—I just can't stand any noise. It grates on my nerves."

Noelle's face dropped. "Daddy, I'm sorry," she said as she went to his side, as if she could help him with her tiny little frame.

"Dad—I didn't know," said Sloane apologetically.

John's expression was grim, but he shook his head as he understood. We weren't accustomed to John requesting silence, so we knew collectively he must have felt awful. "Yes—okay—let's get you upstairs," I said, holding his arm, which was once chiseled with muscle, now thin due to his daily deterioration.

"Girls." I looked at them and no further communication was necessary. They continued their baking with great care.

Once we were upstairs, John attempted to find a position in which he could be comfortable, but it seemed to elude him. "Can you close the blinds?" he asked. "I need darkness."

"John—I'll take you to the hospital. You don't have to suffer like this," I said with my hands across my nose like a teepee.

"No—I don't want that," he said. "As a kid, I went through more tests than you could imagine, and that was all by the age of twelve. I don't want to see the inside of a hospital—I've had my fill. They don't have the answers—they'll just address the symptoms."

I sighed. "Alright but if you change your mind, just ask." I wanted to honor his request; after all, it wasn't my body. I didn't want to be that person who thought she knew what was best for everybody. "Can I do anything else?" I asked as I closed the blinds.

"Can you keep Rouge out of the room?" John asked. "She doesn't understand," he said, as he started pacing the creaky wooden floor of the bedroom.

I scooped her up from one of her many beds and said, "C'mon, girl. Let's go bake cookies." She looked at me with her big, expressive brown eyes. Rouge knew John was sick, and her antidote was to lick him; it was her way of taking care of her pack.

After I closed the door for his needed quiet, Rouge and I joined the girls for some bonding time. Noelle was already covered in flour, and Sloane asked, "Did you separate the eggs?" while she measured the sugar.

"Yes, Sloane, I did, but I'm not sure I did it right," she replied.

"Hmmm—let me see," I said as I made my way to the kitchen island. I saw two bowls with an entire cracked egg in each. A huge smile covered my face, and I said, "Sweetie, did you separate the eggs to keep them from fighting?"

"What? What do you mean, Mom? It said to separate the eggs, so I did."

I chuckled, and then said, "You *did* separate the eggs, didn't you?" My precious, literal daughter had just made a rough week a little lighter.

Sloane said, "Good one!" But Noelle still had no idea where she went wrong. After we explained it to her, she, too, was humored.

After we simmered down, I said, "Girls—Dad didn't mean to be short. It's just that when someone is in intense pain, little things that normally don't bother someone, now seem unbearable."

Noelle, now somber, said, "We know, Mommy." Then she put her pale little hand on top of my hand while Sloane came over and kissed me on the cheek. They were synchronized like a clock.

That night, John could no longer endure sleeping in a bed from the pain of stretching his abdomen, but he preferred the ease of the reclining couch. There were times when he paced the main floor and, at other times, he did not move from the spot on the couch; the great room became his sick room, where it was dark and quiet. It was where I watched him go from bad to worse.

Somehow, I managed to sleep, which was nothing short of miraculous, all things considered. The last day of school, prior to winter break, was normally a time of relaxation, but nothing could have been further from the truth.

While I waited in the long line of cars to pick up the girls from school, my mind was in fifth gear as I searched every aspect of why Tony behaved the way he did. Nothing made sense to me. He had made no attempt to communicate with either Sloane or me, and that looked like a gaping hole in the land of common sense. He had not asked the most basic question: Why don't you want to see me? Tony either knew the answer or simply did not care, but the latter was the most perplexing. It was unfathomable that a parent did not care about his child. If I gave him the benefit of the doubt, and he knew why Sloane was opposed to seeing him, then surely, he should want to mend the relationship and start a conversation. He should begin asking the right questions with the hope of heading toward healing the relationship, but instead, he acted as if it were a joke.

I inched my way up the line and saw Noelle's best friend, Darby Kóbór, with her mom (and my best friend), Bianka Kóbór, waiting for her youngest child, Elijah, to be escorted to the car rider line. The Gáspárs and the Kóbórs had a long history together when both our families lived in Hungary, but it was our Romani culture that bound us through the darkest of times in Europe. A chill ran up my spine for a moment as I thought of my families' past, but I shook it off—one issue at a time. Bianka was more than my best friend; she was more like a sister, and some people thought we were related since our dark features were so similar.

I opened my car window and waved. "Hi, ladies!"

Bianka leaned over to my window and whispered, "Anything new since yesterday?" She scanned the line to make sure no one nosy could overhear our conversation.

I inhaled deeply before answering, "John walks like he's eighty years old—everything hurts, including his joints. He's so weak. I'm not accustomed to seeing him this frail."

"Still won't go to the hospital?" Bianka asked, with hope flecked into her eyes. I shook my head no. "Can't you work on him? You saved his life once before." The line moved again. "Darby, honey, go stand on the sidewalk and wait for Elijah for me. I need to talk to Aunt Katya." Darby complied willingly.

"Hmm—you know John—stubborn cookie." I sighed. "He's determined to do this himself and, if he asks, I'll facilitate if I'm allowed, but you know how this works."

She stared at the ground as if contemplating. "Do you ever tire of explaining that you are not the source of the healing?"

"All the time—because the minute I don't clarify is the time I'm accused of acting like God," I said as I moved my stiff neck.

"Can you"—she raised her eyebrows—"sneak a healing?"

"Bianka, seriously, no—that's not an option." We moved forward again. Bianka was beyond amazing but didn't inherit her ancestors' sixth sense abilities and, therefore, did not necessarily understand. "You know—the Law of Freewill—I can't force my will upon another."

"Right—got it—what about Sloane? Tell me she's not going!" Bianka begged.

"No, she's not going, but I don't know what to expect from Tony. We can't help but wonder if he'll bring Ivy, which could really heat the situation. Sloane can't stand her," I reminded her.

Bianka nodded. "Yeah—and she has a mouth on her. Didn't she use some choice words about you not too long ago?"

"Uh-huh—I don't recall ever behaving that way, even as a child. I wonder what she was thinking?" I said, as if I could figure them out. "Anyway, the lawyer said he can't force it, but that doesn't reduce the gnawing anxiety."

We scooted up another spot, and Bianka said, "What can I do?"

I saw Noelle standing on her pickup spot on the sidewalk, never moving, for fear of breaking a rule, and I said, "I might need a fun diversion for Noelle over break."

"Say no more. Darby would love Noelle to sleepover." Bianka kissed me on the cheek. "Call me after that toad leaves tonight."

Her gaze was drawn to Elijah as he exited the school holding another kindergartner's hand. The school had a buddy system for the children in the special needs class.

———————

Upon our arrival back home, Sloane was especially agitated, but I suspected it was her defense mechanism kicking in. How ironic that she would deny her father when all I ever wanted nowadays were my parents—now both dead.

Sloane paced back and forth prior to his arrival as she made a draft with the friction of her frame. She stopped in her tracks and sniffed the air while she focused her eyes and said, "Do you smell that?"

John and I paused, took a whiff, and I said, "Is that—is that cigar smoke?"

John scrunched up his nose. "I don't smell anything."

I added, "It reminds me of someone . . ." But the answer escaped me, and I became distracted as the sound of the truck approached. No matter. I looked up at the clock and noticed how timely Tony had become in the last week; so—he *can* tell time. Sloane forged forward, leaving the house without a coat, slamming the door in her wake. I caught a glimpse of the gray clouds that had gathered at a strikingly fast pace; when only minutes earlier, the sky was clear and crisp.

She meant business. John and I looked at each other and wondered what Sloane might do if provoked. We stared out the window, watching Sloane lean into the trajectory; she was not about to compromise.

My eldest barreled up to Tony's open window where words were exchanged; whatever was said prompted her to throw her arms up in the air. The interaction didn't last long.

She hurried back toward the house. Then, Tony yelled out his window loud enough to hear inside the house, "See you when I get back, Sloane," sickeningly self-assured. Then he finally backed out of the driveway.

Poor Sloane was livid. Her face turned red, and her fists were clenched while she pushed open the cracked door to the house. "Unbelievable," she muttered under her breath. "They're actually going on vacation—that's how important I am. My message didn't cause even a slight blip in his life— he's not even bothered in the least. Didn't I tell him *twice* I don't want to see him again?" she seethed but seemed to be talking to herself.

Boom! The three of us flinched with fright. It was deafening . . . like a gunshot. Only Tony didn't speed away like he normally did. No—he barely moved at all—in fact, the truck had rolled to a stop.

John's expression changed and, for a few seconds, he had forgotten how ill he was as he pointed toward the truck and said, "Serves him right. Looks like Tony just blew a tire!" John and I snickered, but Sloane was deadpan. She didn't seem to care about the tire.

Noelle, whom we always kept tucked inside away from Tony, came down from her room for an update. Her eyes were wide and her voice shrill. "Sloane—are you okay?" asked Noelle. "What was that loud noise? It really freaked me out!"

"Ask Mom," Sloane said, distracted but unsettled; then she walked into the great room and plopped onto the couch. She simply sat and remained quiet. Even her sister, who was normally very soothing to Sloane, could not get her to come around.

Our adrenaline rush from the shock of the sound started to ebb; I went to Sloane to run my fingers through her auburn hair, and then around her ears like when she was a little girl.

She found it soothing, both then and now.

John leaned over the counter to relieve his taut abdomen since he had straightened up to watch the Tony encounter, and said, "You were right, Noelle. Looks like he'll be gone for winter break; we won't have to deal with him for a while."

Noelle was not the least bit surprised. She said, "I know." And that was the last time I ever doubted Noelle Gáspár Mackenzie's ability to channel.

Sloane started to come around and said, "Did you see how he acted? It looked as if he was trying to bite his lip to keep from laughing," she said stoically. If ever I had any doubt as to the wisdom of the decisions that were made, his utter disrespect for his daughter clarified spot-on.

Noelle peeked out the window and said matter-of-factly, "He's still changing the tire," then glanced at Sloane.

Sloane, mildly amused, said quietly, "Good. That's good."

The snow started to fall and the wind picked up; the weather mirrored the icy way he treated his daughter—cold and cutting.

———

Over the course of the next few hours, the wind whipped as it bounced off the hills of Uniontown, relentless and fierce. Tony had since been long gone and no trace of his presence in the street remained, minus the icy chill lingering in the air. Sloane seemed to recover quickly and settled into her winter break with little effort. The girls got a Wii as an early Christmas gift from *Pápa*. We normally celebrated Hungarian Christmas, at least the gift giving part, in early December. He figured it would be well-used over the course of the next few weeks, and the timing could not have been better since I now dedicated my time to caring for my ailing husband.

Since the girls were downstairs, John was upstairs, as a result of the noise-level factor, which I monitored. Excitement over a video game victory could accidentally cause their hooting and hollering to rise above an acceptable decibel level for John to have some peace.

John, now too weak even to call for me, awaited my frequent check-ins, since he had sequestered himself to the bedroom. I noticed he had stripped down to boxers and shirtless—uncharacteristic of a cold winter day, especially since we couldn't afford to keep our home warm.

"John, what's going on?"

He was in utter agony; he cringed and leaned inward toward a standing fetal position and gasped, "Can you . . . get . . . the scissors?"

I was stunned at his condition, but floored by his request. "Yeah, of course, but why on earth do you want scissors?" I wasn't about to argue.

He couldn't speak for a short time, so I stood for a moment, deeply concerned but silent, since a wave of pain must have torn through him. When he had the strength, he said, "I need to cut the waistband."

I wasn't following. *Now he's destroying his clothes?* I asked myself. I didn't want to seem insensitive, but I couldn't grasp his logic. He saw the look on my face and said, "I . . . can't stand . . . anything touching my skin."

Oh my God. We were now at a whole new level of illness that was beyond my comprehension. I shook my head in utter disbelief, fanned my hands out as if calming the situation, and said, "Oh—okay—I'll be right back." How else could I possibly respond?

I ran downstairs to the kitchen where I nearly plowed Sloane down, and she said, invested, "Mom, what's wrong?"

"Dad is bad—really, really, bad." I covered my mouth and said, "I'm beside myself." She didn't question why I had scissors, either, but she noticed them in my hand.

Sloane had a knack for handling whatever came her way—born with oodles of common sense, and asked, "What do you want me to do?" My daughter had a look of fear in her eyes—uncharacteristic of her. I thought perhaps she wanted to tell me something, but then, didn't. It must've been my imagination.

"I want you and Noelle to quiet your minds, get into the zone, and ask if I need to take Dad to the hospital. Try to detach from emotion—it's possible you may not get an answer," and I was off, like a bullet, back upstairs. I knew they would take care of my question since there was no way I could get clear intuitive information when I felt like a nutjob. Maybe I shouldn't have asked that of my two girls, but I felt I had no choice. I promised myself I would honor whatever John wanted, but that didn't mean I couldn't strongly suggest the hospital—he was well beyond a doctor's visit, especially now.

I returned to the dark bedroom and almost tripped on Rouge, who was too far below eye-level to see when rushing around; luckily, she dodged me, and I said, "Here, I can cut the band."

"No-no—I got it," he insisted and made his shorts looser. He put his arms up to shield his abdomen, creating a safe circumference between his tummy and me. John didn't want me near his core, but I didn't understand what skin had to do with it. He used to have a six-pack, but now he was approaching gaunt.

I let out a soft cry. "What do you need?"

"Just keep Rouge out; close the door." He groaned.

I pulled the door shut to the gloomy room that reminded me of what mammals do when they are dying. They look for a quiet, dark place in which to be left alone while they die.

Rouge had awaited my presence out in the hall and, when I left John in our room, she looked at me with eyes that said, "What did I do?" I kissed her on her furry head and whispered, "It's okay, Girl. Daddy didn't mean anything by it." *Center yourself. Too much is riding on your ability to keep things together, Katya.*

During my training as an intuitive, I cultivated my daughters' abilities. Noelle was advanced, and Sloane did not always trust herself; combined, they were hot cocoa with marshmallows. Noelle was able to tap into the other side almost effortlessly, but Sloane, being older, took more patience to get the psychic wave. Gentle, to not disturb their concentration, I sat down by the girls while they worked and said, "Anything?"

Sloane spoke up first, which meant she was currently feeling confident. "You'll know when to take Dad to the hospital, but the time isn't now." I took a deep breath and let the message seep in.

"Okay." And I looked at my youngest daughter.

Noelle said, assuredly, "Dad's not going to die now. It'll be alright, Mom."

I couldn't read the situation with John, but I was able to read my daughters at any given time. If I was a squeaky violin prior to that moment, the girls' harmonious string section tuned me to the proper pitch. Now that we were symphonic, we could take the cues from the conductor. I just hoped we were well beyond the exposition.

Sloane added, "Mom—there's one other thing," but she hesitated. There was something she didn't want to tell me. "You need to call *Pápa*."

I looked up from having had my eyes closed for longer than a moment, and said, "Huh—are you serious?"

Noelle added, "Mommy, we *are* serious."

My *pápa*, Django Gáspár, was deeply involved in the old ways of my people. He was a *vrezhitóri*, who used magical elements in nature for reasons like healing, but if he felt threatened, he was capable of putting the hex on anyone he deemed deserving. That was where *Pápa* and I deeply disagreed. Our philosophies created a rift in our relationship on more than one occasion. The most recent event was years ago when he was babysitting young Sloane. I came home early from work, sick, and caught *Pápa* engaged in *fármichi* in front of my impressionable child—after he promised to keep that side of him dormant. After it blew over, I knew that was how he was raised, therefore, he saw no issue with it; however, I didn't trust his judgment after that escapade, so I was hesitant to get him involved.

I had to let it go. *Pápa* meant well—and he loved us—I never questioned that for a moment. I'd call, but not until I had to.

———

During the next few days, things only got worse. John's illness consumed him, and my worry consumed me. I ate just enough to maintain functional—but only just. Had it not been for Tony's temporary departure, Bianka's phone calls, and my daughters' assistance at every turn, I would have had a nervous breakdown. Everything about my demeanor was robotic and without thought. I never stopped moving: My days consisted of laundry, dishes, checking on John, cleaning, cooking, peeking in at John, taking care of Rouge, groceries, work, and email. I assured myself that the hospital wasn't far, and often thought, *Is John still alive?* It was never ending.

I dashed, for the millionth time that day, upstairs to check on John and bring him some water, when I saw Sloane texting and laughing silently like she did. I loved how her shoulders bobbed up and down when she laughed. It was good to see her smiling again. I walked into our bedroom, and John asked, "Can you wrap this sheet around me? I thought I heard the girls upstairs and don't want them to see me."

He could no longer tolerate even loose shorts. I sighed and said, "Of course." But when I lifted the sheet onto his back, he recoiled in agony. "What? What happened?" I whispered; my brows pushed up high on my forehead. It was as if I had stabbed him with a knife.

John had to recover before he could answer. He closed his eyes and said, "You touched my back."

I was confused. I couldn't imagine what his back had to do with his abdomen, but then again, I wasn't John. "I-I'm sorry! What can I do to make it better?"

"I'm ready," he said.

I braced my hands on my knees since I was leaning toward him, and said, "Oh—Okay—ready for what?" as I hoped he meant ready to go to the hospital.

"Can you try to heal me?" he asked with great care.

I stood up, somewhat surprised, especially after such a prolonged amount of suffering. "Yeah, I'd be glad to try. Are you able to make it downstairs? I'll need to get comfortable—this may take a while." John nodded and wrapped himself in his 600-thread-count toga.

"Sloane," I said, "You and Noelle stay upstairs, keep Rouge with you, and answer the phone if it rings. I'm going to work on Dad. No interruptions short of a fire breaking out."

She nodded, put her phone down, and got on task. This would take massive concentration and a strong presence. It was imperative that I not disturb the Light flow.

John was no stranger to the technique I used and settled into a cozy spot on the couch, well, as much as his broken body would allow. I nestled into John's favorite seat at the end of the couch, where he was laying, and reclined. I dropped my center of gravity and felt the weightiness of my arms and legs, and soon, my torso followed. My hands and feet felt the familiar tingles of the energy that flowed once the energy centers of the chakras opened. Warmth enveloped me, and the place I loved the most was mine. Before long, the current of energy flowed down into the earth, ready to be cleansed, and then it flowed back up into my body, fresh and clean like a filtration system. The stress and worry left me, but I wasn't left empty; I was instead filled with serenity. More divine than human at that moment—aligned with divinity and permitted to vessel healing as God saw fit.

It was like nothing I had ever experienced, but then again, John's life was hanging by a thread. As always, the telltale flash of Light filled the room. I felt every cell in my body vibrate—I could have been levitating. I felt so ether-like, almost electric. It became more powerful, so powerful that I thought my head might explode. I began to wonder if my body could stand the high voltage that flowed through me and into John. There was no need for physical contact; the energy would have been as powerful had John been halfway across the world. Divinity used me as a buffer since most humans couldn't tolerate direct Light, but I was made differently. I was born the healer, so I was wired differently than most people—like a high-tech circuit board from another galaxy. The Light came in waves, perhaps so it wouldn't kill me, but I couldn't be sure.

I asked John, "Can you feel that?" He nodded and became still and calm, more so than he had been in the last week of his torment.

When the Light tapered back for a less-intense period, my

body drifted off into a gentle sleep, and when it revved back up, I just hoped I wouldn't die. The cycle went on for hours.

John, who could still feel the Light, asked, "Can you look at my intestines?"

He knew that I was not only an empath but a clairvoyant as well. I had the ability to see inside of a body when invited. I likened my vision to a camera—I could pan out for a wider view, or I could zone in for a specific view, and could even change the angle of the camera. And no—I didn't look at people naked.

"Hmmm—there's no nice way to say this, but it looks like Freddy Krueger slashed up your intestines with his razor fingers. They look raw, bloody, and inflamed," I said flatly.

John, much more functional now, said, "It's incredible, but the pain's gone—I still feel awful, but I can breathe now."

Fate would not snip his thread of life today.

———

A few days later, John was well enough to join us in the great room, where a fire roared in efforts to keep the room comfortable, since he preferred to remain shirtless, as the idea of fabric against his abdomen was not an option. Sloane stared at John and asked, "Dad, can you move toward the lamp?" with a curious look on her face.

"The lamp—no Sloane—I feel icky. What's wrong?" John asked.

She got up and said, "Hold on. I'm going to get a flashlight." And moments later, she shined it on John's abdomen. "What's *that*?" She gasped.

He looked down while his jaw dropped open, touched his skin lightly, and said, "Katya," stunned.

I tripped over the blanket that was wrapped around my legs, lost my balance for a second, and bolted toward the two of them. Noelle sat paralyzed from fear. I thought I was seeing things. On John's abdomen was a raised, red-hot bulge the size of a softball. "Can I touch it?" I asked, befuddled. I needed to gather data because his body was showing disturbing signs that something was still seriously wrong. The paunch was as hot to the touch as it looked. Something horrific raged inside John's body.

That's it! I can't do this anymore. I looked into John's green eyes and said, "I'm losing it."

"I know, I am too," he said, defeated. After a long pause, he added, "I think I'm ready to go to the hospital."

"Just ask and we're there," I said, greatly comforted that he had finally given in.

Unfortunately, it was time to call *Pápa*.

CHAPTER 7

THE TOWER

It had been a long day, but I was determined to finish the bracelet I'd been laboring over. Nightfall emerged, and the lighting at The Crow's Nest was not as bright as my old eyes would have liked, so I pushed the lamp closer and strung wire through rose quartz, *twisting* and *snipping*. The numbness in my thumb was annoying me. I put the pliers down and rubbed my wrist to get some feeling back; but I felt no relief. I was a metalworker by trade, but I had taken a liking to jewelry design since my younger sister, Jeta, introduced me to the art. We owned a storefront in Uniontown, not too far from where my *nepáta*, Katya Gáspár, lived. We sold our wares, but we also provided Romani services to those who asked. The gift was strong in the line of Gáspár.

"Django," said Jeta, over the Romani violinist playing Czárdás while we worked, "you almost finished? I'm tired and ready for upstairs." She stretched as she spoke. Jeta and I, when alone, always spoke in a hybrid of our native Hungarian, laced with *Rrómani-ship*. She was a good-looking woman, like all Gáspárs, with soft wrinkles and a slightly pointed chin. Her once dark brown hair with traces of red was streaked heavily with white, and she wore it in a loose braid down her back.

As a good Romani, Jeta dressed in solid-colored vibrant skirts down to her ankles. When weather allowed, she wore a bodice with bells, but the coolness of winter and age brought practical matters. Sister often added a sweater. And, as a matter of formality, her head was always covered with a *diklo*. We had been working around the clock since shopping season was ripe with anticipation. Jeta and I were the only ones left since our family had been wiped out in Europe. I thought about my beloved son, Katya's father, Nicolae, every day, but I shook off the sadness as best I could.

"Goulash has stewed all day long—time to rest," she said. I put the tools away and swept my workbench clean from little pieces of wire that had accumulated and doused the incense while Jeta shut off the lights and locked the front door. We headed up to our apartment.

The aroma of my sister's stew greeted us upon our entrance. The inviting scent reminded me how I forgot to eat lunch that day. I turned the knob of the faucet in the washroom to tidy up my work hands, and then I looked in the mirror. My face was engraved with deep lines from weathering, but it was still a handsome face. I kept my beard trimmed short and, surprisingly, there was still a bit of mustache that had not grayed yet. My nose was prominent; my eyebrows were still dark and full. After all these years, I maintained a lean physique, probably from so many years from going without. Django was not taking a chance, so we rationed food.

"I'll get the bread, Jeta," I said as I moved toward the cutting board. The absence of bread at the table of a Romani would not go unnoticed. We had been a team since we moved to America, but we often had little to say since we saw so much of each other. Jeta ladled out the steaming goulash made of potatoes, beef, paprika, and tomatoes. Our food fell into two groups: *baxtalo* or neutrally lucky. We considered foods with strong flavors to be in the *baxtalo* group because it nurtured body and spirit, so Jeta used red and black pepper for *baxt*.

I rubbed my hand again, and Jeta, having noticed, piped up: "You should have Katya work on your hand—she helped Bianka." Just then, the phone rang, and Jeta said, "That's Katya," without looking at the phone. My sister was a *drabarni*; she provided that service to the *gazhe*.

A huge smile covered my face, since my Katya and I hadn't spoken in weeks. Delighted, I said, "Katya! How is my dear one? How is your John?" John was what us Romani people referred to as a *gazho*, a male non-Romani. Typically, a Romani female who married a *gazho* was highly controversial, and it could result in expulsion from her Romani family. It was considered shameful and against our laws. However, with my luck to have any family, coupled with my new tolerant Americanized status, I was willing to overlook *Nepáta's* infraction. She wasn't the first rebel to be born out of the Gáspár family; probably not the last one, either.

"Oh, *Pápa*—I need to take John to the hospital." And she told me about the calamity, but it got worse. Katya also spoke of the jackass, Tony; I was incensed that he upset my Sloane. How dare he!

"Jeta and I should have taken care of him a long time ago!" I said, actually speaking to Jeta. But from my resentment, she knew I wasn't speaking of John; she crossed her arms in front of her, waiting to hear more. We had restrained ourselves on more than one occasion when it came to Tony, and if it hadn't been for Katya's insistence, Jeta and I would have put a tiny curse on the troublemaker—nothing too painful.

"No, *Pápa*! You leave the old ways out of this. Tony might come around, eventually," she said indignantly. I wasn't going to push. John was the priority. "I want you to come with us to the hospital—I'm going to need you."

"What about the girls?" I asked, then reached into my shirt pocket and pulled out the tobacco pipe.

"I'll have Bianka watch them. I don't know what to expect," she raced. "We could be there all night."

"Do you want me to drive?" I asked, but really, I was scared to death of driving. The police knew me by name—apparently, I had a reputation for "reckless driving." So, I got a little nervous, ran a few red lights! I patted my pockets to look for my lighter, but I couldn't find it.

"Hmmm—John can't sit up straight anymore, and I'm afraid the seat belt may cut him where the red paunch sits—it's in a bad place for traveling in a car," she pondered.

"Get an ambulance, Katya," I said, as I knew from experience, health care was better in America. "Which hospital is he going to?"

"Uh—let me ask him," I heard a garbled interaction, and she said, flustered, "He doesn't know—he's too sick to care. And I can't think straight right now."

Jeta said, "Tell her to take John to the White Tower. They'll help him." But then Jeta muttered so Katya couldn't hear, "I'll get the amulets." Then she gave a wink.

"What's that, *Pápa*?" she asked.

I reached for my cap and said, "That white tower—Three Rivers Hospital—but it will be a long ride." Jeta found a spare lighter and handed it to me.

She sighed. "Alright. And *Pápa*—thanks." Then we hung up.

Jeta said, "I will get the salt for you, Django," and she scrambled to equip me for the task ahead. She said, "It's dark—no one will see."

"Burn incense, will you?" I asked. "John will need *baxt*."

Jeta nodded, and I was off, but not before I attached bells to my shoes for protection. I flicked the lighter and lit the pipe when I got outside.

The snow on the ground and the darkness concealed the salt I spilled in a massive circle outside Katya's home—a defensive measure to protect the family from Tony's *bi-baxt*. After I walked into the house, I kissed Katya, but she saw my medicine pouch and said disapprovingly, "*Pápa!* Don't blow our cover, now. They don't know who we really are."

I stroked my beard, took off my cap, and said, "*Nepáta!* I know better than to expose our secret." Then I patted the medicine pouch. "This is for when the *gazhe* aren't looking," I said mischievously. Looking around, I added, "Where's my beautiful great-granddaughters?"

"They left already. Now, where's Rouge?" she said to herself, and found the furry rascal sitting obediently on the carpet, hanging her head. She knew her mama was leaving.

Katya was all over place. She had too many things to do; she ran upstairs. "John, are you ready? The ambulance will be here soon," she said as she rounded the corner upstairs, looking to see if she had forgotten anything.

John insisted on managing steps without help—he was a stubborn man, especially after he caught me gazing at his ravaged body. He moved like he was older than me—deliberate, slow, and guarded. I was appalled—I hadn't seen him for several weeks since he didn't want visitors, but this—this I did not expect.

"John," I muttered faintly, as I was at a loss. It took time, but John finally got downstairs and sat down, as he had to rest.

"Thanks for coming, *Pápa*," he said, and sat awkwardly, leaning back. I walked toward him, making a *ching, ching*, sound with each step, to give him a pat on his arm since he looked so ill.

"Django—are you wearing bells?" asked Katya, stopping to listen. She called me that when she wasn't happy with me.

My bells replied with a *ching, ching*, and I almost ran into her; "Of course. How else will I scare off the ghosts?" Katya gave me a look, but she stayed silent.

The ambulance men arrived, took his vital signs, blood, and gave John fluids through an IV, but they were confounded by his questionable condition. They had never seen anything like it. Lying flat on the gurney was out of the question, so they had to work around his most comfortable position for transport.

"Will you be meeting us at the hospital, Ma'am?" asked the older paramedic.

Katya took her purse. "Yeah—we'll travel behind you?" She kissed John and said, "I'll see you soon. It's going to be fine." He nodded, but I got the sense he was anxious. John was normally quiet, but he now spoke only when necessary.

I was relieved Katya drove, since I wasn't comfortable going outside the confines of Uniontown. We never needed a car when we lived in Europe. "How are you, *Nepáta*?" I asked while I squeezed her shoulder.

"To tell you the truth, *Pápa*, I'm relieved," she said as she hit the brakes for a light. "It's been a heavy burden. Going to the hospital relieves me of the responsibility of keeping John alive."

I fussed with my beard some more while I pondered. "What about his family? Are you going to tell them after they called you a *vrêzhitórka*?"

The turn signal clicked off after she turned the corner, and she said, "No, John doesn't want me to call. It's up to him." But I could tell she was still hurt.

"You know, Katya, it's not an insult—not really. Some of the greatest *fármichi* means great things—you are a Romani—be proud of your magical heritage!"

"It was meant as an insult, *Pápa*. I have never dabbled in dark magic—not ever," she said, indignant. "It's different here than it is in Europe—sometimes there is a Puritanical mindset here."

I added, "They might blame you if he dies."

"Yes, that thought crossed my mind," Katya said, "but John's a grown man."

"I understand, but the *gazhe* might see it differently—might say you should have dragged him to the hospital," I warned. "Some think their way is the best way." I worried about the many weights Katya shouldered. And I wondered what God had in store for her . . .

———

The three of us waited, uneasy, in John's hospital room. I especially hated hospitals—too many hungry ghosts roaming the halls for an unsuspecting host. It was my responsibility to keep them away; I pulled my incense and lighter out of my medicine pouch and lit it. Katya jumped up and said, "*Pápa*—no—you can't burn that in a hospital!" She was on edge.

I said, "Why they so afraid of a little smoke?" and rolled my eyes. I had to do something—sitting there for hours, unprotected, was foolish, so I placed satchels full of protective herb concoctions, to repel ghosts, around the room.

Nepáta said, "Just so long as you stay out of trouble, *Pápa*." We learned there were five murders the day before—five—all of which were shootings. Since John's life force was still with him, he was pushed aside like small potatoes. John slept lightly until one of the many garbed in a blue tunic uniform entered the room. Finally.

The *gazho* carried a clipboard and asked many questions. Sometimes, he said, "Hmm," and liked to gnaw on the end of his pen. He asked John, after putting rubber gloves on, "Can I take a look at your abdomen?" He agreed, but he was apprehensive. *Gazho* said, "I need to press on it." I wasn't sure who recoiled more, John or Katya. Poor John—he clenched his fists while he pulled the sheet on the hospital bed. *Gazho* continued, "We'll have to run some tests before we know more." Then he left the room. But that was only the start.

Two more in the same blue tunics came in and asked questions, reworded, but basically the same. And they also insisted on pressing on the angry red ball of pain that used to be John's stomach. But it didn't end there. John flinched in silence while Katya scrunched her hands up over her mouth. It was hell.

That routine continued on for hours. New *gazhe* repeated the process, and some even came in multiple times, taking notes and talking amongst themselves, as if we weren't there. Sometimes, they tossed out possible diagnoses, but they missed pieces of the puzzle. It was Jeta who warned me about that. She said *gazhe* focus on the body, but they forget about the spirit. Without all the pieces to the puzzle, it was like putting duct tape on a leaky pipe—a short-term repair.

I lost count of how many tunics poked John—some of them were older and some younger. I pulled *Nepáta* aside and asked, "Why so many? They all ask the same thing. Don't they listen?" But I didn't care if they heard. I didn't trust them.

"*Pápa*, some of these doctors are residents," she whispered as she raised her eyebrows, hoping to shush me.

I said, "Residents? You mean some don't live in America?"

One of the residents overheard as he glanced my way, then looked away. Katya said, "No, *Pápa*. Resident means—uhhhh—an apprentice doctor."

"Oh," I said, as it all made sense, "so they are little doctors." But the residents didn't like that either. "Where is the big doctor? Boss doctor?" Just then, a blue *gazho* walked in—he was older than the rest and wore a toupee on his head. These questions had gone on too long, so I asked him, "Are you the boss doctor?"

He adjusted his glasses, blinked, and said, "I'm Dr. Massic, the attending physician." But he wasn't interested in me; he wanted to speak to John. Katya gave me a look again. Sometimes, she forgot that I was the elder of the family.

Dr. Massic saw one of my protective satchels around John, picked it up like it was dirty underwear, and moved it aside. "That's mine!" I said, but he acted as if he didn't hear me.

Katya wrapped her arm around mine, turned her face so the *gazho* couldn't hear, and said, "*Pápa*—this is not the time." What could I do?

The boss doctor poked John some more, which really seemed unnecessary since the wound was so obvious. Then he said, after he twitched, "I'm going to order a CT scan. That will give me an idea of the size of the protrusion."

Within a few minutes, a blue tunic *gazhi* gave John orange liquid. She said, "Drink this, and then we'll wheel you down to radiology, where the technician will take a picture of your abdomen—it's similar to an X-ray."

John said very little, but he was agreeable. He, too, wanted to know what anger brewed inside his body.

Once the pictures were developed, the boss doctor called Katya out into the hallway to show her the results, but I followed anyway, *ching, ching.* He adjusted his glasses, twitched again, and used a pen to point to the computer screen. I wondered why he was twitching so much. Maybe it was a nervous habit? I forced myself to focus on the screen instead. The boss said while he circled the dark mass on the screen, "I don't know how John is still alive—I've never seen anything quite like this. The mass is the size of a grapefruit." He looked at Katya, who gasped, and he continued to ignore me as he said, "He should be dead by all medical standards."

I chimed in and said, "I know why. My granddaughter is a powerful *drabarni,*" but he didn't listen.

"I cannot offer a medical reason as to how John survived. It is unprecedented, at least from my experience," he said, perplexed. He wasn't comfortable with the unknown. He twitched and said, "We need to find what material makes up the mass. The answer to that will determine whether or not John will have to undergo major emergency surgery tonight."

I watched *Nepáta* wrap her arms around her waist for comfort. She was petrified, and I along with her. I just hoped we could trust him, but it was not in the Romani nature to trust *gazhe.*

The three of us reentered John's room where the boss doctor intentionally left out the part about the survival bit. I could see why. Throughout the evening, the residents continually came in and out of the room. John's case was so fascinating to them. But this time, a new tunic appeared, but he was not as young as the others. Massic, after another twitch, said, "This is Dr. Levi Rosen. He's a colorectal surgeon and will be monitoring your case with me."

After another painful examination, Rosen, an unassuming man, the kind you pass on the street without looking at twice, said, "We're going to have Dr. Massic continue as your attending physician for now, unless there is a need for major surgery, in which case, I'd be the surgeon."

John asked, "What do you think it is?"

Massic said, "We are going to have the radiologist perform a procedure where she will insert a CT drain into the protrusion in order to attempt to drain it. Currently, there is only a resident radiologist on duty, so we will need to wait for the chief radiologist's arrival. It may take some time."

The *gazho* didn't want to guess. John was unusually quiet, and Katya fidgeted with her hands. I thought I'd call Jeta to give her an update and ask her, without Katya listening, to talk to the spirit guardians and respectfully ask for help. *Ching, ching*; I walked down the hall while the blue tunics looked on. I wondered why they were so plain, like a glass of tepid tap water.

It wasn't easy to find a pay phone, not like it used to be. No—I didn't trust those cell phones. News Lady said they have cameras and can find someone, like on a map. I don't understand how, but it doesn't matter. Not taking chances. Django didn't want to be hunted like an animal. Next thing you know, they'll round up my people and gas us. No—not Django—I got this far on instinct. *Oh, over there—by the elevator. Good thing Django's got change—no credit card for me!* Like News Lady said, "Stay off the radar." Don't have to tell Django twice!

After the pay phone ate the coins, Jeta finally answered, "Hello." She sounded winded.

"Jeta, what are you doing?"

I heard the sound of a lighter *flicking* repeatedly. Jeta said, "Having problems catching mugwort—I don't think it's dry enough." Romanies used a combination of dried herbs for protection and for visions. Sister was preparing for our sacred ritual. "Ah, well—I'll fix it. How are things?"

"Not good," I said, and gave Jeta the news on John.

Flick, flick. "I'll get the guardians. Tell Katya I called Bianka too. And Django?"

"Yes?"

I heard a sniffle. "Kisses from *Bibíyo* Jeta."

Jeta was worried—not a good sign.

As I headed back toward John's room, his door opened, and the tunics rolled him away. *Ching, ching, ching;* I quickly tried to catch up with them. Luckily, I'm a spry one! Once I caught up, I asked Katya, "Where we going?" I looked at the hands on my watch that told me it was close to 3:00 a.m.

She wrapped her sweater tightly around her. The tower's halls were icy cold. She said, "The radiologist is here. What did Jeta say?"

"Jeta is making the arrangements on her end," I said, smelling antiseptic in the tower's hallway. *Nepáta* acknowledged, but she looked tired, with dark shadows under her drooping eyes. We walked behind John far enough for me to ask, "How is he holding up?"

She whispered, "He's scared."

The *gazhi* radiologist, who had probably been sleeping just an hour or so earlier, explained, "We're going to deaden the skin with a topical solution and, using the CT scan, insert a long plastic tube into John's abdomen where we will allow the matter to drain into a bag, assuming it is an infection. If it isn't, Dr. Rosen will have to perform emergency surgery."

They had already moved John to a surgical table under an array of bright lights; he struggled to lie flat in a face-up, vulnerable position. I was overwhelmed with pity as he turned ashen white. There would be no anesthesia for John—my poor grandson. I held his hand for a moment—*Nepáta* squeezed his hand—but they ushered us out. Blue tunics wanted to get started. To my dismay, John groaned loudly as they applied the topical solution.

Nepáta and I are the only ones in the waiting room—thank goodness! We drew no attention, and each of us worked for the same mutual purpose, but alone. To the untrained eye, Katya appeared to be resting her eyes while seated, but I saw something different. Colors bloomed like an artist's palette, brilliant and unyielding. It reminded me of the beautiful brazen skirts that dancing Romani women displayed when twirled about. Color filled the room and moved through the walls into the area where we left John. Space didn't matter— Light couldn't be contained.

A good *vrezhitóri* created sacred space, so I spilled salt around Katya and me in a large circle. No harm there, it could be vacuumed up. After having arranged the talismans and crystal grid around the waiting room, I summoned the guardians telepathically. Katya seemed to be a million miles away—focused. Jeta burned the sacred herbs, since I dared not. Django waited patiently for the vision granted by the guardians—at first, it was fuzzy, but then it became clear. I saw a long, winding road that extended so far, that no end was in sight. The next scene was a bridge over water; this meant a huge transition riddled with emotion. I then opened my eyes at the same time Katya opened hers. The clock ticking on the wall revealed we had been in ceremony for over an hour, but it had seemed like minutes.

Moments later, the boss doctor entered the waiting room and said, "John is resting. The procedure was successful, but he has a raging infection. The radiologist suctioned out large amounts of pus; the bag connected to the drain will continue to collect it, but he is very ill. The good news is that there will be no major surgery this evening." Boss paused, like he was holding back on telling us more.

I asked, "What is it?"

Katya sat on the edge of her seat. "Do you know what's wrong?"

Boss *gazho* twitched. "We don't have enough information just yet to know the cause. Your husband's case is quite unusual." Again, he stopped. "Did either of you experience a flash of light during the procedure?"

"What do you mean?" my granddaughter asked.

"Was there a power outage or a light anomaly? Something unusual?"

Katya looked at Django; the look that said, "Not a word."

She shook her head. "Uhhh, no, we didn't notice anything strange."

"Must have been limited to the operation room, then," Boss mumbled.

Katya fidgeted with her sweater. "Do you know how long John will be hospitalized?" She wasn't going to let the boss doctor go until she had more information.

I noticed he had a blue shower cap over his toupee and wondered how he kept it on. He said, "First we have to get the infection under control, so I'll guess a week, but that could change. We are giving him the strongest possible dosages of multiple antibiotics, but he's not out of the woods yet."

"Come with me. You can see him now," said the boss.

I breathed thanks to the spirit guardians for their intervention. We followed Boss down freezing hallways, deeper into the belly of the place where *gazhe* cut people open. How would John recover in such a sterile, cold place?

John's face told of great anguish—he was shaken and pale when he normally had ruddiness to his complexion. Katya was upset when she saw his condition, but she tried her best to hide it. She said, "It went well, John," but his discomfort was so great that Katya treated him like a fragile egg.

His eyes were bloodshot, and his face strained. John said, "The topical solution did nothing. It was so painful." I wondered if he would get any sleep that night.

We stayed with John a little longer, but he insisted we go home to get some rest. I left a satchel with him, and he nodded as a means of thanking me.

I decided to keep the vision to myself; it would only trouble my *nepáta*. There was still hope, but the bridge over water was an ominous omen. Would John survive?

Maybe.

CHAPTER 8

THE EXPERIMENT

Lick, lick, lick. Why was my hand tickling—and wet? It stopped—I must be dreaming. I heard *sniff, sniff,* but near my face. I felt a cold, wet nose on my cheek! "Hah, hah, hah!" I laughed straight from my belly. I opened my eyes so big and found Rouge trying to wake me. "Girl—that's enough loves." But I had a hard time being serious with my cute little dog. She was so happy. It was her way of telling me, "Time to wake up, Sleepyhead!"

I rolled over on the bed to see my best friend in the whole wide world, Darby Kóbór, starting to wake up in a tangled mess of golden blonde hair. She was the pickle in the middle. Sloane was on the far side of the bed, fast asleep. That was what Sloane liked best about break—sleeping in—but I decided I wouldn't be like those lazy teenagers when I grew up. Rouge had other plans for Sloane and went in for a sloppy kiss. Then Sloane put her arm over her face and said, "No, girl. Go away." Rouge didn't even care, and she kept nudging, licking, and sniffing my sister. The ruckus fully woke Darby, who sat up and said, "Get her, Rouge!" And my pup got so excited and wagged her tail, clapping against the nightstand every time she wagged left.

But Sloane was cranky—she liked her sleep, and she commanded, "Get the dog out of here."

Darby looked at me and said, "Is she serious?"

I nodded and said, "C'mon Rogue. Let's go see Elijah," annoyed that my big sister was no fun in the morning. I tried to get Rouge, but I wasn't very commanding, so Darby snatched up my vivacious puppy, and we headed toward the kitchen. We tried to giggle as quietly as possible, but we simply found Rouge too adorable. I loved that Darby found Rouge as fun as I did. Auntie's kitchen looked like a delicious green apple, crisp green with hints of white. The appliances were stainless steel, which made it so easy to clean off our fingerprints and Rouge's wet nose splotches. Darby and I would pretend to film HGTV commercials in the kitchen like the "after" shots of home makeovers. I love being here with them!

Elijah sat at Auntie's kitchen table with his sippy cup and his ankles crossed. He was swinging his legs forward and backward, forward and backward, with his eyes zoned in, straight to the TV. He liked anything that moved, especially electronic devices like cell phones, iPads, and computers. *Dora the Explorer* was his favorite cartoon, but he especially liked the monkey, Boots. "Boots" was one of the few words he could say at six years old. My mom said I spoke a lot more when I was six. Elijah had darker hair, like Auntie, but he had big gray eyes, instead of her dark brown ones.

"Good morning, ladies," said Aunt Bianka, in her fuzzy bathrobe, as she flipped pancakes. Auntie had taken off from her family business over break to take care of the four of us cousins. *Pápa* had taught us that it was normal for Romanies to own their own businesses, and Auntie was no different; she owned a used car dealership. *Pápa* had always said that Romanies, a long, long time ago, traded horses, but over time turned to selling cars. I'd rather Auntie had a bunch of horses to sell; that would be so fun to see all those pretty horses! But dealing cars was traditional for Romani men, yet it seems we broke all the rules, anyway. That's how Tony met my mom, through Auntie's business. She used to shop at Tony's auto shop to repair some of the used cars they bought to sell all fixed up until she realized he was ripping her off. I wasn't sure what that meant. "Breakfast is almost ready—have a seat." She yawned. "Where's Sloane?"

"She's still in bed, being lazy," I said as I looked at Darby, and we laughed some more.

"Teenagers," said Darby as she pretended to disapprove, and I smiled. We liked to act older.

Elijah, who was an early riser, had already finished breakfast, so Aunt Bianka shut off the television. He picked up one of his man-dolls, babbled to it, then ran to the corner of the kitchen, turned his man-doll face out, and babbled as if someone was standing there.

"There he goes again!" said Darby. "Why does he talk to nobody?"

I thought he was a cute little kid, but Darby didn't always think so. Elijah ran to the other side of the kitchen and repeated the babbling with his man-doll, but I was too busy eating my pancakes, soaked in syrup, to pay attention. Just then, the phone rang, and Aunt Bianka turned off the stove and answered the phone in a serious tone: "Katya, how's John doing?" And then she looked at me since it was Mommy.

Daddy! I hoped he was feeling better. She motioned for Darby to look after Elijah, but she just made a face. Auntie kept the phone in place with her shoulder and said, "Uh-huh," as she scooped food into Rouge's bowl. "Can he eat?" she asked, but she shook her head to tell me "no" and mouthed "too sick." "Does he want visitors?" After she listened to my mom's response, she whispered to me, "She said 'later.'" But then she went down the hallway to speak to Mommy, so I didn't hear any more of the conversation.

Elijah brought his man-doll to me and said, "Play," but then he ran away again and babbled some more.

Darby said, "He's so annoying!" and continued to chip away at her pancakes. Then she said, "Too much syrup."

"You have too much syrup?" I asked Darby, shocked because we loved drenching our food with sweet stuff.

"No, I mean Elijah had too much. He's going to bounce off the walls now," she said and rolled her eyes. But as I tried to zone Darby out, something moved and caught my attention.

Elijah headed toward the space that seemed to move and started babbling again. Only this time, I didn't think he was acting like a silly little kid—he was actually speaking to someone. I looked away with my eyes because I could see better when I looked at something boring, like the tabletop. It helped me to concentrate, and he became clear as I got into my mode. The little boy looked like he could be Elijah's age, only he was able to speak in sentences.

Addressing the spirit boy, I said in my mind, "Do you play with Elijah a lot?"

He looked at me and said, "All the time, when he's not busy doing other stuff."

"What's your name?" I asked, and that's when Rouge saw him too, but she just stared.

"I'm Enoch," he said, smiling.

"Oh—I'm Noelle, Darby's friend," I said.

He nodded, "I know."

"Well, it was nice to meet you," I said, since I didn't know what else to say; but then he disappeared.

Clink, clink, clink, and Darby tapped her fork on her plate, "Hey! I'm talking to you, Noelle. Sometimes you don't listen." I had to switch gears from the see-through Enoch to my muggle friend, Darby.

"Sorry—I must have been daydreaming again," I responded. What could I say? I didn't want her to feel bad. Just then, Auntie entered the kitchen and said, "Where's Elijah?"

Darby's eyes got big, and she said, "Oh, Mommy, I forgot," but then got off her chair quickly and said, "I'll go see what he's up to." I could tell Auntie wasn't pleased, but she wasn't angry either. She came back a minute later and said, "He's sitting on his bed with the sheet pulled over his head, playing on his iPad."

"He's going to ruin his eyes," Auntie mumbled while she loaded the dishwasher.

I waited until I wasn't interrupting and said, "How's Daddy?"

"Oh, right, I got distracted and meant to tell you. Your mom said he's really weak—but wants to see you and Sloane. She said it would cheer him up." But I could tell she was worried.

I felt sorry for Auntie—she looked so tired, so I gave her a big hug and said, "Thank you for everything." I don't think she was used to being thanked, and she hugged me back. "I would like to see Daddy—when he's ready."

"Okay, Peanut. Why don't you see if Sloane is up?"

I loaded my dishes and said, "I'll go check," and headed to the bedroom, but Sloane was already up and texting. "Who are you texting?" I asked.

She glanced up and barely heard me enter the room. "Oh, hey Noelle—it's Zariah. Her texting is happy-go-lucky even this early in the morning—unbelievable."

I laughed. "Sloane—it's eleven."

"Dude—like I said—it's early!" But then she remembered

why we were here and said in a serious tone, "Have you heard any news about Dad?"

Picking out my clothes for the day since we packed for several, I said, "I think he's really sick. Auntie didn't actually say, though." But I trusted my gut feeling.

Just then, Auntie stuck her head in the door and said, "Sloane, can you keep an eye on Elijah? I need to take a shower. It looks like we're going to visit your dad today."

"Yeah sure," she said. Then she pushed down on the bed with her hands and added, "Is this a Tempur-Pedic mattress?"

But she was already walking away, and I heard faintly, "Maybe—I think so."

Rubbing her chin, Sloane said, "Hmm—I have an idea," but she left the room without telling me.

A few minutes later, Darby and Elijah came into the room and sat on the bed, but it didn't take long to start bouncing. We were getting wound up and slap happy—it was the first fun day we had on break. Pretty soon, we were fully jumping on the bed, and Elijah let out a cute and funny squeal. In walked Sloane with a glass of white wine, and we all stopped jumping, except Elijah, because he was in his own little world.

Darby said, "Sloane, *what* are you doing?" I said nothing because I wasn't about to cross my sister.

Sloane had a big smile on her face. "Haven't you ever seen the Tempur-Pedic commercials where they have a glass of red wine sitting on the mattress and people bouncing up and down and the wine doesn't spill?"

"Yes!" we said in unison, and then we laughed hysterically. "I think we should see if that actually works," said Sloane, "only I couldn't find red wine, so we'll have to settle for white." We pulled off the blankets and the sheet to make it more real—we wanted to see the actual mattress, just like in the commercial.

Elijah had lost interest and wandered out of the room. It was probably best that he wouldn't jump too high, anyway.

"You two can test it out," said Sloane. "I'll stay on the floor— I'm too tall, anyway. I'll hit my head on the ceiling."

So, Darby and I jumped, hooted, and nearly cried from laughing so hard! We couldn't believe the glass didn't spill, so we jumped harder to give it a fair test. "Nobody is going to believe this. I'll use the video on my iPhone to get the proof so we can show everyone at school," Sloane said, pleased with herself. Darby and I thought Sloane was the coolest.

Sloane was looking at the screen and said, "Hold on—no way," and her smile was replaced with a scowl. "I can't believe it."

Darby and I took our howls down a couple of notches; and I managed to ask, "What's wrong, Sloane?" But we kept up the jumping. We couldn't seem to get the glass to tip.

I could see her eyes scanning the screen and she said, "How did he get my phone number?" but her face turned scarlet with anger.

"Who, Sloane?" asked Darby, who was now really concerned.

She had that look that only Sloane could get when super aggravated, and she said, "That Hutch Markovic!" But then she clammed up—too furious to speak—as if she were about to blow like the Death Star in *Star Wars*.

And then it happened.

The white wine that stayed full and upright through that ridiculous amount of jumping shattered! Wine and shards of glass showered the room like a firecracker—it was like slow motion—but sticky and dangerous.

We screamed and attempted to cover our faces, but it was too late—our reaction was delayed. Sloane got her wits about her first. Her almond eyes were wide with disbelief, and she put her hands out, as if willing us to freeze. Her voice boomed,

"Nobody move." There was silence for a moment while we heard the shower in the background. "Good—she's still in the shower. You two—scan the mattress for glass until I get back with the vacuum cleaner. I'm the only one wearing slippers." Then I heard her say something about how it was good that Elijah was in his room down the hall.

Darby and I looked at each other with open mouths. "What just happened?" Darby asked. "Do you think the bouncing really broke the glass?"

"Uh—yeah—probably. We did get pretty wild," I said doubtfully. I tried to get over the shock factor, but my brain was way ahead. I needed to speak to Sloane in private, because I noticed weirdness lately, and I usually don't notice anything. Sloane called it "la-la land."

Darby was too preoccupied with cleaning, so the subject got dropped. We were lucky that Auntie liked long showers *and* that she was out of red wine. I never got into trouble, but this was a close first.

———

Bibíyo Jeta came to babysit Darby and Elijah; Auntie felt better about her taking the long drive to the hospital to visit my dad. Mom was already there. Auntie didn't know who was worse at driving, Jeta or *Pápa*. *Bibíyo* Jeta was not actually their aunt, but in the Romani culture, nearly everyone is an aunt or an uncle. Since Mom was born in America, she stuck with certain traditions to keep *Pápa* and *Bibíyo* happy. But she was not "right off the boat" like they were—whatever that meant. When I heard that expression I thought, *I love boats*!

———————

Sloane, Auntie, and I arrived at the hospital, but I felt confused. I was looking forward to seeing Daddy, but the hospital was a little creepy. I sensed I wasn't taking in deep breathes of air. There were gross odors there, and people seemed serious and sad a lot of the time. While we went up into the white tower on the elevator, a lady dabbed her eyes with a tissue and sniffed. Maybe she had a cold. I knew I'd better wash my hands when I got home. Something else I noticed—they all wore the same color blue, and sometimes they wore white, but I wondered about their fashion sense. A little splash of color would have helped.

We passed a friendly man who flashed his gold-toothed-smile while pushing a silver cart full of trays. He hummed and did a little dance while he pushed his cart, and he said something like, "Nothin' like work release." I guessed he was happy to go home after work released him. I smiled and nodded in agreement.

When we were outside Daddy's room, Auntie said, "Your dad may not look good—he has tubes coming out of him, so try not to look if you can help it. Focus on his face, instead, okay?" Sloane and I nodded, but nothing scared Sloane. I held her hand—tight.

First, we had to walk past his roommate, who sounded like he was in a hot tub. Water *swirled* and *gushed*. It *gurgled*—loudly. I tried not to look, but I couldn't help but wonder why he had a Jacuzzi in his room. It turned out that the noises came from a little machine next to his bed. Maybe Daddy had a *gurgle* machine too.

I saw Mommy first, sitting in a chair with her head against the wall, eyes closed. Her French twist was a little messy for

Mommy; pieces of hair had popped out. That wasn't like her. She hadn't seen us come in. But then I saw Daddy sitting upright in his hospital bed, wearing the same thin gown as the rest of the patients. White sheets covered his legs, and he had tubes all over him, which were connected to a machine with a computer on it. The machine made a consistent *beep, beep* sound. He heard us somehow over the *gurgle* machine and opened his eyes. I had never seen my daddy cry before, but his eyes welled up with tears. He lifted his arm (that was free of tubes) and motioned for us to come over to him. He strained to lift his head off the pillow to kiss me on the cheek and did the same with Sloane.

"Girls," he breathed, and tears ran down his face. He must've been hurting, and I wanted to cry. He said, "I'm glad you're here," but it took a lot of energy for him to speak. We looked at Mommy, now awake, who was beaming from ear to ear to see us. Dad looked at her to signal that he wanted her to explain.

"Are you getting rest, Dad?" asked Sloane, but I could see he was exhausted. Mommy answered for him.

"It's hard for Dad to get rest—he has a fever and a raging infection. Between the nurses coming in frequently to check on him or his medications and the constant flow of residents asking questions, he gets little sleep." Mommy always helped Daddy, no matter what.

I nodded, and Sloane asked, "What do the residents say?" She knew what to ask since she was thinking of going to college to be a doctor or something, so I listened, but I liked art better.

"They have differing theories and won't know for sure until they run tests, but right now, Dad's infection is too serious to stir up," said Mommy.

"What does that mean?" I asked.

"Well," said Mommy, "do you remember the red paunch on Daddy's abdomen?" I nodded. "It turns out that was an infection the size of a softball. The doctors think that Dad's intestine burst, like an appendix, but his body accumulated all the yucky stuff in one spot. Most of the time, the body releases the contents of the intestine, and it goes into the bloodstream—"

"And kills the patient," Sloane interrupted.

"Yes," said Mommy. "We are very fortunate we didn't lose him."

"But then," said Sloane, always curious, "what caused the intestine to burst?"

She looked at Daddy and said, "That's where it gets fuzzy. It could be something as simple as a fishbone, or something as serious as cancer."

I may not have known what all that medical stuff meant at that time, but boy, I knew the word "cancer." I knew that things could get worse for him.

"What's that bag, Dad, on the outside of your leg?" Sloane asked.

He moved the sheet to show a rubbery-looking bag with gross stuff inside, and said, "There is a tube inside my abdomen that drains the gunk into the bag." I wasn't going to get too close to it. It grossed me out a lot, but I also felt bad for what he was going through. Daddy closed his eyes. Maybe he was even embarrassed for us to see his gunk bag.

Sloane, always thinking, said, "How do they know if it's working well?" But she addressed Mommy this time.

She crossed her legs to switch the angle she was sitting, and said, "As disturbing as this sounds, the surgeon came in earlier and suctioned gunk out, measured it, plus the contents of the bag, and keeps a record of it," Mommy said as she cringed. "That was rough."

"Oh—I can see why." Sloane wrinkled her brows.

I wondered, "Daddy, do you get to eat?" I put my little hand on top of his.

He opened his eyes like slits and said, "I'm not hungry," and closed them again.

Mommy said, "Dad's on a liquid diet—only clear broth and Jell-O right now. Oh—some good news! Daddy was able to walk to the hallway and back to his bed," she said proudly. "It wasn't easy, though, because he had to drag that pole and all the bags with him."

"Good job, Daddy," I said, but it broke my heart to see him like this. It was like he was a little kid, and I was his mommy. This didn't feel quite right to me. He squeezed my hand.

"Well girls, I think Dad needs to rest. Sloane, could you ask Aunt Bianka to come in?"

Sloane went to the waiting area to get Auntie, but I stayed with Daddy and patted his hand gently. I could tell he liked I was there, and I saw a tear fall down the side of his face. My eyes filled up too—I just couldn't help it.

Auntie and Mommy chatted while Daddy slept, since he couldn't keep his eyes open. They weren't really sisters, but they both had the long, straight dark hair and the Romani olive skin. They even shared clothes, especially the colorful maxi skirts. I smiled to myself when I noticed that they both talked with their hands. She kissed Daddy on the forehead, and they exchanged hellos.

Auntie whispered to Mommy, "What do you want to do about tomorrow?"

Mommy had a blank look—she didn't know what day it was at first because she had been "camping out" at the hospital for days now. Her eyes got big. "Tomorrow's Christmas! I have lost all track of time. This was not what I had planned," she said sadly.

"You need to be here," Auntie said, looking at Daddy but speaking to Mommy.

"Mom," Sloane said, "we can hang out at Aunt Bianka's house. We understand," she said. And I nodded in agreement. My parents always put Sloane and me first. We could do this for them.

"Yeah, okay. I've already got the gifts wrapped. Can you stop at the house and pick them up? They're in my usual hiding place."

Sloane added, "I know where they're at."

Mommy said, "You do?"

"Under the stairs," said Sloane.

"Oh, brother!" said Mommy with a slight grin. "Would it be possible to bring the girls for a visit tomorrow so John can see them?"

Auntie said, "Of course, and I'll have Django and Jeta come for dinner to my house, instead."

"You're a lifesaver!"

"I figured when John wasn't getting any better, I'd be ready to have Christmas dinner, just in case," said Auntie, always on top of things.

"Alright—time to rest." Mommy kissed us goodbye.

"Don't forget to put cookies out for Santa tonight," Daddy said, clasping my hand. My heart felt warm and happy—Daddy was okay with us having Christmas, even though things weren't normal, even though it would be without them. I knew he loved us.

We blew kisses his way since he was too weak.

That night, Christmas Eve, we had yet another fun sleepover. Elijah zoomed from corner to corner with his plush Boots doll in one hand, and one of Santa's cookies in the other, but everyone was either half asleep or lost in

It's a Wonderful Life. Sloane texted. Darby was sleeping in her mass of blonde hair, and Auntie was going on and on about how she loved the movie and how life was so fragile. The kids in the movie came close to not having a daddy, so I realized how lucky I was to have a daddy, even though he wasn't going to be with us for Christmas.

Darby and Elijah weren't so lucky.

Our visit to the hospital on Christmas Day was better than the first time we saw Daddy with his tubes—maybe because I knew what to expect. He had eaten an entire green Jell-O, and Mommy seemed less frazzled. Her hair was smoother—that was good. He had gotten more rest than usual because the hospital had just enough people to run it, and the residents were gone for the day, so they didn't bombard Daddy with dozens of questions every hour. Mommy said they were like a beehive and traveled in groups—always lots of buzzing, but no answers. They still knew nothing, and Mommy got frustrated.

We exchanged gifts. Sloane and I got video games that we planned to play later in the day, after we had dinner at home. I liked the idea of being home alone with my sister—it was exciting—like we were pretend adults.

Bibíyo Jeta and *Pápa* were on their way to Auntie's house for Christmas dinner; we had been preparing all morning long. Darby and I were on cleaning duty while Sloane and Auntie cooked. We decided it was best that I stay out of the kitchen after the egg incident. Elijah kept himself busy playing with Enoch; only this time, he had just water in his sippy cup. Auntie thought it best that we keep Elijah sugar free for as long as possible.

Ding-dong. Whoa! That's all Rouge had to hear. She raced to the full-length windows, which were on each side of Auntie's front door, to get a better look. Her claws *clicked* as she ran with excitement against the wooden floor. It didn't take much to wind up Rouge! Once she saw *Bibíyo* and *Pápa*, she pushed herself up on her hind legs and smashed her cute little wet nose onto the window, tail wagging like crazy. Sometimes, I wished I was a little dog. Then, in walked my *Pápa* and *Bibíyo*. Mmmm! They smelled so good. *Pápa* smelled like his pipe—It was supposed to be cherry tobacco, but I didn't know how tobacco could be flavored like fruit. It didn't make sense to me.

Bibíyo—mmmm—*Bibíyo* smelled like heaven. She used her favorite perfume, Chanel N°5, for special days. Today was special. Just in case it wasn't enough good smell, *Bibíyo* wore a tiny green bottle of that perfume around her neck on a chain. Luckily, she and *Pápa* made jewelry; I thought it was a cool idea.

"*Nepáta!*" *Pápa* said as he took off his cap and gave me a big bear hug. He didn't like to wear coats; he said weathering the cold reminded him of the "old days," whatever that was. *Pápa* wore a blue dress shirt with the sleeves rolled up—he always wore baggy-sleeved shirts. I saw a funny tattoo on *Pápa's* left arm, Z-2178, but he never talked about it. *Bibíyo* had one too, Z-2179, but I pretended I didn't notice. I liked his vest best. It was dark brown with little stripes, and it matched his pants. I giggled—*Pápa* had one of his homemade satchels attached to his belt loop. The satchel was like bug repellent. Gotta keep those ghosts away!

Bibíyo put her jiggly arms out for me to give her a hug. "Merry Christmas!" she said, and kissed me once on each cheek. "Be a good girl and take *Bibíyo's* coat." I gasped when

I saw how pretty she was in a burgundy-colored long skirt and pink hip scarf. *Bibíyo*'s corset belt was laced with ribbon. Her bodice was white, and her *diklo* was burgundy. Each finger had a ring. *Later, I will ask her if I can try them on.* I loved jewelry too.

Auntie's house buzzed with excitement, especially from Elijah. He proudly showed them his man-doll while babbling something to Enoch at the same time. *I wonder if he found the sugar!* Sloane and Darby came out from the kitchen to hug *Pápa* and *Bibíyo* while Auntie said, "I'll be right out!"

Pápa and *Bibíyo* arrived with tins of gingerbread cookies and a pot of *ukha* that was so ugly, it had to be eaten by candlelight. *Ukha* was a Russian soup that *Pápa* made in memory of my great-grandmother. I figured if I ate the other food and played with the soup, no one would notice; at least, that was my plan. I'd stick with the stuffed cabbage Sloane helped make, even though I didn't like it much. It was better than the ugly soup.

Our Christmas with *Pápa* and *Bibíyo* was like they do in Hungary. We exchanged gifts in early December on St. Nicholas Day. Then we had the typical American celebration on Christmas Day, with a big meal and lots of cookies and desserts. Sloane and I loved the early gifts! The kids at school always hung out at our house, the Mackenzies, for school breaks. We were "the house" to go to for sleepovers, homemade pizza, and movie night. Most of the time, the kids didn't want to go home. We had a fun house!

After we finished dinner, Auntie's phone rang, but I could tell by the look on her face that something was wrong when she checked the caller ID on her cordless phone. She scowled, looked at Sloane, and said, "Oh no, it's Tony." She pursed her lips together.

I saw a part of *Pápa* I had never seen before. He got red in the face, leaned forward, and growled. "What does he want? He has no business calling here!" At first, I wondered what *Pápa* meant by that, but then I realized we weren't at home. *How did he find Sloane?*

Auntie was flustered and said, "Should I answer it? I don't want to make matters worse." But I noticed my sister stiffen—somehow stand taller—like she was not afraid of him in the least. But then something happened I didn't expect: *Bibíyo* Jeta, too, had transformed into a force that I had never seen before today. She was no longer the jolly *Bibíyo*; she had become much darker and serious. She said, "Go ahead, Bianka, answer it," but her eyes flitted toward *Pápa* for a split second.

Sloane took the phone from Auntie Bianka as if confronting a bully and snarled, "What do you want?" She paused, listening to his answer, and then, like a smarty-pants, she said, "What do you think—caller ID," with a grimace. *He must have answered Sloane.* My sister then said, "I don't care! It isn't 'very nice' that you called me after I told you to leave me alone." There was another pause, but she was harsh. "How did you know I was here?" she demanded, and even Elijah stopped his playtime to watch Sloane in action.

By this time, Auntie was past the shock and had joined in the heated mood of the room. "Yeah—ask him how he got this phone number! I had to change it once before because of him," she said with her hand on her hip. Even Darby's blood boiled as she got up to stand next to her mom.

I watched the entire scene with awe since I was the smooth sour cream to my family's spicy, sharp paprika.

Sloane covered the phone with her hand, angry, but hurt, and mouthed, "He's laughing."

Pápa tightened his fist and shouted at the air, "*Rúgjon meg a ló!*" He was so angry!

It was as if a shadow was cast over the room, and, at the same time, *Bibíyo* and *Pápa* made eye contact. Then we heard shouting on the other end of the phone—his voice sounded garbled at first, but later, it got a bit clearer.

"What are you people doin'?" he cried. "Stop it!" I could hear him yell.

Agitated, Sloane said, "What are you talking about? Stop what?" There was more garbled noise that came from that cranky Tony.

"The smoke—there's smoke coming from my phone!"

Sloane rolled her eyes. "What smoke?"

He was yelling at this point. "You crazy people—did you do this?" My eyes met Sloane's for a second. I thought something silly, but then I thought Tony was being a baby. Maybe he had too much eggnog.

"Maybe you'll think twice about calling me again," she said, eyes on fire, and promptly hung up a little harder than she should have, considering it was Auntie's phone.

"Whoa—what was that all about?" asked Darby, who already thought Sloane was cool, but she now reigned supreme in the spectrum of coolness. Elijah took his sister's cue and ran around in a circle as if he were chasing an invisible tail. Comically, Rouge was concerned she had done something wrong, and her tail dropped low to the floor.

Bibíyo became animated and said, "That *gazho* no good! He always trouble—trouble for Katya, trouble for Bianka, and now trouble for you, Sloane."

"He won't call here again," said *Pápa* confidently. Hopefully, that would be the end of Tony the Troublemaker.

Darby wouldn't let it go, though, and said, "Did you do that Sloane?"

Sloane and I looked at each other. "Do what?" she said.

"Aunt Bianka," said Sloane, "we should probably check to make sure your phone still works." She readily agreed. To no surprise of mine, the phone still worked fine.

———————

Later that evening, when Sloane and I were home waiting for Mom, I said, "Sloane—seriously—did you mess with Tony's phone?"

My sister took me by my hand and said, "I'm not sure, Little Strawberry," and I knew she was telling the truth.

CHAPTER 9

DEBATE

I sat digging my fingernail into the end of my eraser; the tip of my thumb turned white each time I pressed it. Somehow, it comforted me while I sat and waited for my classmates to cast their votes for the winner of the debate. It was entirely possible that I could have eased up on Rayce Rinehart, but I was brutally competitive. I made sure I knew my material inside and out. What if I bruised his ego? I could have let a few points slide by, but he was ridiculously presumptuous. He didn't think a girl could beat him, so it only provoked me to prove him wrong.

English class buzzed with a flurry over our debate topic: legalization v. decriminalization of marijuana. Mr. Chapman was clever to have scheduled a stimulating and controversial topic the week back from winter break—a sure fire way of getting our attention, and boy, did it ever.

"Alright, cast your vote for whomever you believe presented the best argument: Mr. Rinehart for legalization or Ms. Barzetti for decriminalization. Yvette—would you collect the votes? The plastic container on my desk will do," he said as he wedged the pen behind his ear.

With cheeks flushed, Yvette beamed at the opportunity of

being asked to help—she was the wannabe teacher's pet. "Absolutely, Mr. Chapman," she said, and then her ears turned red. When she walked past me, she casually brushed up against my arm to get my attention, and then gave me the thumbs up. I wasn't sure if she thought I did a good job or if she thought I'd won. Yvette meant well, yet I couldn't help finding her kissing up to Mr. Chapman unappealing.

Our debate caused even the somewhat-reserved Jason Pham to vocalize his siding with his boy, Rayce. "Barzetti—I still don't get you. How could decriminalization be better than legalization? It's like a buy one, get one free deal, but passing up on the free merch." *Did I miss something? Is today national kiss-up day?*

"Dude—weren't you listening?" I tossed one of the balled up blank ballots at him, which Yvette found hilarious.

He returned the favor and threw it back, hoping that Rayce was impressed. "Enlighten us, Sloane."

"Bottom line—the country isn't ready for it," I said. "People don't like change, and that's why change has to happen in smaller doses, so they aren't left choking."

Rayce jumped in, "Are you saying you'd choke on legalized weed?"

I rolled my eyes. "No," I said, "but that's beside the point. The legalization of weed needs to happen smartly, not necessarily quickly."

Jason nudged Rayce and I overheard him loudly whisper, "We should test that smaller dose theory." Rayce laughed.

But Mr. Chapman, the most chill, self-proclaimed hippie, said, "Let's save that for another time, avid debaters. I've tallied the results, and the winner, by a margin of one, is Sloane Barzetti!"

The class hooted and bordered on unruly, but it was all in

jest. No one was actually angry, just wound up. Mr. Chapman enjoyed stimulating thought—he said he didn't want us to turn out to be parrots no matter what our stance on the issues of the day.

Rayce sauntered toward me, and with each step, my heart skipped a few beats. Should I have let him win? It would've been difficult—I didn't like to back down when I knew, in principle, I was right. However, he was at least willing to speak to me. It would've been worse had he given me the cold shoulder and left without a word. It's not like I crushed him with a landslide vote. Awkwardly, as he slipped into place, right next to me, I realized I was holding my breath. I was being so absurd! So, I counteracted my stupid reaction and took in a deep breath, recognizing I've never stood this close to Rayce before. His scent was appealing, so much so, that I inhaled deeply several times so I wouldn't forget it; it reminded me of walking past the storefront of Abercrombie or Hollister. The scent was always too overwhelming while in the store, but if you were walking past, it was the perfect formula to be hypnotized.

He had a twinkle in his blue eyes, and he said, "Barzetti, what are you doing?"

What am I doing? "I am just taking it all in," I said. Probably looking like an idiot!

He leaned on the desk with his full focus on me. "Oh—taking in your victory." He nodded his head like he'd be doing the same if he were me. "Don't gloat too much—next time it'll be me." My face turned warm. It was almost a compliment, and I found myself slightly flustered.

"Thanks Rinehart," I said, since I guessed we were on a last name basis. Best to keep it impersonal, so he wouldn't think I was crushing on him. "Your points were well taken. I can see you did your homework," I added as we started walking out of the classroom together. It's possible I may have heard Yvette and Jason in the background, but they may as well have been miles away while I inhaled his Crombie-passer-by fragrance, trancing myself into a high . . . cannabis aside.

He held his books along his leg just below his low-riders. "We'll do this again Barzetti," he said as he sauntered off, leaving his scent behind, which continued making me dizzy with possibilities.

Let's hope so. Debate was now my new favorite—hands-down. It would take a deluge to ruin the sunshine I currently basked in. I soaked up the sun's essence that Rayce left behind, but soon enough, Yvette's short strides caught up to me. It's not as if I was trying to lose her as much as I wanted to fully absorb the Rayce moment, uninterrupted.

"Sloane, hey, way to go! You beat The Franchise—yeah you did!" said Yvette wide-eyed as we headed to Zariah's classroom to pick her up for lunch.

Mentally, I lingered back in the moment with Rayce, which is why it took me a couple of seconds to get my bearings. "He, I mean, *it* was amazing, always good to stir things up. So—what's *your* debate topic?"

The side of her mouth inched up into a nervous smile. "I had to pick something less controversial, or my parents would have contacted Mr. Chapman, and I would've just *died* of embarrassment." *I bet! Her mother's completely neurotic.* She checked to make sure Yvette was in bed in the middle of the night, like Yvette was a tot who might wander away. "Don't laugh—it's the best I could do."

"So, what is it?" I asked, trying to remain composed.

Yvette rolled her eyes and said, "Social media is a venue for pedophiles."

"Hmmm—so do you get to pick which side of the issue you want to argue?"

"Technically—yes, but I might make sure I don't bring it to my mom's attention, or I'll never hear the end of it," said my rebel friend. I wondered if I was starting to rub off on her. Honestly, I thought that would be a good thing for her; she needed to build a backbone, one vertebra at a time. With a mother like hers, I wondered if her spine was only a coagulation of cartilage.

We stood outside Zariah's closed classroom door, waiting. I said, "No kidding—your mom insisted on becoming one of your social media followers?" But I contemplated further, "However, the pedophile issue is valid. It could happen if it hasn't already."

"Right, I know. But I could still use some breathing room from my parents." The only chance this poor girl had of living a little was going off to college someday. Her parents smothered her more than cream cheese covering a bagel, and that was saying something. Just then, Zariah's classroom door opened, and, for a moment, I stole a glance. I was surprised she was the only student. Had I always assumed there was a classroom full of students, or had it always been this way? Normally, her class let out earlier, and she would meet us halfway. I almost felt as if I was intruding on the mystery classroom.

Yvette said, "Hey, Zariah!" She was still pumped from my Rayce victory. I wondered if at times Yvette lived through me. "You ready for lunch?"

I expected to be blinded by her dazzling white teeth, but instead, she barely cracked a smile. "What's up, girl? I gotta go back to my locker for a minute. Why don't you go on ahead and save my seat?"

"Sure," I said, hesitating. "Everything okay?"

She looked straight ahead and said, "Yeah, I'm fine," but

Zariah, the extrovert, was anything but social at the moment and continued down the hall, alone. Weird.

Yvette pulled my sweater sleeve, forgetting my need for personal space, and said, "Gotcha covered, Zariah." But I wasn't in the mood to lecture Yvette. I'd give her three strikes before that happened.

We headed to the cafeteria along with the hungry herd while the stench of room temperature lunch meat sandwiches hovered over us all. Today was pizza day, thank God, and Yvette and I lived for it. While we scooted closer to the cashier, I said, "What do you think's going on with Zariah?"

She pulled off a greasy pepperoni, popped it into her mouth, and said casually, "She's probably struggling with her grades," and shrugged her shoulders. "I don't think school's ever been easy for her, ya know?"

"Mmm—could be—I just don't remember ever seeing her bummed out about it before, that's all. She's so talented—I guess that always seemed to make up for it," I said as I swiped to pay the cashier. There were few people who knew that Zariah had repeated one of the early core grades before she moved here. It was then that I saw him standing there, raking his fingers through his mane, two down from where I stood. Hutch hadn't been in Algebra, so I had forgotten about his text over break.

He had trouble written all over his face; he turned toward me at the same time I'd realized his presence. The first thing I laid eyes on was his mouth—more specifically, his lips. I hated myself for it. Why did I always notice his mouth? Ugh—probably because I was expecting something stupid to come out of it. "So, Sloane, why didn't you text me back?"

I could feel my body tense. I wanted to deck him, but it wasn't a good idea. I shouldn't let him affect me so much. He's just a guy—an annoying guy. And that's just screwed up—he's concerned I didn't text him back? "How'd you get my number, Hutch?" I asked with restraint.

He raked his hair again and said, "That's why you're bothered? Because I got your number?" Then he laughed, which only agitated me further. "Do you have any idea how easy that is?" He wasn't kidding, either. *Should I be creeped out?*

That's when Logan Kumar stepped from behind Hutch, adjusted his dark-framed glasses, and said, "Yeah—easy." Unlike Hutch, I actually liked Logan. He was some kind of technology guru who typically kept to himself, but he'd earned my respect while he was my lab partner last year in our science class. He kept up with me, and for once, I didn't have to tell my partner what to do like some puppy in training. He understood not only what needed to be done, but the quality of work necessary to earn an "A." Apparently neither one of us liked half-assed work.

"You two know each other?" I asked incredulously.

Hutch interrupted, "We do."

But I cut him off and said, "Not talking to you." *He better not get under my skin this soon after winter break.*

Logan cleared his throat. "Look, Sloane, it was my idea for Hutch to text you, although I'm beginning to think that was a bad idea." He swiped to pay for his pizza. "I didn't realize you two had a contentious relationship," he said, glaring at Hutch, who once again found humor in the situation. I wondered why Hutch didn't tell Logan . . .

I'm beginning to question my precise perception skills now that these two seem to be friends, but there must be a story in it. My curiosity proved to be stronger. "You think? So, what's so interesting that you two are creeping on me?" This better be good.

Logan answered, "We have a proposal. The Science Department asked Hutch and I to participate in a competition to represent the school. Each team consists of four students, and at least one has to be a female. That's where you come in."

I looked at Hutch and then at Logan. "I'm not sure if I'm supposed to be offended."

"No—Sloane—it's not like that. We're asking you because you're the smartest girl—you know—good at math and science," Logan said. In all fairness, guys actually did score higher in math and science on the ACT and SAT exams, but I felt confident I could easily keep up.

I snickered a little. "You're starting to redeem yourself—so—who's the fourth member?" The conversation seemed lighter now.

Logan added, "Do you know Kem Zelenko?"

"Yeah, I know Kem—a little," I remarked. He was also Romani, although our families weren't close, so I didn't know him like the Kóbórs. Other than passing him in the halls at school, my only other exposure to his family was at weddings and funerals. Those were the two occasions where every Romani from within hundreds of miles traveled to either celebrate or pay their respects. It wasn't only tradition, it was expected. Nobody married and died quite like the Romanies.

Hutch raked his hair again, which put me in a salty mood. *If he does that again, I'm taking scissors to it.* "So—you in?" Logan asked.

It was an interesting offer. I liked the fact such a smart group of guys asked me to join their team; they must've figured I could carry some weight. However, I had reservations. Addressing Logan, I said, "Why don't you text me the details since you already have my phone number." Then I turned to Hutch and added, "And I'll let you know," with a pinch of salt.

I had to acknowledge that I had much to ponder. Working with Logan would likely be a thought-provoking experience, and I didn't know enough about Kem, which kept me impartial. It was Hutch that concerned me. Would I be able to work with him voluntarily? I wrapped my arms around my waist in an effort to keep warm while I stood outside in the car rider line, looking for Noelle and waiting for Mom. It was gusty out, and it seemed the wind bounced off the hills, blowing my hair with it. It was this kind of day that I wished we had uniform pants rather than skirts, but I guess it was a small price to pay to attend such a prestigious school. Noelle and I were fortunate that our scholarships allowed our entrance into the school, where otherwise there was a wait list and a sizable price tag.

As Mom pulled up to the curb in the Ford Explorer, I hoped she had time to make warm soup for dinner. It was that kind of January day that made me crave warm comfort food. Noelle scampered out of school with perfect timing and beamed her everlastingly happy face at me, but Mom's presence brought her back to reality. "How's Dad doing?"

"He's stable. I had to go into the office today, so I haven't been home; *Pápa* is staying with him, just in case," Mom said. "I'm behind at work." After a solid week in the hospital, Dad was allowed to come home yesterday, but still no diagnosis. The "not knowing" piece was a killer for us all.

Mom shut off the radio and said, "How'd the debate go, Sloane?"

I smiled unusually big and said, "I beat Rayce Rinehart by one vote! First, I was kinda concerned that the guys would vote for Rayce based on the fact that he was for legalized pot. Second, I was worried that the girls would vote for him just because he's The Franchise."

It was my mom's turn to smile. She said, "Good job, honey! Isn't Rayce the boy that called 911 in first grade during a field trip on a dare?"

"Yep—same one," I said. "He's an idiot."

Mom laughed. "I'm sure. How was school today for you, Noelle?"

She bubbled up and said, "I have to create a mask of my favorite President for Presidents' Day, but I have to say why he's my favorite." Noelle had that distant look in her eyes; she looked that way when she was getting a creative download.

Mom didn't see her face, though, so she asked, "Do you know yet what you want to do?"

Her eyes seemed to scan space. "I have some ideas, but nothing I'm ready to talk about now. First, I have to decide which President is my favorite." My sister preferred to allow the creative process to ferment—nothing could be rushed with her.

Upon our arrival home, a fresh layer of snow blanketed the ground and *Pápa*'s car; he must've been here all day. I could hear Rouge well before we opened the garage door leading into the house as she barked her familiar cries, asking, "Where have you been all day?" Noelle said, "Hi, Girl!" But no one had an empty hand to pet her since we were loaded down with weighted backpacks and Mom had her laptop, work bag, and purse. Rouge was sure to lick my hand once I leaned over to drop my backpack on the floor near the closet. The good day got even better when we saw that not only did *Bibíyo* Jeta tag along, but she also made my favorite soup! Rosemary lingered in the air, and knowing *Bibíyo*, I was sure it was fresh herbs.

Dad sat in his familiar sick place on the reclined couch.

It seemed that loose cargo pants worked best to pocket the collection bag of infection. He had lost so much weight that the pants hung off him, although oddly, it worked out, since the long thin tube that snaked out of his abdomen required room at the waist. The tube stayed in place by a mere few pieces of surgical tape that Dad guarded like Fort Knox.

Mom beamed at *Bibíyo* and *Pápa*, and asked, "How's our patient doing?" I could tell she was grateful for them.

"He doesn't move from that spot," *Bibíyo* said sadly. "I take his temperature every hour to check." *Bibíyo* hovered like a worried mother hen. "Always the fever."

Pápa added, "It's no good. His energy is low—this sickness has sucked the life out of him." Dad couldn't get a word in if he wanted.

Dad managed to say, "Hi, girls," but it took effort.

I asked, "How are you, Dad?" Then I headed toward him in the family room.

He mumbled, "Icky," but that much was obvious. Noelle flapped her angel wings and went to Dad's side to hold his hand.

Bibíyo lifted the lid and stirred the piping-hot potatoes that reminded me of the days *Pápa* used to watch me. The aroma of the baking bread was tantalizing and warmed my heart. Mom ran upstairs to change her clothes while *Bibíyo* said to Dad, "John, you want soup?" He just nodded. It was too much of an effort to do much else, so *Bibíyo* brought him a tray. By this point, I couldn't even remember the last time Dad sat at a table. It took a long time for him to make his way anywhere in the house; *Pápa* could now move faster than Dad.

Each of us dipped into our sumptuous bowls of soup with freshly cut bread and butter. *Pápa* asked, after wiping his neat beard with a napkin, "Sloane, you hear anything from the *gazho*?"

"No—only that stupid phone call on Christmas," I spouted with sarcasm, which was my new favorite.

Bibíyo, cutting the bread, flourished the knife that doubled as a sword. "He only cares about Tony—he never wanted to be a parent." She sputtered with vinegar, "Vacation . . ."

Pápa asked, "Did he go with the *gazhi*—Ivy?"

I said, "I don't know—she walked out on him the same day." I pondered, "But he probably wouldn't let that stop him from enjoying himself." I had to admit, even though the last several weeks had been awful because of Dad's illness, I didn't miss Tony, and I certainly didn't miss Ivy.

Bibíyo asked my mom, "You hear from *gazho*, Katya?"

"No—nothing—and I can't get his smug face out of my mind," Mom responded. "Tony hasn't even attempted a conversation with me." I guess that wasn't too shocking since I'm sure Mom didn't try to converse with him either.

Pápa rubbed his hands together, creating friction, and said, "That *gazho* is a bad egg, Katya. His heart like tar—John is sick and dying—you see? *Gazho* do this! He brings *bi-baxt* to John—that's why he's sick."

The Romani are a highly superstitious people, so illness and bad luck were essentially tied together, as were health and good fortune. Most cultures, even my Italian side, had superstitions in regard to the "evil eye," which usually stemmed from jealousy or envy, and could be either intentional or unintentional. *Pápa*, who was well versed in everything "luck" related, was a luck ninja, and *Bibíyo* was no slouch, either.

A memory from Tony's house came flooding back from when I was little—maybe as young as six. He had given me a plush doll for my birthday—it was a male because I remembered distinctly the doll wore a suit and tie like the "Daddy" doll. There were other dolls, too, but this one was special.

Tony said, "Why don't you give your dolls names? You can name them whatever you want, but I'll name the doll with the tie."

I was thrilled Tony wanted to play with me because he never did. I'd gladly accept whatever name he gave the doll, and I said, "Sure!" If I was an extra good girl, he might not ignore me today. Maybe I had to earn his attention.

He said sweetly, "Let's name him Giovanni," and I readily agreed. That day we played more than I can remember. He suggested we turn my playhouse into a pirate ship. Luckily, he had some of Grandma Aurelia's knitting needles that we could use as swords. Giovanni was the bad pirate, and Tony's doll was the good pirate, so he stabbed Giovanni with the knitting needles because he was plundering the treasure. For good measure, he also made Giovanni walk the plank. My goodness had paid off, and for once, I wasn't left alone all day as a small child.

As I sat, gnawing on some bread, I wondered. Normally, I never took my phone out at dinner, but the impulse was too strong. How do I know? *It.* I Googled "Giovanni" to see if there is an English version of the name—there must've been a reason Tony wanted to play that day, and *Pápa*'s insistence on the evil eye somehow made sense.

Anxiety inched up as I waited for the blue circle to stop searching, and I found it. Giovanni was Italian for John! My own father had fashioned a makeshift voodoo doll and tricked me into some warped way of hurting Dad. Was it actually the cause of his illness? I knew not to tempt the fates—Mom drilled it into me, never to dabble in black magic. She had heard too many stories from the old country.

Mom didn't want to argue with *Pápa*, so instead she said, "Sloane, did you remember to get the mail today?" She started to stack the dishes.

"No, I'll do it now," I said, putting away my phone. There was no sense in telling my story. It couldn't be proven and would only fuel *Pápa* and *Bibíyo* into yet another ritual. *Bibíyo* headed toward Dad, and I could feel her good intentions all the way into the kitchen, knowing she was up to something. The mail could wait a few minutes—this was bound to be epic.

Swish, swish, swish. *Bibíyo*'s long skirt sashayed toward Dad. She said, "John, you want more? We need to fatten you up. Skinny no good." It meant bad health, but in this case, it was true. He shook his head and said, "Thanks, Jeta."

"You know, John, I need your pants," said *Bibíyo*, apathetically, like it was a normal request.

Once again, he was the armed guard at Fort Knox, and he said, "Wh-What do you need?" His eyebrows may have been as high as his hairline.

Here we go.

Mom had her eyes closed, and she shook her head, wishing away *Bibíyo*'s bizarre request. *Pápa* waved my dad on like he had one more lap to do at a Formula One race, and Noelle crinkled her nose; she'd like to disapparate, like Harry Potter, to anywhere but here. Even Rouge's ears perked up.

"John, your pants polluted. We destroy them."

"Whoa—Jeta—you lost me."

Bibíyo sat down next to Dad, looking like a schoolteacher, and explained the rules to him as if he were a young kid who simply didn't know better. "You see, we have laws. The sickness pollutes the pants—so to keep the family healthy, we destroy."

Dad gave Mom the 'Is she serious?' look, and Mom said, "The Romani believe that all sickness is contagious. Infection is considered unclean, and uncleanliness pollutes all who are near. It's her way of protecting the household."

"But Jeta," Dad clarified, "I know I'm not contagious."

"No, no, no," she said, "you are *marime*. I get the gloves." Then she went out to the car, where I knew she kept a stash of latex gloves for *marime* emergencies.

Pápa showed his encouragement, but left the dirty work for *Bibíyo* to take care of. Being a red-blooded Romani, *Pápa* was content with *Bibíyo* forging forward with her traditional female role. So much for equality!

Our household, honestly, was watered down so much with Americanism that Mom didn't follow the Romani Laws. It wasn't out of disrespect; it was simply the fact that she had fully immersed herself in American culture.

I think Dad was too sick to care; besides, he had a place in his heart for what he called their "eccentricities." He didn't want to admit he'd married into a family of crazy Romanies. Each tradition, no matter how strange it seemed to the outside world, endured for a reason. Dad respected that notion even though he didn't always get it.

"What am I supposed to do for pants?" asked Dad.

"Oh, Jeta took care of that. She got you new ones," said *Pápa* proudly.

Dad gingerly started his routine to get out of the couch; it took time and skill to not upset the tube. "You realize I don't know if I'll get better."

"It's okay, son; we work a little magic." Then he winked at Dad. I wasn't sure what that meant, and neither Dad nor I were about to ask. Noelle just stood there, taking in the entire conversation while Mom readied the shower with adequate towels. She already knew Jeta would insist on a set of towels for the upper half of his body, and another set of towels for the lower half—Romani Law. It was the whole cleanliness concept, again. No point in upsetting them, especially because Dad was a *gazho* and *gazhe* were considered unclean, regardless.

It was then that Dr. Jeta came back into the house with her hands carefully covered in latex. She looked as if she had prepped for surgery. She even had a garbage bag, which she also likely kept in her car, so that she could dispose of the pants. Mom intervened to give Dad some privacy, but I'm pretty sure I heard him cursing under his breath. Once Dr. Jeta captured the pants, she took them out to her car for proper destruction, only I wasn't sure what that meant, either. I again chose not to ask.

Since it seemed I encapsulated the essence of the three-ring circus, I thought I'd best get the mail before I completely forgot. That blanket of snow was now bordering on several inches deep, but I was too lazy to change into boots. I liked how most of the lighting came from the snow since the days were shorter now. No matter how dark it got, the snow seemed to illuminate the outside, plus it made everything prettier. It turned out to be a great day for once, and I felt the apples of my cheeks push up toward my eyes into a smile. There was a good chance that everything would turn out right—I mean—at least I had a fanatically loyal family.

I reached into the mailbox, which let out a squeak, catching in my peripheral vision, the sleeves of my new teal sweater. *Bibíyo* Jeta bought it for me for Christmas. Wrapped inside all the junk mail was an electric bill, a reminder notice from the dentist, and something official-looking from the Court of Common Pleas Domestic Relations. It took a second to register, but the apples on my face fell to the ground and splashed into applesauce. I ran back into the house, flung the door open, trudged snow into the house that had caked on my shoes, and ripped open the offensive envelope. *Bibíyo* and *Pápa* scooted over to see why I was so flabbergasted. Noelle grabbed Rouge to keep her from getting trampled by the chaos.

It was a summons to appear in court! Anthony Barzetti filed charges against Yekaterina Gáspár because he wasn't seeing me. This was the same guy who never spent time with me—who just went on a vacation after I walked out on him, like it didn't bother him in the least. I had to keep myself from shaking; I was so irate, and I wasn't the only one.

"That *gazho*!" steamed *Pápa*. "*A ménkű csapjon beléd*!" he screamed, shaking his fist furiously in the air.

Bibíyo Jeta couldn't keep her cursing PG-rated; she said something in her native tongue, but I think it meant the equivalent of his plumbs shriveling up into raisins. She crowed, "Sloane is for our Katya, not that Tony!"

Our blood bubbled with fury under our skin; we all were united in our revulsion for Tony. Then something caught my eye as I held the reprehensible piece of paper—a spark! A split second later, the paper burst into flames, lighting my hand up like a fire ball, but my brain didn't register fast enough for my hand to let go. I heard screams, but they seemed so distant. It seemed like an eternity, although it was probably only seconds passing, when *Bibíyo* sandwiched her "*swish swish*" skirt over my hands to smother the inferno. The pain receptors kicked in—I was locked in silence—it couldn't have been real. I was smiling in the sparkling snow only moments before this.

Scenes appeared in black-and-white as if a reel of film played in my head in slow motion. I heard no sound. *Pápa brings his face close to mine and mouths something to me, but it's too slow to understand.*

Charlie Chaplin mouths something to me, but it's too slow to understand.

Pápa.

Charlie Chaplin.

Pápa.

Charlie Chaplin.

Then the film gets stuck in the reel.

Fade to black.

CHAPTER 10

UNHINGED

My body swayed to the left as we turned a corner. I'd have to plant my feet better if I wanted to avoid falling on my face, but that was the least of my problems. The silver tin can reminded me of what it would be like to be a sardine—squeezed into a tight container with peculiar nauseating smells. I cupped my hand over my nose and mouth to reduce the fumes that gagged me. Claustrophobia was a past life issue I had dealt with before. Many lifetimes ago, I contracted leprosy, a once highly feared contagious disease. My village's solution was to pile the lepers into a cave, seal it up, and leave us to die. I felt like I was in that cave again. It was warm—too warm—and I wanted to vomit. I could feel the life drain out of me—that sense of light-headedness coupled with the cold clamminess of my skin.

Somewhere in the ethers, I heard a disembodied voice tell me, "Focus." *Focus on what?* The deafening sound of the siren grated on my nerves, but it had a rhythm to it. *Focus—focus on the siren—the siren.* It was repetitious and slowly brought me back to reality as I looked at my daughter strapped to a gurney. She looked smaller, childlike, and vulnerable. I'd have to bridle my dire need to exit the ambulance and run for the free air if I were to be the pillar that Sloane needed.

The paramedic said something to me, but his lips moved in slow motion, and I couldn't discern any words from his moving mouth. My brain and ears were not in sync. Still fighting nausea, I said, "W-what?"

"It's a good thing her burns are isolated to her hand and wrist," he said as he glanced at the monitor. "This is a second-degree burn, which means it's going to be very painful—that's why she blacked out earlier. It's the body's way of coping with pain. To keep her more comfortable, we've administered morphine. Because we don't know the extent of the burn, we are taking her to Three Rivers Hospital—they have a burn unit that will take good care of your daughter."

He seemed to know what he was talking about—but he's so young! I was hoping he knew what he was doing—he looked like a kid. *Maybe that's good.* He seemed sharp, at least. *Did he say Three Rivers? Isn't that the same as The Tower—The White Tower—didn't somebody say that earlier? I know that place, right? Burn unit—that's serious.*

My mind was like a padlock with a lost combination. Slowly I said, "Burn unit?"

"Right now, it's hard to say the depth of the burn. The doctors will assess the damage, treat her, and manage the pain," he said while looking out the window. "We're almost there. Do you have someone meeting you? You're pale, and it's going to be a long night."

I could hear the driver communicating with the hospital. They're awaiting Sloane's arrival. Did I have someone meeting me? Who? "Yeah—I think so—yeah," I said, barely present. I wanted to hold Sloane's hand, but the burn was dressed, and her good hand was near the other wall of the ambulance. I watched her breathe in and out as the oxygen mask on her face fogged up and then cleared again each time.

"Ma'am—Ma'am—she's not going to lose the hand," he said. "Look at me," he coaxed. "She's going to be okay."

She had lots of life in her—Sloane would be okay.

After the ambulance rolled to a stop, the driver opened the doors and brittle, cold air frosted my lungs. No longer imprisoned inside that sardine can, I inhaled deeply to revitalize my senses. I was like a wilted celery stick rehydrated by a glass of water. My cognitive abilities started to return. I saw the familiar structure and realized, yes, this was the hospital that treated John.

The paramedic put a warm blanket on Sloane but was careful to leave her entire left arm free. Medical personnel from the hospital streamed out to assist. "Get the other IV pole," commanded the young paramedic. The jolting had stirred Sloane; her eyes batted at an attempt to open, but she fought against the effects of the morphine.

"Luckily, it's been a slow night, and we have room in the pediatric burn unit," said a female dressed in pink puppy scrubs. She multitasked while we walked briskly, grabbing a clipboard en route. "Oh, and your husband and father are waiting for you."

"Grandfather," I said, concerned. That meant one of them drove like a maniac, and I wasn't sure which was worse, my ill husband on painkillers, or my rule-resistant grandfather. In fact, I was starting to question whether *Pápa* had a valid license anymore. He wasn't big on compliance.

Sloane was starting to come to. She blinked and her eyes watered, but I wasn't sure if it was from pain or from the stark brightness of the hospital lighting. The paramedic, who was pushing the gurney by her head, said to the nurse, "The morphine's wearing off, and her hand's in bad enough shape where that can't happen." I tensed up.

She asked urgently, "What's her height and weight, Mom?"

Think Katya. "She's 6 foot and about 150 pounds."

"Got it," she said, and was off like a bullet. Sloane started moaning and turning her head from side to side. "Mommy," she cried softly. She rarely called me that anymore.

I was helpless to make it better; my heart shattered into pieces. Nothing is worse than to see your child suffer. "Hurry," I said aloud, willing the puppy-print nurse Godspeed.

We turned into the unit as the nurse met us with a syringe full of medication. Sloane's body relaxed as the morphine worked its way through her veins and she slipped into a drug-induced sleep. Having a moment for formalities, the nurse said, "I'll be with Sloane all night—my name's Kelly—I'm going to triage her right here. Have a seat and I'll have someone get your family." She had big gray eyes and honey-blonde hair, and she exhibited a warm confidence. Kelly conversed with a new arrival, a male nurse, and the paramedic. They were deep in discussion about the "resuscitation formula" they planned to continue to administer based on Sloane's weight and the burn area. It sounded like the paramedic was right on point with his estimations—the IV volume was crucial during the first forty-eight hours after a burn.

Pápa and John, who had his collection bag stowed into his cargo pants pocket, came into Sloane's triage area, and asked in unison, "How is she?" I told them what little information I knew.

I said, "Wait, how did you get here so fast?"

Pápa said indifferently, "I drive fast." He made a motion with his hand, slicing through the air.

I looked at John and asked, "How fast?"

John looked like he was about to betray a secret pact. "Beat the ambulance fast," he said under his breath.

Oh my God! "Django—were you playing 'Race The Ambulance' again? I told you it's not a competition!" *Pápa* knew he was in deep when I called him "Django."

He held his cap in his hand. "Katya—you worry for nothing. Django get the job done."

I'd have to look into the license situation when things settled down. I was beginning to wonder if he had insurance . . .

Just then, Kelly came and sat with us as the male nurse examined Sloane's hand. "I need to know more information—the burn is not a chemical burn, correct?"

"That's right," I said.

Kelly countered, "Did anyone see her get burned?"

Pápa chimed in, "I see." Oh boy! I'm sure the hospital has probably never heard of a story of spontaneous combustion caused by supernatural abilities. I tried to warn him with my eyes: "*Pápa*—keep a lid on it." I desperately hoped my thoughts streamed into his Hungarian-Romani noggin.

"Can you tell me what happened, Mr.? . . ."

"Gáspár," he said. Is this where they lock him up and throw away the key? Don't say it—don't say it.

"I'll tell you. My great-granddaughter opened a piece of mail, but she stand too close to the gas stove and the mail catch fire," he said, proud of himself. I wondered if John had a talk with him in the car. Django can be quite cavalier. Kelly wrote furiously on her clipboard while she nodded her head. It made sense to her.

"The flames caught her teal sweater sleeve on the end—it was probably synthetic fiber, which melts easily and burns quickly, making it worse," she said.

I held my breath. "Did the fiber melt?"

She put the pen behind her ear. "It did, and it made the burns worse. But the surgeon can take care of that while she's under."

John asked, "Sloane needs surgery?"

"I'm afraid so, but we'll know more once the surgeon arrives," Kelly clarified and scooted off to attend to other patients, since Sloane was now somewhat comfortable.

We went closer to her, and I brushed her hair around her ear, feeling its silkiness. I never got the full story of what mail burned or who was responsible. Both Django and Jeta were genuinely gifted in the metaphysical arena—it ran in my family going generations back. I took this moment as my first opportunity and asked *Pápa* quietly, "What mail burned?"

He sighed deeply and didn't want to answer. "Sloane was very upset—that *gazho*, Tony—he take you to court." Oh, no! What did he hope to accomplish? I didn't have time to digest the implications. I asked him about the details of the document, but *Pápa* didn't understand legalese.

Quietly, I asked, "Who caught the mail on fire?"

Pápa again hesitated, fiddled with his cap, and said, "Not me. Not Jeta."

"And John and I were upstairs; that leaves Sloane or Noelle," I said, unsatisfied.

John said, "Do you remember when Tony's tire blew?" I nodded slowly. "Remember how angry Sloane was with him?" I did recall that now that he mentioned it. *Pápa* added, "She angry right before mail burst into flames.

My eyes popped out of my head. "What are you saying?"

"Katya—Sloane very powerful!" warned *Pápa*. He showed a slow-motion explosion with his hands.

I wanted to scream! "No, no, look at her! She's a little girl— she couldn't possibly have done this." My head was swimming with the possibilities. I bit my knuckle to keep from bursting because the nurse looked over our way.

John said, "Katya, you can't be that surprised—look at your abilities—think about it. Think about Noelle, and how easy—how natural her gifts come to her. What makes Sloane any different? She's a Gáspár too." He had to sit down, as this must have taken a tremendous toll on him.

Could it be that her abilities sat dormant until triggered by anger? Was it possible for a human to manipulate matter? I suppose it was possible—anything was possible.

"*Pápa*, you're sure you didn't accidentally do this?"

"I promise, *Nepáta*; I did not do this thing." And there was no lie in his eyes. "There's one more thing we must consider tonight," he said, referring to John.

John vacillated, but said, "The court is involved now. There's no way you can hide that burn. And doesn't he have a visitation tomorrow night?"

My mind raced. I didn't have time to process the Tony factor earlier. Sloane was in bad shape from the burn, but to think of adding more emotional turmoil to the equation, like Tony, was inconceivable. But John was right. Tony was looking for trouble. My lawyer wasn't available in the evenings for advice, so I'd have to decide.

On top of that decision, there was no way I could act as healer—it was hard enough with my husband but, for my child, it would be unbearable. I was too emotional, and emotion can cause a lack of presence—something a healer cannot afford. Since we were still waiting on the surgeon, I'd need to move quickly.

"Okay, John—I'll handle Tony. *Pápa*, do you have your medicine bag?" I was going to put the Luck Ninja to work. "Call Jeta, John, so *Pápa* can have her get to work on her end of things." At times, I barked out orders when under duress, not to mention, *Pápa* didn't have a mobile phone; technology tended to freak him out. I was leaving nothing to chance.

I never took my eyes off Sloane but stepped away, beyond earshot, to contemplate.

The legal obligation to inform Tony about the accident ate away at me—it was ridiculous for me to choose Tony's legal right over Sloane's health, but ironically, he's the one that put me in this bad position. I knew she wouldn't want him here—that the emotional upset would make matters worse. But Sloane was unconscious and couldn't speak for herself. I thought Tony would've dropped the matter, but instead he pursued it. I didn't get to read the court document that burned, so I didn't know Tony's specific complaints, but I was sure the main complaint was that he wasn't getting his visitations. If I didn't inform him of the accident, I'd likely be in deep trouble, but to what degree? Could I argue what my daughter wanted?

I glanced at Sloane, felt sick at what I had to do, and dialed Tony's number. *Ring, ring, ring* . . . He'd pick up any second. *Ring, ring, ring* . . . I was holding my breath as it went to his voicemail. *How much do I say? I hate this.* "Tony, it's Katya. Sloane has a bad burn to the hand—it's possible she'll have surgery tonight—just letting you know." *Jerk.* Click. With any luck, his phone is off. I walked back, just in time, as John and *Pápa* returned from their phone call to Jeta, along with a beehive of medical professionals.

The queen bee, in her late thirties, wore navy-framed eyeglasses with her hair stuffed into a scrub cap. Her eyeliner was smudged—she looked like she'd been in surgery all day. She said, "You're Sloane's mom? I'm Dr. Nora McDonald—one of the pediatric burn surgeons." This Queen Bee chose not to introduce her resident hive. "We're going to keep Sloane heavily sedated while we examine her hand, but first we have a few questions." And the hive buzzed with a fervor for learning.

They were very discreet, but I was certain they looked for evidence of child abuse. It was unimaginable, but I'm sure they saw many awful incidents. Dr. McDonald had the residents triple check the resuscitation formula while Kelly, and a male nurse, gently unwrapped Sloane's dressing as if she were an antique ceramic doll.

I stood at Sloane's head, followed the swirls of dark peach fuzz near her ears, yet fought looking at her injuries. Torn between my motherly duty and squeamishness, I stole a glance. Some of the skin was red and blistered, but most of it was white. I didn't know much about burns, but I was pretty sure white was a bad sign. I put my hand over my mouth and shuttered. There, on Sloane's wrist, I saw clotted teal sweater fibers imbedded into her skin! I felt a wave of nausea hit me. *Pápa* saw me flinch, so he took a look himself; *Pápa* crossed himself while I quivered.

I heard the residents talking amongst themselves, saying, "White looks like second-degree full thickness burn—probably from the sweater catching," and "looks like the red skin is second-degree partial thickness." Dr. McDonald took off her glasses and spoke with them, "Sloane is going to need a skin graft for a portion of her burns." Just then, Sloane's eyes started flitting. Dr. McDonald then said to Kelly, "Nurse, I want this patient ready to go to surgery within the next ten minutes, and you'll have to monitor her pain closely. We need to move on this." Kelly and the male nurse moved simultaneously, and I got the sense that Dr. McDonald intimidated them. "We'll take skin from her buttocks—it's cosmetically the least objectionable."

"Wait," I said, "that means she'll have two places to heal. Can't you take my skin?"

"No," said Dr. McDonald, "there's a good chance her body will reject donor skin from another, even her mom. We have a much better chance at success if we use skin from Sloane's own body. We won't have to use too much—the area will be relatively small."

"Oh good," John said as he put his hand to his abdomen, unconsciously checking to make sure the tube hadn't moved. "How long will Sloane's recovery be?"

She put her glasses back on. "The lesser-burned areas will take about two weeks, the grafted areas may take two months, but considering she's young and healthy, and that the more severe burns are limited to the hand and wrist, it may take less time if she's lucky." *Pápa* leaned over and kissed Sloane on the forehead. She added, "You can see her when she comes out of surgery."

I was overwhelmed; Dr. McDonald noticed my apprehension, but I suspected it was an inconvenience. "Sloane really is going to be alright," she said vehemently. Ugh—she took my reaction to mean I lacked confidence in her prognosis.

John placed his hand on Sloane's foot, and then I took a moment to whisper, "I love you, honey," into her ear. Then they wheeled her away. At least Sloane wouldn't have to see Tony before the surgery. Just then, I felt my phone vibrate in my back pocket.

1 New Text Msg: Tony

Let me know how she is.

"Sounds like he's not coming," I said aloud.

"Good!" said *Pápa* as he *chinged* while we walked, warding off bad spirits. "That Tony *bi-baxt*."

John said, "Let's go to the cafeteria, where we can talk. I'm hungry and need to sit." Good—any appetite was a good sign. At this point, I'd get John a Thanksgiving feast if he asked for it. *Pápa* mulled around the cafeteria, looking for something he considered to be untainted. He inspected numerous items, giving them all the sniff test. He finally settled on a pre-packaged lunch dessert, which must have appeared innocent enough. Their appetites made up for my lack of one.

"So, what did he say?" John asked while he dug into a piece of apple pie. I showed them the vague text.

I played with *Pápa's* cellophane wrapper—I liked the way it crinkled and never remained creased, but for a moment—fleeting and unpredictable. "I'm glad he's not here; it would have made things much worse," I said.

"But?" John added, knowing me too well.

"But—what's his excuse?" I wondered. "Sloane's his only child—what reason could there be?"

"There's no one to impress," John clarified. "There's no audience—he'll never see that surgeon again, so it doesn't matter to him. He figures he's covered since he asked you to keep him up to date."

Pápa interjected, "He a showboat—like American game show host."

I managed to turn the cellophane into an accordion but was unwilling to let it go. "I see what you're saying, but I don't comprehend that line of thinking. Could it be that the court might find his absence tonight an issue?"

"They might," said John, eyeing the cafeteria for more food. "But we don't know what Tony is charging you with—you'll have to call the lawyer tomorrow—she should have it." I nodded and fiddled more.

Pápa wiped his beard and said, "He know not what he asks for. What happen to *gazho* if he makes Sloane angry?" He stacked the coffee creamers on top of one another. "She can't control," he said, and the creamers toppled over. I trembled.

How many other instances of telekinesis have occurred that I was unaware?

John tossed out the garbage and said, "I'll dial Jeta for you, *Pápa*. She and Noelle will want an update." The men in my life looked for somewhere quieter to call.

"I'll meet you back in the waiting room," I said, distracted. I was worried I'd miss the surgeon.

Pápa was animated more than usual and said, "Jeta said Sloane be okay—she saw it," he said, smiling. Good—but then did she mean the injury, Tony, or her abilities in general? Visions were subjective, and I wasn't certain that even Jeta knew the answer. *Pápa* then mumbled, "Jeta teach Noelle the trade." And he was most agreeable after he heard the family trade had not been lost, and I'm not referring to jewelry design.

I wanted to object—it was just like team Gáspár to forge ahead with or without my permission—it wasn't like I was the mom or anything. Django had a skip in his step and was already several paces ahead of John and me. So, I gave John the "can you believe it" look, but he said, "Let it go—Noelle's gifted anyway—she can decide what to do with it when she's older."

"I guess," I said reluctantly. I tried to fit my family into a traditional mold and live incognito, plain and blanched, like boiled cabbage, but the bold flavors were always present. There was nothing normal about my family.

After a short wait, Dr. McDonald came out from behind the operating room area with a pleased expression. She said, "Sloane's surgery was successful. I'll know in a few days if her body accepts the donor skin, but I'm pretty confident. I'm expecting that to take six to eight weeks to heal, but the rest of the hand should be significantly better in fourteen days. She's very lucky. It could have been much worse if her sweater hadn't been snuffed out so quickly. We're going to manage her pain with narcotics. You can go back to see her now, but she'll be in a drug-induced coma."

"Did you say coma?" I panted. Suddenly, I felt light-headed and nauseous—that sickeningly out-of-body feeling that sent me reeling into no-man's-land. I lost my bearings and felt the blood drain from my head.

"Nurse," commanded Dr. McDonald, "get this woman some water right now." She grabbed an arm, and John, who wasn't strong yet, grabbed my other arm; and somehow, I ended up in a chair. My eyes rolled back into my head. I felt someone take my head and push it down between my legs. "Is she diabetic?" I hazily heard Dr. McDonald ask, but she sounded far away.

"No," John answered, "but she passes out. She might be dehydrated—that combined with the coma thing," he muttered. *Pápa* knew the drill—he started fanning me with a newspaper. Somehow, that always seemed to help.

I never fully lost consciousness; nonetheless, the partial loss of consciousness was guaranteed to be awful. I started to come back. Eventually, I no longer felt warm but cold and exhausted. "Too much excitement," said *Pápa*. "I get chocolate," and he *chinged* toward a vending machine. I must've resembled Harry Potter. Harry passes out from the effects of the dementors, so Professor Lupin gives him chocolate to revitalize him. Funny—it actually did work.

John was in charge of the water sips, and *Pápa* fed me the chocolate. To my dismay, I was the person of interest in the waiting room, as all eyes were on me. Dr. McDonald had more pressing matters to attend to, so she had instructed the nurse to allow us back when I was feeling better.

After I no longer resembled Raggedy Ann and regained use of my noodle legs, we headed into the recovery room. Monitors *beeped* rhythmically while a nurse attended to the chart. He said, "She's looking good. We have a private room for her—we'll wheel her down shortly."

Pápa wiped a tear from his eye. "It looks like she just sleeping."

The nurse nodded and said, "For all practical purposes she is, don't let the 'coma' word be frightening—it's purely an artificial means to keep Sloane comfortable." But he could sense our trepidation. "Sloane has one of the best burn surgeons in the Northeast—she's tough. In fact, we call her *The McDonald*." Humor was good medicine, and I grinned with a comforting relief while I stroked my child's hair.

I pulled out my phone and cringed at having to update Tony. It was a matter of time before he, and worse, that tart girlfriend, came to visit. *Pápa* placed protective satchels around Sloane while John was visibly uncomfortable. He was past due for his medication and needed to rest his infection-laden body. John checked the volume of his bag and said, "What are you going to tell him?"

I groaned and rubbed my index finger along my lip. What to say—what not to say? I can't dodge the coma piece. The problem is—he *should* be here—I mean, any good parent would at least try. But I don't want him here; he is acidic—I can't believe he offers no explanation. There was no answer—no amount of wisdom seemed to suffice as we mulled it over, but I decided to err on the side of full disclosure. The situation automatically meant a lengthy, expensive hospital stay, and those facts couldn't be hidden.

Nearly two weeks had elapsed, and I barely left Sloane's side other than to shower and grab a bite at the cafeteria. I slept in an overstuffed chair that turned into a bed in Sloane's hospital room. Dr. McDonald and the medical team took great care of her. I became braver with the passing of time and could catch longer glances of Sloane's wounds when the dressings were changed—her body had accepted her repurposed skin, and she was healing. But she still remained in a coma.

Liz, the lawyer, who was punctual at advising my legal needs, said in her nasal voice, "Don't panic about the court charges— it's routine—not a big deal. He just wants his visitation and for you to pay his legal fees. There are a few other charges, but they probably won't happen, so don't worry about it." She reminded me of a switchboard operator from the 1940s, and I wondered if she wore the headphones with the mouthpiece.

"What do I have to do?" I hated relying so heavily on her.

"Think of it as a meeting. You're going to arrive at court on Monday—I'll meet you there. You and John can wait in the hallway while his attorney and I meet with Magistrate Schluser and discuss the relationship."

"I'm assuming you'll clarify Tony's lack of concern for Sloane?"

Liz cleared her throat. "He still hasn't been to see her?" she said with an air of surprise.

"No, he hasn't. Says he can't take time from the shop. He's been a real pill about it too—he acts as if her injury is an inconvenience. He says things like, 'When's she gonna get better?'"

"You're kidding?" she said.

With each passing day of his indifference, I grew dead set on revealing Tony's apathy regarding Sloane. The magistrate would hang him out to dry for his negligence. He was making it obvious why Sloane didn't want to see him in the first place.

Liz asked, "How is he communicating that?"

I had to pause to think. "Those kinds of comments are over the phone."

"Not a text or an email?"

"No—texts and emails are usually more like, 'Tell her I'm thinking about her,'" or "'Hope she feels better soon.'"

"Hmmm," said Liz. "I bet—keep him informed of any changes, especially for the worse. Also, track all your medical expenses—he'll owe you for half, but you'll be lucky to get anything."

Just like Tony to get away with something, yet I owe him loyalty. Maybe *I'm* the switchboard operator.

"How's John?"

"His appetite is better, and he's put on weight—his abscess continues to drain, which is a good sign. We see the surgeon today—luckily, we're already at the hospital." Jeta and Bianka acted as the tag team taking care of John and Noelle while *Pápa* ran the errands (and likely the traffic lights too) and took care of Rouge—she was his little buddy. How I missed Noelle! A burn unit was no place for a child—it would have traumatized her. She continued to amaze me—such a small child exhibited such strength and maturity.

Jeta drove John to the hospital for his appointment. She was dressed in her traditional Romani garb and received many stares. Up until this point, it wasn't obvious we were Romani. The men were much harder to identify, and I wore tailored clothes, like an actuary, fitting in like a Muggle. Most of the time, when Romanies were hospitalized, it caused a flurry of activity. Hospitalization was a family event—like a funeral or wedding—but to a smaller extent. Since our family was pared down considerably, nearly extinct, we were the exceptions to the rule.

Jeta glided to Sloane with her skirt *swishing* in brilliant emerald green. "My sweet little Sloane," she said. Then she kissed her grandniece on the cheek. "How does she eat, Katya?" I tried to explain, but I knew *Bibíyo* would take it up with the nurse on duty. Maybe he could explain better than I, but John and I were out the door when I remembered something. I stuck my head back in. "No burning anything, *Bibíyo!*" She waved her hand as if to shoo me away. I hoped she planned to behave.

Dr. Massic, after a twitch, said to John, "It's been . . . what . . . three weeks since the surgery?" refreshing his own memory. "Let's have you lie flat on your back. I'd like to examine the drain site." He said while he pushed on John, "It's significantly softer and there's no sign of infection like there was originally." He pulled out John's chart. "Looks like the last blood test was yesterday—your white blood count went down—another good sign. How are you feeling?"

John was uneasy with Massic being too close to Fort Knox, but what choice did he have? He said, "Icky most of the time."

"Any fever?"

"Every afternoon—it usually stays below 101 degrees, but I have no energy."

Massic nodded. "Let's see how much matter is in the bag since the last appointment." Massic removed the tube from the bag and poured the milky putrefying substance into a graduated cylinder to determine the volume. He added the measurement to the chart, did some math, and said, "We've removed over two liters of substance from his abdomen." Ugh!

"Where's that coming from?" I asked, repelled.

He twitched again and said, "We still don't know the reason, but it's quite possible it'll resolve on its own." Then, while John was still lying flat in a vulnerable position, Massic pulled the tube from his abdomen much like a magician pulls handkerchiefs from his sleeve—a never-ending array of surprise. I'm not sure who flinched more—John or me—but Fort Knox had been breached! I gasped aloud. The tube was a foot long and had a curly pig's tail on the end.

John held Fort Knox while wincing—in too much pain to utter a sound, but I made up for the two of us. "Why—why didn't you warn him? How will he drain without the tube?" After the initial shock, I was upset.

Massic taped gauze to John's abdomen where the tube vacated. "I couldn't because he would've tensed up, and it would've been worse. There's no reason to keep the drain in when the infection might abate on its own." I hoped he knew what he was doing because I wasn't comfortable with it. "I'll send the nurse in to give instructions on how to keep it clean. If anything changes, call me right away, and if in doubt, take him back to the hospital."

Just like that, he left to continue his office hours.

John's pallor was telling. "That was excruciating," he said, and he was forced to remain still until the pain subsided. The nurse instructed John on changing his bandages and reminded us of what symptoms prompted a call or hospitalization.

"Did you take a painkiller before leaving the house?" I asked.

"No, but I wish I had," said John. "I was concerned Jeta's driving would be questionable. This new turn of events should keep her busy burning all my pants."

"You're not only a *gazho*, but an infected one!" I winked.

"She means well—they both do. Think about it—the Romani laws and ways have kept the race alive for over one thousand years of persecution and turmoil. It only makes sense that they keep doing what's worked for so long," he said.

I supposed I didn't always take my people as seriously as I should've, but John was right. I'd try to be less critical. But I had to admit, I really wanted to blend in, but the two ideas seemed in conflict with one another.

For the first time since Sloane's hospitalization, I stayed at home Sunday night and slept in my own bed since we had court the next morning. I didn't want to leave her, but Liz insisted, since Sloane was stable and under hospital care.

The glowing clockface of my alarm indicated 5:00 a.m. *Good! I'm going back to sleep. Sloane's in the front yard. The neighbor says to Sloane, but using Ivy's voice, "Do you want to know why we're moving?" Sloane nods. The neighbor spits, "It's entirely your fault."*

I awoke with a start, sat up in bed, and pondered the dream. Could it have something to do with court today?

Rising early after the disturbing dream, I made my way downstairs, took Rouge out, who was exceedingly happy to have her mama home, and made coffee. I'd need plenty of time to make my way to the courthouse. I hadn't officially met Liz—all our conversations had been over the phone. I kept in mind what she said so there seemed no reason to get worried; besides, I had more than my share of worry already.

Noelle awoke early to cuddle with me. She looked like a larger version of her Barbie dressed in her nightgown, holding her Barbie in a duplicate nightgown. There was only a small window of time since Bianka would be by to take Noelle to school.

John called downstairs, "Katya—come here!" John was normally laid back, but his sense of urgency gave me goosebumps. I put my coffee cup down, squeezed Noelle, and scooted Rouge off my lap, so as not to upset everyone right after our first decent night in a long time.

"What's wrong?" I asked as I bolted up the staircase toward the bedroom.

He had his shirt off, turned around, and said, "Look!" Within three days of Dr. Massic having pulled the tube, John's red paunch was back—red, hot, and hard—screaming like a siren.

With my hand to my mouth, I uttered, "Oh, no! Not again." I actually had hoped that Massic was right—that it would resolve itself. That explained the daily fevers—it wasn't resolved, just draining.

John was too sick to think clearly. It was up to me. "Okay—this fits as a reason to go back to the hospital." But it hadn't occurred to me that he might refuse.

He held his gauze bandages under the old drain site, collecting the pus that churned out of it. "Yeah . . . okay," he said reluctantly. "What do you think they'll do?" John was concerned and rightfully so. Surgery, on a large scale, had been an ongoing option, but Massic didn't want to risk stirring the infection. This new development might change his mind.

I shook my head and bit my lip. "I don't know—probably another CT scan for starters." John hated the contrast they made him drink in order for the scan to work. The contrast had radioactive components—not the best choice for someone who is über health conscious—but he had been too close to death before to continue playing that wild card.

John took fresh gauze and tape off the dresser to re-cover the wound, and said, "You've got to get me to the hospital." His eyes were dark pools of fear.

My mind raced. I heard footsteps and Rouge's collar jingling as Barbie Noelle made it up the stairs with her canine sidekick.

"Dad, what's wrong?" asked Noelle, dropping little Barbie on the bed. Rouge instinctively made a beeline for her bed nestled on the floor. She knew something was up; she always did. Rouge's soulful eyes met mine, expressive and concerned.

John didn't hear Noelle. He was concentrating too hard on covering Fort Knox, or more like, the Great Pyramid, considering the paunch's growth factor. What if today was the day? Was John supposed to survive? I couldn't let that thought enter my head—push it aside—that's nonsense. Stop thinking, Katya!

I stared at Noelle. I'd have to call Bianka. She and Jeta would have to sort out caring for Noelle and Rouge. I had to get John to the hospital.

"Mommy?"

"Yeah—sweetie—Daddy is sick again," I said, but I was a million miles away. "I'm going to have to take him back to the hospital."

"But Mommy, remember? You were about to get dressed to go to court."

My mouth fell open, and an exhale escaped. *Court? I'm supposed to go to court!* I had forgotten. *That cannot be! I can't be in two places at once!*

I stared at my youngest—the cherub in a human's body. My eyes welled up with hot tears streaming down my face. I was lost—hope draining as each moment trickled down the sewer of despair.

She may have been small, but her presence was mighty. I saw a flash of light that I couldn't explain. Instantly, Noelle seemed to emit radiance, like Christmas lights emitting a warm glow on her little face. As she became more radiant, her eyes beamed with confidence, no—knowledge—the kind that eight-year-olds don't normally own. She stood a little taller, lost the twinkle of innocence, just for a moment, and exuded maturity beyond all reason.

My child's mouth opened, and with the utmost grace, she said, "You know where you must go."

Only it wasn't Noelle. For an instant, she was a channel for a high vibration divine being. We called it trance mediumship. *Where did she learn to do that?*

CHAPTER 11

FLOTSAM AND JETSAM

Up and up—I felt like a balloon full of helium—light and airy, free, and buoyant. I could've been bobbing on the surface of the ocean, for all I knew, staring into the dazzling sun; unaware of my body, yet whole and bursting with vitality. I was not sure I wanted to head to the sun, as tempting as it was. It beckoned me—taunted me. I was sentient of how perfect it was without submerging myself into the glow of what should have been blinding but wasn't. But—I didn't *have* to do anything. I could decide for myself. *It* told me I had a choice. I had too many unanswered questions in that snapshot of time.

Mom was right there—in that chair—maybe she stepped out. I sensed a disconnection from her—that felt strange—I didn't like that. She hadn't left my side since I burned myself, but I don't feel pain anymore. I like that. It was time to take advantage of my new freedom—get out of this room already. I saw them sitting on my nightstand; the brilliant colors and freshness of the scent gave life to the otherwise dead space. Nice thought—according to the card, the flowers were from Zariah and Yvette—but I'm not a fan of cut flowers. I don't like it when something living is sacrificed. I'll have to mention that the next time I see them. They do make the sterile room aromatic, though, like passing by a Bath and Body Works.

I seriously didn't know how long I'd been here—there's not enough information in my room. I'd have to check out a computer and dig around a little to find my records, so I pushed my door open to enter the hallway. *Whoa! What's with all the insanity?* The nurses were rushing down the hall. *What's that?* The intercom system—code blue—I learned that from *Grey's Anatomy.* It was probably an issue with an older patient. *Okay—got it—getting annoying with the repetition. Kinda loud!* Feel free to turn it off! Good—the nurses' station in the hall was empty—this way I could mess with the computer without causing a coronary.

Technology was so easy to navigate. I pushed a few keys and found my records so easily that it was ridiculous. *What? That can't be! I've been here for two weeks—long time.* The nurses rushed into my room . . . wonder why? Probably shouldn't set myself on fire again. How'd that happen, anyway? *Oh, right—I got heated—good one!* Now I've cracked myself up—at least I could laugh about it.

I was still a little discombobulated . . . Maybe Mom left to get bottled water. I checked out the waiting room since it probably had vending machines. Someone was in there. Not her—some guy. *Wow—Dude! Ever hear of a robe?* He just burned out my retinas—way too much exposure of a hairy butt—thanks a lot, man. *Note to self: take "nurse" off the list of potential careers. Gross! Okay—recover Sloane.* There had to be a better way. *What time was it?* Just then, I whizzed around the counter, directly facing a clock. Poof! Cool! Just by asking, I found myself in front of a clock; it was 10:05 a.m. *Wait a minute. Shouldn't time and space affect me? I should be limited.* What was different? *Hmmm . . .* I wondered if that worked for everything. *Time to test time—and space. Ha—I haven't had this much fun in a while!*

Where was Mom? *Poof! Ahhh!* Everything around me was blurring so fast into lines of color. I had to steady myself—get to a point of equilibrium. My body moved faster than my mind could comprehend. Okay—readjust—and get a grip. *Maybe this time, the movement was extreme—like a larger distance because I'm no longer in the waiting room. Where the hell am I?* Check it! There she was—right there, by herself, sitting on a polished wooden bench that looked like a church pew. But it wasn't a church. It seemed like I could will myself to be somewhere, and voilà, there I was. This building was old and stale; I didn't like it. *How tall are these ceilings, anyway?* I sat next to Mom, but she didn't react.

"Mom!" I said, putting my hand on her shoulder. She flinched, but slightly, and kept her head down as she wrung her hands. "Mom—it's me, Sloane!" But she didn't respond, so I slid right next to her, shoulder to shoulder, so our bodies were touching. She stopped wringing her hands and wrapped her arms around herself, rubbing her hands up and down her arms, creating friction trying to warm herself. She shuddered and, for a moment, I could see her breath, like when stepping outside on a frigid day. *Why doesn't she see me? Maybe I can get her attention by texting something on her phone. Oh—wait a minute—I don't have my phone.* She seemed really sad—but—stressed out. *What's going on?* She looked thin too.

Oh, right, there's Tony and Ivy—more like Flotsam and Jetsam. It's coming back—I bet this is the courthouse. Looks like Ivy's got more ink—this time it's climbing up her neck like a vine of ivy—how original, Ivy! Maybe it will choke you—I can only hope. Her hair is now a dark shade of blue—what a surprise. Who's the guy with them; the one with the big beefy purple lips? I'll call him Beef. If Mom couldn't see me, there's a good chance they won't see me either. What do I have to lose? Nothing. I'll spy on them while they're in that huddle, at the end of the hall, like it's some kind of football game. Poof! Like a genie, hurled by lines of color through space, I was down the hall by the mere thought. *Wait*—I had to steady myself first. *Okay, I'm good.*

"Look," Tony said to Beef, "I got no intention of payin' child support for a kid I don't see—I pay enough already. I'll cut off payments—see how that Gypsy likes it." He was antsy and kept shifting his weight from leg to leg.

"You need to stop talking smack about your ex-wife—that's not the tactic I want to use. You'll get no sympathy from Magistrate Schluser that way," said Beef, adjusting his suit jacket. "We need to be clever. Say that Ivy caught Sloane stealing—you know—they're known for their thieving ways. Ivy punished her, and now Sloane doesn't want to deal with the consequences. This way, we keep you out of it, Tony. We say that it's Katya's fault for having raised a thief—that you've suffered financially and emotionally from the loss of your daughter." Beef had unusually white hair—not gray, but white-blond. Both his nose and chin were unusually pointy. I couldn't take my eyes off him.

Liar! I've never stolen a thing in my life!

"Okay," said Ivy, crossing her arms over her thick top. "What did I catch the snot stealing?" She chomped on her gum like Rouge gnaws on bones.

"Think of something," Beef directed to Tony. I could see Beef's reflection in his shoes—they shined like mirrors.

Tony adjusted his nub of hair on the back of his neck. "How 'bout—Sloane rifled through my desk and stole cash out of it."

Ivy chomped, "Nah—you keep the desk locked."

"How'd you know?" Tony asked while he furrowed his brows.

She stammered, "I-I clean, ya know."

Tony was mad. "We'll talk 'bout that later."

Beef looked at his watch and said, "The magistrate must be running late. We'll go with that story. Now, what was the punishment?"

Ivy laughed. "The usual—Tony leaves, doing God knows what, and sticks me with the kid."

Tony turned beet red. He looked for his cigarettes, but then realized he couldn't light up. "Like you don't enjoy that!" he said, But Beef was losing his patience. Tony added, "Uh—the punishment was she was grounded to her room for the next four weekends at our house. Sloane didn't like that, so she didn't want to come back."

He wishes. If I had to stay in my room for punishment, I would've been all the happier to stay away from them.

Beef checked his watch again. "Hmmm—have a seat."

I was deflated—I had hoped that he'd actually leave me alone. But he wasn't just indifferent toward my existence, he was also a bigot. I may not have felt physical pain anymore, but I still felt emotion. I had to go see Mom.

Mom was speaking to a woman with flaming red hair that stuck out with a ton of product. Her designer heels were dope, and once she stood up, they gave her an added boost because she was tiny yet round. I missed some of the earlier conversation because of Flotsam and Jetsam. With a cell phone in her hand, she seemed to speak with it, and said nasally, "This shouldn't take long." Both Beef and Nasal headed toward what I assumed was the magistrate's office.

Poof! This was getting easier each time. C'mon Nasal! Kick Beef's ass!

The plaque on the marble wall said, "Magistrate Schluser." His chambers looked a little bit like my room—cluttered and full of paper, everywhere. Only he was worse. There were stacks and stacks of files, both on his desk and on the massive wooden conference table. It smelled dusty and old, sort of like him. He also stooped with a hunch, but that wasn't his defining characteristic—Schluser had combed all his dyed black hair, (well, at least those strands that were left on his head) to a point in the middle of his forehead, in a lame attempt to hide his baldness. He was fascinating. Schluser took the file on top, glanced at it, and said, "Anthony Barzetti v. Yekaterina Gáspár. This divorce took place forever ago. How old is the child and what is the problem?"

"Your Honor," jumped in Beef, "the minor is fourteen. My client, Anthony Barzetti, has not seen his daughter for over a month and wants his visitation rights back."

Schluser fussed with the file and cleared his throat. "Why isn't he seeing his daughter, Mr. Hoyt?"

"Apparently the child stole from her father, wanted to avoid punishment, so has avoided his household as a result," said Beef, proud of the story. "We believe the mother is at fault for having done a poor job of raising the child."

"And your client, Mr. Hoyt, is completely faultless?" quipped Schluser.

Beef adjusted his tie. "Oh yes—he and his girlfriend dote on his child."

Whaaaat?

"I'll tell you what, Mr. Hoyt, we're going to avoid the blame game right out of the gate, understood?" said Schluser, agitated.

"No blame assigned, Your Honor."

Schluser focused on Nasal and said, "What's your client's story, Ms. Kaminski?"

"Well, Your Honor, most importantly, I'd like to state that the child is currently hospitalized at Three Rivers Burn Unit for second-degree burns to the hand," stated Nasal, but not without a glare at Beef.

Beef was flustered, so much so that his head became red even under his stark blond hair and pasty skin; the magistrate noticed.

"Ms. Kaminski—what is the prognosis?" asked Magistrate Schluser.

She adjusted her stance, probably because her feet hurt. She said, "The child is in a medically induced coma, and has been for two weeks for pain management. And, by the way, there hasn't been a single visit from the father." Nasal spoke more to Beef than to Schluser.

Shocked, Schluser asked, "Is that right, Mr. Hoyt?"

Beef composed himself. He said, "I don't have enough information to answer that, Your Honor. But—I noticed Ms. Kaminski never addressed the theft."

Nasal started to fume; her red hair looked like flames. "Mr. Hoyt, first, I've never once heard of any theft, and second, why is your client neglecting his daughter? I take issue with it!"

Beef towered over Nasal, attempting to intimidate her. He said, "How do I know the child is actually hospitalized? Your client is lying."

"Lying?" said Nasal. "Hospitalization is easy to prove; don't go there, Mr. Hoyt." She gritted her teeth.

"Then prove it!" snarled Beef.

"That is quite enough," ordered Schluser. "You will both simmer down while you're in my chambers, is that clear?"

Beef and Nasal nodded.

"Now, because the situation is extenuating, this will have to be monitored with reasonableness, Mr. Hoyt," said Schluser. "However, Ms. Kaminski, I am bound by time constraints; therefore, once the child has been discharged from the hospital, I am ordering the child and her parents to attend counseling to get to the bottom of this. How much longer do you expect the child to be hospitalized?"

Nasal pulled out her cell to check a calendar. "There's a possibility she'll be out in a week or two. To clarify, whom do you want in counseling?"

Schluser restacked his file. "Which parents are a concern?"

"My client has concern with the mother," said Beef. "By the way, Ms. Kaminski, where is your client's husband?"

"That's not really your business, is it, Mr. Hoyt?" said Nasal insolently.

"And you?" Schluser asked Nasal.

Nasal in reheat mode said, "We have issues with both the father and the live-in-girlfriend," addressing Beef.

"Fine—get them into counseling—whatever counselor they can agree on, and get this ironed out," said Schluser. "And Mr. Hoyt—your client's lackadaisical attitude toward his daughter's injury is distasteful." He glanced at his watch; Schluser seemed to be on a tight schedule. "Dismissed."

I wanted to stick around and listen in on Beef's post-game conversation with Tony and Ivy, but something unavoidable happened. I found myself catapulted, once again, through time and space, with lines of color whizzing by, blindingly. It was as if I snapped back into my body, like a rubber band. My eyes opened wide, my chest ached, and a stranger—a woman with blue framed eyeglasses and curly dark hair—stuck her face near mine. "Sloane—you're in the hospital. We just gave you a shot of adrenaline to the heart—you were in cardiac arrest—we lost you for about fifteen minutes. You may feel disoriented. I'm Dr. McDonald—I've been attending to your burns."

Within moments of reclaiming my body, I bolted to a sitting position in the hospital bed and vomited uncontrollably. I wasn't sure if it was from the blurred lights from my travel or if it had something to do with the fact that I was reanimated—kinda like Frankenstein's monster. Once the sick stopped, I noticed I was surrounded by several nurses, one of which held a defibrillator in her hands. Right—made sense. *Grey's Anatomy* paid off.

"I feel awful."

Dr. McDonald said, "Yes—but you're alive—most people don't make it without a heartbeat for more than five minutes. You're a medical miracle, Sloane."

I'm alive right now, right?

"Can you be specific about what feels awful?"

My mouth tasted dry and thick. "I feel weak, got a headache, my heart's pounding, and my hand hurts."

"Those are all normal symptoms—and of course the hand hurts from the burn. We replaced skin on your hand and kept you in a medically induced coma to keep you from feeling pain, but that's no longer an option," she said. "We'll manage that pain differently now."

"What happened?" I asked, trying not to vomit.

"Nurse—get some diphenhydramine for the nausea and ice chips—now," she said with a cutting undertone, her face turned away from mine. "We'll talk about that later. Right now, we're going to try to get you more comfortable and monitor you closely." Dr. McDonald addressed another nurse and said, "Have we found her mom yet?" The young nurse shook her head, fearing she had failed.

"She's in court," I said flippantly.

Dr. McDonald just stared at me for what seemed an eternity. She searched for the right words, trying not to upset the girl that was dead moments ago. "Sloane, you've been unconscious for weeks." She bit her lip, hesitated, and said, "Do you know what day it is?"

It was hard to think with my head pounding. "Uhm, it's—uh—January 20th."

Dr. McDonald's jaw dropped. She turned to look at the small dry erase board on the wall that had no date on it whatsoever. I recalled from Dad's hospital stay that the staff usually wrote the day, the date, and the names of the nursing staff for the patient's reference. She slowly asked, "How . . . do you know . . . your mom's in court?" She looked afraid of what I might say.

I'm just going to say it—what do I have to lose? "I was just there."

The doctor just stared, patted my hand, and said to the nurse without taking her eyes off me, "Find her mom—where's her dad?" The remaining nurse shook her head no. The turn of events displeased Dr. McDonald, so she headed to the hall, indicating the nurse ought to follow. They spoke in hushed undertones, but I could hear everything—I shouldn't have been able to hear, but it was amplified, like a bat's strong sense.

The nurse whispered, "Her dad's inpatient here at Three Rivers."

Not again!

She added, "I don't know how to tell you this—her mom *is* in court."

I wished I could have seen Dr. McDonald's expression, but she had her body turned the other way to help the mute factor—which made no difference since I could hear them breathing.

The doctor said, "Get Dr. Nostrum in here."

The nurse asked nervously, "Nostrum—Nostrum—I'm not familiar; what discipline is Nostrum in?"

"Neurology," Dr. McDonald said; then she added, "And he's a psychiatrist." And with that, she walked down the hall.

Great! Now they think I'm bat shit crazy—the bat part might

be true, though. I need to get my head around this. It was all just too much to take in.

Just then, the puppy-print nurse came over and said, "I'm Kelly—I've actually been one of your nurses since you arrived. Your hand and wrist are healing nicely—in fact, I've never seen anyone heal so quickly. Dr. McDonald made the same comment just the other day. What's your secret?" She smiled at me and gently touched my arm. "Do you eat lots of veggies or something?" Kelly had a honey-blonde ponytail and big, gray eyes. Her demeanor was opposite that of Dr. McDonald.

I appreciated her attempt at lightening the mood. "Probably no better than anyone else my age," I said.

Kelly, who typed away on her portable keyboard, said, "We're working on getting ahold of your mom."

I nodded. *No worries—I can hear her down the hall—she's here, speaking to Dr. McDonald, trying not to freak out about my dying.*

"How's the upset tummy?"

"It's better."

Mom wanted to know how that could've happened.

Kelly said, "How's the pain on a scale of one to ten?"

"Hmmm—it's about a five. My chest bothers me more—feels like I got run over by a bus or something."

"That's because we had to plunge a syringe into your heart to get it going again. Once I get the orders, we'll take the edge off the pain," said Kelly as she *clicked* away.

Dr. McDonald was avoiding giving a reason for the cardiac arrest. This was getting scandalous—Dr. McDonald's clever— she just told Mom they were trying to locate her.

"Does your heart feel like it's racing?" asked Kelly.

Hold on—Mom responded that her cell phone had been off because she was in court.

"No—my heart feels more normal now."

Dr. McDonald mentioned the neurologist and dropped the "shrink" bomb—she said it's common to have brain damage during extended periods of cardiac arrest from lack of blood to the brain. Mom wanted to know if I was responsive—never mind—she'll see for herself.

The door opened wide and in walked Mom. "Sloane!" she said as tears welled up in her eyes. "Can you speak?" The welled-up tears slid down her face, seeping mascara in the flood. "I can't believe it! I can't believe it! I leave you for one night! I should never have done that—I'm so, so sorry!"

"Yeah—I'm okay, Mom," I said in the split second after her regret poured out. She hugged me gently, as if I'd break. "I'm more than okay—bruised up, but fine." I'd have to tell her about what I'd overheard in court when we had time alone, but Kelly had orders to never leave my side. She stared at me for what seemed an eternity—it was as if she couldn't absorb the fact that I came back from death and could speak coherently.

Mom covered her nose and mouth in her hands and pressed on the bridge of her nose. "How's boo-boo hand?" I was still her little girl. This would normally annoy me, but when I'm not feeling well, she knew I enjoyed it.

I managed a smile. "It's tolerable."

"Let me check on your pain medication," said Kelly, sticking her head out the door. Somebody had likely screwed up my coma medication—I could hear Dr. McDonald in the hallway—something about heads going to roll.

I paused a split second and said, "What happened to Dad?"

Mom caught me up on the whole paunch incident. She said, "Wait—how'd you know?"

"Long story."

"Dad's going in for another surgery today—Dr. Massic's

waiting for an operating room to open," said Mom. "I'm waiting for Dad's text." She was starting to fade from all the stress like a piece of vintage fabric, thin and worn.

My ears tingled—*ching, ching, ching*—that could only be one person. *Pápa*! I heard him well before I should've, as he was making his way toward my room.

Mom's cell vibrated. "It's Dad—they're taking him to surgery any minute," she said, and the color drained from her face.

"Mom—you have to go—you're the only one who'll be there for him. I'll be okay—I've got Kelly here." Kelly looked up from her work and smiled. Then I added, "And *Pápa*'s on his way."

As he stepped through the door, she asked, "How'd you know?" She was bewildered. "Maybe I need to eat," she added, thinking she missed something.

With his cap in one hand and flowers in the other, *Pápa* squeezed my hand and smiled. "*Nepáta*, you're awake!"

Mom said, wringing her hands, "*Pápa*—John's going into surgery right now—can you stay with Sloane? You have a lot of catching up to do."

"Of course!" he said jubilantly, assuming I'd be the more fun patient to visit right now.

"And *Pápa*—don't leave her side!" resolutely.

He shrugged. "Where else would I go?"

"Noelle got to school, okay?" Mom asked.

He nodded, still pleased at my awakened state. "Jeta take care of little one."

"Good," Mom said. She kissed my good hand, and then she kissed *Pápa* on the cheek. "I love you, honey," she said. Then she whispered in my ear, "Don't leave again, okay?" and exited as quickly as she entered. I heard her mumble something about being a bad mother as she left my room.

I told *Pápa* as much as I could without creating too much

of a disturbance; I was sure to leave out the medical mistake piece. There was the possibility he'd flip out; regardless, he kept his cool. He was simply glad I was awake and getting better. Since Kelly already heard some of my story, I didn't care if she overheard, and I told *Pápa* about the court conversations. He believed me without question.

"*Nepáta*, it must not have been your time." He patted my healthy hand. We sat quietly for a while, absorbing the mystery of it all.

Then a pack of doctors wearing white lab coats interrupted our family time. The oldest doctor, who had a full head of hair, peppered with gray, and a short, well-trimmed beard, said, "Hello, Miss Barzetti—I'm Dr. Nostrum. You've had quite a morning—we wanted to ask you some questions to see how you're feeling." He kept his hands in his coat pockets, thumbs sticking out, and continued, "Is it okay to speak in front of this gentleman?" He had a refined accent that I couldn't place. Normally, I'm sure they had to do this with the patient alone, but since I wasn't eighteen, I suppose it was my choice to have others with me. Plus, what had I to hide? From *Pápa*, I mean . . .

"Yeah—this is my great-grandpa—no problem," I said. He must be the shrink. I made sure I left that out when telling *Pápa* my experience.

"Can you tell me if you're experiencing any headaches, blurred vision, or pain?"

"No—only my hand and my chest hurt, but my head feels fine—I did have a headache earlier, but it's gone now."

Dr. Nostrum took his pen flashlight and checked my eyes. "Look at that wall straight ahead." Then he touched the white part of my eye. The doctor snapped off his gloves, stroked his beard, and said, "You have recovered remarkably—your pupillary and corneal reflexes are good—you seem to have your full faculties. As a precautionary measure, I will order an electrocardiogram of your heart to see if there is any damage." But the pack of doctors couldn't contain themselves much longer and began shooting questions my way. It was beyond enthusiastic.

My curiosity got the best of me. "Were you expecting something else?"

A pack member said, "Not this," but Dr. Nostrum shot him a look.

Dr. Nostrum examined my reflexes and ordered blood tests. "We will need to do a CT scan of your brain to make sure everything is functioning properly. But don't worry—that doesn't hurt. It's like taking a picture." I nodded. "So far, everything looks normal."

The younger doctors seemed intrigued, taking notes with everything that was said, but they, as a pack, were still holding back.

"Miss Barzetti," said Dr. Nostrum cautiously, "Dr. McDonald mentioned you felt as if you left your body when your heart stopped."

Pápa stayed unusually silent. "That's right. I can describe the courthouse in detail if you'd like," I said. I could hear the pack's pens scratching on their clipboards; it sounded like mice scratching on wood, but louder. I described all I could remember about the courthouse, but I left out the conversations.

One of them asked, "Is it possible you have been there before?"

Pápa had his hands on his knees and said, "You don't listen—my Sloane told you she was never there." There was more than one skeptic in the room—*Pápa* sensed it too.

Dr. Nostrum wasn't happy with the young pup that had just

upset the almost dead girl's family; however, he had oodles of charm. He said, "There are documented cases where patients who have near-death experiences note increases in psychic abilities, and this may be the case with you, Miss Barzetti."

I nodded. "I could describe the lawyers, too, if you'd like. And, no, I never met them either."

"Yes, go right ahead," said Dr. Nostrum. He was genuinely interested; however, I could feel the dissention from the pack skeptics. I wouldn't let that stop me, though. I'd prove I wasn't lying. It wasn't something I'd do anyway, but they didn't know that about me.

I described the physical characteristics of Beef, Nasal, and Magistrate Schluser, but then added details regarding their personalities, including why I gave them nicknames. Dr. Nostrum was humored, but he took me seriously—I hated being discounted—Tony and Ivy had seen to that.

"Miss Barzetti—I've worked with patients before who've experienced this kind of phenomena, but these resident doctors haven't had that opportunity yet. Would you be insulted if we searched online for a photograph of these attorneys?"

"No—go ahead." It was my turn to be humored. *Pápa* crossed his arms over his chest—he was proud as a peacock.

Dr. Nostrum nodded to the skeptic resident. The resident said, "May I?" to Kelly, who sat at a computer on wheels. Kelly readily stepped away and gave me a covert wink.

The skeptic resident easily found each attorney since I knew their actual names. This created quite a stir in the room! *Pápa* couldn't have been more satisfied.

The psychiatrist said, "Miss Barzetti, that's impressive." At that moment, Dr. McDonald walked into my room and said, "I think that's enough for today, Dr. Nostrum. Sloane needs to rest."

He didn't want to give up that easily, and added, "We will

talk further tomorrow." The residents followed him out, still talking as they left my room.

I could hear them continue while they were in the hallway and should've been out of earshot. Dr. McDonald said, "What do you think, Viggo?"

"I think Miss Barzetti would have had to have gone through a lot of trouble to pull the wool over our eyes," Viggo Nostrum said. "Unless she had prior knowledge, and for whatever reason, needs attention, but I think she's telling the truth. I'll know more tomorrow. What do you think, Nora?"

She let out a sigh. "This girl's been in my care for over two weeks. She expired for fifteen minutes and came back, with only side effects from the adrenaline. She had no time to surf the internet, no cell phone, and no contact with her family during the incident. Do you see any signs of brain damage?"

He huffed, "No—none so far. We'll need to run routine tests, but I seriously doubt we'll find anything to be concerned about. I'm interested to see if she still has the ability to leave her body. Anyway, you have bigger problems. Nora—what happened?"

"I'm not sure—could have been the pharmacy for all I know. We'll have to follow protocol in case of a lawsuit—the mother was pretty upset."

He added, "The grandfather strikes me as confident—he wasn't upset in the least about his granddaughter's abilities. There's something I can't quite put my finger on. I know it wasn't as extraordinary of a reaction as I would have expected from him."

She remarked, "Hmmm—I can tell you the family is Romani if that matters."

"Are they? Well, yes. It *does* matter."

The two doctors were now too far for me to hear. *I wonder if Pápa should've acted shocked. I wonder if I shouldn't have said as much as I did. Why does being Romani matter? More importantly, what do these doctors think about Romani people?* I was getting nervous and regretting all I said.

Just then, Dr. Nostrum returned to hang my chart on the end of my bed, which he took out of the room with him by mistake. His penetrating gaze met my eyes, as if he were sizing me up—questioning me—but for what? Or was that just what he wanted me to believe? Maybe he was judging me, looking for signs of Romani on my physical body. He saw *Pápa*, though, and *Pápa* was pure Romani. Any lingering doubt in Dr. Nostrum's mind vanished when he saw Django Gáspár, who was the poster child of the Romani race.

CHAPTER 12

LAZARUS

lick down, click up, click down. I liked how the pen felt between my fingers as I pushed down on the spring-loaded retractable pen. The steady beat gave me the sense of control I craved, yet it often eluded me. I fixed my eyes on my graduation picture. What an idealist I was back then! *Click up, click down, click up.* On top of the world—top in my class after medical school, a residency to die for, and the ride hadn't stopped until the other day. It came to a screeching halt when, regardless of my brilliance and dedication, I could have—should have—lost a patient to someone's idiotic negligence. I hated feeling out of control. *Click down, click up, click down.* There was no choice but to sit by and wait for the hospital to investigate the death of Sloane Barzetti—my patient—my surgical success until somebody had to screw up her meds.

Say what you will about obsessive-compulsive disorder, but it saved my ass on many occasions. I didn't make mistakes—other people did. After the incident, I had poured over the patient's record with a fine-tooth comb and found . . . nothing—my orders were on point, and I stood by them—it wasn't me. The problem was, I couldn't be there 24-7, although

I certainly tried. Today was my day off, and where was I? At the hospital—I would've been there anyway, checking on my patients, but the situation had left me with no choice but to find the answers. If I couldn't perform an investigation, I'd have to at least research Sloane Barzetti's remarkable recovery. I could make an attempt at speaking intelligently about the phenomena, but if I hadn't witnessed it myself, I wouldn't have believed it. Not only should Sloane Barzetti have been clinically dead, but she also shouldn't have had exceptional cognitive abilities immediately thereafter.

I was not sure I believed the weirdest piece of all—the claim that she somehow traveled to a courthouse dozens of miles away while she was lying dead in my burn unit. C'mon—she was only a kid—maybe she'd been on the internet prior to her accident. Although, Viggo certainly seemed willing to entertain that there might be something to it. He was one of my few colleagues that was worth his salt. He was a gifted neurologist, but he also got his doctorate in Psychiatry from the University of Edinburgh in England—not something we talked about much. Europeans tended to see things differently, so I tended to avoid the subject—I respected him too much to get into a debate about nonsense. I was all about hard science. *Click up, click down, click up.*

I fluffed up my still damp hair and rubbed the wet on my jeans. The door to our suite of offices creaked. *Hmmm—not many of us hang out in the office on Sunday. It's probably Dr. Patel—he and I are both the unit workaholics.* Most people are home watching the Super Bowl. The hospital was like a ghost town today. I didn't bother turning my light on—the computer screen gave off enough light, but it was in sleep mode now. *Yeah—I'm sure it's Patel—his office is right next to mine. I can hear his footsteps coming this way.*

My door opened. "Dr. McDonald—what are you doing here?" asked one of our most diligent burn unit nurses, Kelly Lamont. She flinched from the shock of seeing me with her gray eyes.

"Thought you were Dr. Patel," I said, adjusting my glasses. Then I exhaled before I added, "I'm here for rounds."

She had a stack of files in her hands. "I thought you'd be kicking back with a few beers at the party—that's where I'd be, except I couldn't get anyone to switch my shift. Anyway— update—the Steelers are losing."

Lamont must not know me as well as I thought—no time for a social life.

"You have something for me?" I asked.

She said, "Just putting this file back."

My thoughts were a million miles away. "Thanks," I said, without giving it much thought.

"No problem," Kelly said, leaving me to attend to my thoughts.

My fingers found the home row on my keyboard; I pulled up Google and typed, "Lazarus Syndrome." We had touched on extreme cases back in med school, but the phenomenon was rare with only thirty-eight documented cases; but it was likely underreported. Granted, spontaneous resuscitation after a prolonged period of cardiac arrest, hence the term Lazarus Syndrome, named after the biblical event, when Jesus raised Lazarus from the dead after four days, was extraordinary. I still couldn't explain Sloane Barzetti's psychic abilities—I didn't necessarily buy it—but I couldn't deny what I witnessed either.

After much searching, I found two documented cases that zeroed in on psychic abilities after the commencement of Lazarus Syndrome. First, was a case that dated back to 1943 at the Auschwitz II concentration camp. Horrific medical experiments, without the consent of the prisoners, left many disfigured, mutilated, traumatized, or dead. The Nazi Party, and in particular, Heinrich Himmler, was obsessed with the occult. It had been the Third Reich's fascination to reign and govern supernatural powers, as they believed it was essential to their success. Apparently, one prisoner who had resuscitated on his own exhibited unusually advanced psychic phenomena, but unfortunately, his name remained classified for the privacy of the family. Although their methods were abominable, I wished I could get my hands on the records. I was sure I could poke holes in the methodology and the conclusions.

The second documented case was a Peruvian male who was said to have become a healer after his Lazarus experience. His residence is remote, placed somewhere in the Andes, so there wasn't much to go on. As far as I could tell, he was still alive since I couldn't find a date of death. *It makes no sense to rely on documentation from a third world country—I consider Peru atypical, anyway.*

Alright—enough time wasted—back to the real world of fact. I know better than to get carried away with such nonsense. Click down, click up, click down. There's a reasonable explanation for all of it—moving on. I pulled my lab coat over my Banana Republic T-shirt and jeans and tapped the light switch down.

I headed to Sloane Barzetti's room and ran into Viggo, exiting her room. "Nora," said my colleague and friend.

"Just the person I wanted to see. Any change in our patient?" I asked.

Even on Sunday, Viggo looked refined. "Certainly no changes for the worst—I'll keep a close watch on her these next three days, which are, as you know, typically crucial for cardiac arrest patients, but my prognosis is exceedingly positive."

I adjusted my glasses and said, "Good. Anything back yet from the scans?"

There was a hesitation—something he didn't want to reveal. He stroked his beard and said slowly, "Nothing to be concerned about, however, there's lower activity in her frontal and temporal lobes."

I looked into his eyes. "And what does that mean, Viggo?"

"Let's walk," and we moved away from Sloane Barzetti's closed door. "It means she has decreased brain activity—when she desires—but it's similar to seizure phenomena."

"So, I'm unclear. Are you saying she has brain damage?" I could feel my heart rate increase.

He put his hand inside his pocket. "No—it means she has the ability to alter her state of mind—change her brainwaves from beta to a slower steadier rate, but . . ."

"But what, Viggo?"

"But—it's a phenomenon found in psychics."

I crossed my arms over my chest. "Are you testing our patient beyond normal protocol? I just want to make sure she's going to be okay—I don't need any more complications."

"Come, let's keep walking," he said.

What's he doing? "Viggo—do you need a vacation?"

He laughed. "No—I'm just piecing this puzzle together. Miss Barzetti made some enormous claims, but her exceptional recovery coupled with her scans are leading me to entertain the idea that"—he paused, then continued with a smirk on his face—"there is more to this than meets the eye."

"I don't have time for this," I said impatiently. "Just answer my question."

"No—I haven't tested her beyond normal protocol—yet."

"Wait a minute—I'm the attending physician, Viggo."

"Just let me see if she can replicate her out-of-body experience while I scan."

I cleared my throat. "My job is to keep that girl healthy—not to mention there's an investigation going on," I said, lowering my voice. But I struggled to make the call—he'd been a mentor to me, but that was out of line. "No—no testing beyond the norm—I mean it."

Defeated, he replied with a sigh, "Oh, Nora, you can be so stubborn. She's fine—actually more than fine," like the diplomat he was.

"I don't care—I can't allow it—you know this puts me in a bad position."

He gave me that fatherly look. "I'll respect your decision, but it doesn't mean I have to like it." He left me standing in the hall.

How could such a brilliant man succumb to such tom-foolery? I guess it was his slightly eccentric side that made him so intriguing. I smiled as he headed down the hall and wondered what others thought of me—eccentricity probably wasn't on the list.

I needed Sloane Barzetti's chart. *Where's Lamont?* I looked down at my watch and realized it was time for the nurse's shift change—great—by the time they got each other up to speed on their patients, I could have done my rounds and made it home to catch up on more sleep. Seemed like that was all I did—work and sleep. I'd get the chart myself; it'd be faster that way. I backtracked to Sloane Barzetti's room and peeked in for an instant, but the chart was gone. Maybe Viggo had it. No—he wasn't carrying anything. *Did I leave it in my office? Maybe—I've been scattered since this incident—I won't feel settled until I know I'm absolved of blame. Click up, click down, click up.*

I made it back to my office, and there it was, right on my desk. I snatched it and headed back to her room—the hospital really was quiet. *Oh, that's right; it's Super Bowl Sunday.* I didn't know who made it to the Super Bowl besides the

Steelers—no time to follow sports. I heard chatter inside of her room, opened the door, and saw the aunt dressed in her flowing Romani clothing. Her bangle bracelets jingled as she spoke with her hands. At least there weren't twenty visitors at once—that had happened before with another Romani patient—illness was a well-attended custom with them, I guess.

The aunt acknowledged me in her graceful way, with a smile and a nod. Good—I don't think she blamed me—maybe with any luck, the rest of that family felt the same way. I mean, I had done a beautiful job mending Sloane's hand.

"Hello Sloane—how are you feeling today?" I asked.

Sloane was sitting up in bed with color in her face, relaxed and almost jovial. She said, "I'm feeling pretty good, Dr. McDonald, but I'd feel better if I could get some real food!"

"Real food? Are you hungry?" I asked, pleased. She really was rare.

"I brought this," chimed in the elderly aunt, showing me what looked like chicken paprikash. She beamed utter happiness at having helped her family. She explained that traditional Romani folk often brought their own food to hospitals in order to prevent contamination from us non-Romanies. How . . . *thoughtful*?

"That looks delicious. But I'll tell you what—let me examine you, and then I'll make the call," I said.

"*Bibíyo* Jeta, I think I'd like dessert too. I'm starving—feel like I haven't eaten in weeks."

The aunt pointed down to her bag silently—she had already thought of dessert, and I wondered what delights awaited my patient. She was sweet—not a word I used too often and always sparingly.

"My Katya be here soon," said the aunt, addressing me

while I examined Sloane's eyes. It was a compulsion to double-check everything, and even Viggo's work wasn't exempt. "She goes back and forth between rooms—her husband had surgery. He's not a Romani you know—I guess that's okay." She shrugged her shoulders.

I nodded. It wasn't for me to get involved with other doctors' patients.

The aunt jingled from her jewelry. "I'll visit John later—that's his name—it's a good name, John. He's got a new tube—a bigger one—no bag this time. He uses, what you call—bandages—thick and lots of tape." She shook her head. "I take care of John—he's like a father to Sloane."

Interesting. I thought that was her father.

"How's the pain in your hand?" I asked.

"Ummmm—it's about a three," she said.

Interesting again—her recovery has been off the charts in every single way. I couldn't explain it, and that really bothered me. "You know—that's unusual. Most people have much higher pain for a longer period of time."

"We help," added the aunt.

What did she mean by that? Hmmm—best not to ask. There are too many variables already with this patient.

I collected the items I needed for a dressing change—sterility was essential and our state-of-the-art burn unit provided my every medical need. "Let's take a look at your hand—try to relax." I grasped the sterile scissors and gingerly removed the dressing. "Ahhh—it's nice and pink like new skin—the donor skin has taken nicely," I boasted.

Sloane looked perplexed. "Donor skin? Who donated it?"

"Your buttocks," I said. "Lean over onto your hip—I want to check that next."

"No wonder it felt thick lying on my side. Couldn't you

have used spray-on skin or something less gross?" Sloane complained.

Not much got past this young lady. "No—the technology's currently undergoing clinical trials, but we are hopeful it will be fully approved by the FDA. We've been using grafting over the last thirty years, and this would be a welcomed change."

Her donor skin site was also healing well. "Any pain on your butt cheek?" I asked.

Her stomach grumbled. "None—I never would have known."

Just then, the door opened and her mom peeked in, fatigued. I knew the look—the bloodshot eyes, the drawn facial muscles, the sluggish movement. Her rational ability was sapped, making her mind work slowly.

"I'm back," she said while attempting a smile, acknowledging the three of us.

Sloane's eyes reflected pity. She said, "How's Dad?"

She sniffed. "Not good—his white blood cell count is dangerously high, and his fever hovers around 104 degrees. He shakes too."

"Polluted," said the aunt.

Interesting word choice, but she's right on the money—sounds like sepsis—I'd hate to be the surgeon who's forced to delay surgery. Yet, surgery would stir up the infection—probably kill him—but that might happen anyway.

"Has Noelle been in to see Dad? She'd cheer him up," Sloane optimistically suggested.

"Not since this second surgery—he doesn't want to upset her."

"I could go," she added with a smile.

"No!" cried the aunt and the mom in unison.

"Absolutely not—neither of us would put you at risk," said the mom, attempting to compose herself.

Sloane argued, "Dr. McDonald—Tell her how well I'm doing."

Foxy—yet I was humored—she reminded me of me. "You're healing fast—textbook unusual case study fast—but I want your new skin and your heart where I can keep an eye on them."

"Okay—fine, but I can sleep here by myself tonight. Dad needs you."

She nodded—too depleted to argue.

Hunger pangs echoed loudly from Sloane. She said to me, "So what do you say about real food?"

I tripled-clicked my pen, then triple-checked her chart and vitals. "Considering Dr. Nostrum and I are pleased with your recovery, I think you can enjoy your aunt's cooking."

The aunt added, "Katya, you eat too. I brought enough."

Sloane smiled.

In two shakes of a lamb's tail, Sloane Barzetti's heart rate increased—unprovoked. *Beep, beep, beep* . . . faster and faster on the monitor.

"Sloane—can you tell me how you're feeling?" My mind raced as I could see no scientific reason for it. I looked for the pulse on her neck in case the machinery was faulty.

Her jaw was clenched—so were her fists. She shook her head—no—but I couldn't identify it. Then two unfamiliar people walked into the room. The male was tall and jittery, with dark hair slicked back. The female was thick with blue hair, breathing heavily, and carrying a cellophane-wrapped bouquet of flowers. *Beep, beep, beep* . . . Oddly, the timing couldn't have been worse.

"What are you doing here?" bellowed my previously content patient. She leaned forward in her bed.

"Okay, Sloane—take it easy," I coached. *How the hell did she get upset before these two walked into the room? I didn't hear voices, and I know the sounds of the burn unit only too well.*

Syrupy, the male said, "We've come to visit you, Sloane.

Don't act like that." He looked at the mom with a smirk, and then the aunt scowled at him, saying something in a foreign language that I'm pretty sure was derogatory.

I stepped away from Sloane and toward the male in question. "Excuse me—who are you?" But he ignored me, as if I were invisible.

"Don't tell me how to act! You have no business being here," she growled.

Whoever they were, they weren't on good terms with my patient. There was no way I'd allow my Lazarus to be put at risk. I stepped closer to the offending couple.

"Sloane—we love you. Look—we brought you some flowers," said the female sweetly. I swore she giggled, but raspy. *Hmmm . . . asthma?*

I'm not sure how this was remotely funny. What a bizarre reaction; nonetheless, I wasn't going to tolerate it a minute longer. I put myself as a barrier between Sloane and the intruders, and her mother joined me like a wall while her aunt stayed closer to Sloane. I said firmly, "You need to leave. You are upsetting my patient, and I need her to maintain a stable heart rate."

"Yeah—get out—I don't want you here!" shrieked Sloane. *Beep, beep, beep.* I looked back at the monitor, then back at the hair-slicked guy.

"You can't tell me what to do. I have a right to be here—I'm her father!" he fumed.

Oh shit. I was in a bad position—I just lost Sloane yesterday. I needed to attend to her—but I had to deal with these two first. *Where's the nurse? I thought I had been clear on my orders . . .*

"I'm entitled!" he claimed, turning deep red. "That's *my* daughter in there!"

Right—you're entitled to my fist. I grew up with four older brothers, so I knew how to protect. My first inclination was to deck this guy; it was a fleeting thought, but I had to admit, it would have been immensely satisfying.

"See how you've riled her up. Now—you listen to me. I'm the attending physician here. If Sloane doesn't want you here, you have to leave. We can do this the easy way or the hard way." No one was going to compromise her delicate cardiovascular system.

They weren't budging.

While the aunt continued to curse in her native tongue, the female let out a shriek as she tried to decipher what was happening while looking at the wrapped bouquet in her hands before dropping it out of bewildering fear. The crinkly cellophane encasing the fresh flowers melted before our eyes. The room filled with the odor of melted plastic.

"*You* did this," screamed the female, breathlessly, to the jingly aunt. "You dirty Gypsy! I knew you were into black magic, you . . . you . . . you freak!" *Beep, Beep, Beep, Beep . . .*

Thank God the female dropped the melting cellophane before she got burned. I didn't want that corrosive woman in my burn unit.

I had no choice but to leave the room, seeking out the first employee I set eyes on. "Get security!" I yelled. *Where are they? Probably watching the damn game on somebody's phone—crap!* I bellowed, "I need help in here," to whomever could hear me within those quiet walls. I, fortunately, heard commotion a little down the hall and hoped they were on their way.

I saw Bert, from hospital security, in the corner of my eye, come barreling down the hallway. I entered the room right before Bert. The monitor wailed—*Beep, Beep, Beep!*

I scanned the room to find my priority—she was still in

bed, gripping the sheet with her good hand, shaking, only I wasn't sure if was from anger or from shock. Sloane, along with the others, were staring at the floor—some spectacle drew their eyes there.

Sprawled on the floor was the female with the pair of scissors I used to cut Sloane's bandages; only now, they were lodged in her trachea, and her flesh was turning blue like her hair.

No time—need to perform an emergency tracheostomy so she can get air. I yanked the drawers open to our supply cabinets, one after another, to find a piece of tubing—but there was nothing. *Of course, there's no tubing; we're in a burn unit.* The female's eyes were rolling back into her head. She was losing consciousness. There wasn't much time. And then—I saw it—the answer to save her life. It was not ideal—not sterile—but it was something. My retractable pen would do the trick. I plowed the father over to grab it in time—unscrewed it—took out the ink tube and the spring. I looked through it to make sure there were no more parts left inside. She was unconscious and blue—no choice. I carefully pulled out the lodged scissors, wiped the blood, and inserted the hull of the pen into her neck. I waited for air to enter her trachea, filling up her lungs with much needed oxygen.

Color began to return to her face, but now she must learn to breathe differently. She struggled—gasped—even gurgled.

I hadn't even noticed, but Bert and two other nurses had entered the room during the incident.

"Give her space!" I barked. Her eyes fluttered—she was coming back. My solution was merely temporary. "This woman needs emergency surgery," I told the round-faced nurse. She nodded, but one of the others had already grabbed a gurney. Carefully, it took four of us to lift the female onto the gurney; she sputtered and struggled for air, and the staff quickly rolled her away.

Bert said, "What happened?" Bert was a formidable man in his younger days, but he still packed much muscle, coupled with an abundant beer belly. He had been on the Pittsburgh police force but now worked for the hospital part-time during his golden years.

The father seemed far more angry than alarmed. He snarled and pointed to the mother, "*You* did that—I don't know how—but I know it was you."

How was it possible the father didn't know? He was in the room!

"What do you mean, you 'don't know how'?" Bert asked.

Exactly!

The father became rattled. "She did some weird Gypsy voodoo mumbo jumbo," he spewed, and shook with rage.

"What do you mean?" I asked the father, but I was blatantly ignored.

Sloane shook her head vehemently and said, "No—No," choked up. "Mom didn't do anything!" said Sloane, teary-eyed.

None of this made sense. How scissors ended up in the throat of the female should be obvious when there were so many witnesses.

"Sloane," said the mom, shaking her head to indicate she should speak no more.

Not again. I couldn't let him upset her. My eyes scanned my patient for signs of arrest, and my ears perked up to listen to the monitor—*beep . . . beep . . .* The aunt's jeweled fingers rubbed Sloane's temples while the round-faced nurse double-checked Sloane's vitals. She communicated something to Sloane in an attempt to soothe the distraught teen.

Another individual from hospital security entered the room.

Bert asked him to escort the father out. The father looked like a pressure cooker ready to blow. He bellowed, "You did this—Katya Gáspár—I'll see you burn for it, Gypsy witch!"

That was uncalled for!

Beep, beep, beep! Sloane boiled over in an instant, quaking in her bed, forward and back, forward and back, forward and back.

"Get him out of here!" I yelled and motioned for security to move. Everything in the room started to shake—*now what?* The round-faced nurse started screaming. It must be an earthquake—but in Pittsburgh? That doesn't make sense. The aunt, with hands together, seemed to be praying in her native tongue. Could it be an act of terrorism? Perhaps a gas-line exploded? My mind blew through the possible scenarios, but none seemed likely. We each looked at each other, eyes wide, with the hope that it would stop. There was no choice but to hold our stances.

As quickly as the shaking started, it dwindled down with each step the father took, moving him further away from the room; I'm sure it was a coincidence, but it seemed he wanted to get the hell out of there. It took several minutes, but we each regained composure—some more than others. The round-faced nurse ran out of the room and down the hall in a panic. The aunt continued to pray, and Bert, being an ex-police officer, seemed to have the most command of his faculties. Luckily, Sloane calmed down as the father exited. The mom, however, looked defeated—even gaunt.

Bert said, "Doc, there's gonna have to be a full investigation here; I've gotta get the police involved." He pulled up his utility belt since his belly pushed it down. "That pair of scissors didn't enter that woman's neck on its own. I'm not a believer in hocus pocus, ya know?"

I didn't believe it either.

"Right," I said.

"I'm gonna have to get statements from each of ya's, individually."

Just then, the mom looked at Sloane and cried, "I did it! I stabbed Ivy in the neck!" She lowered her eyes to stare at the foot of the bed.

Both Sloane and the aunt let out a sob. Something was awry. I mean, beyond all the other crap going on already.

"Bert, I need to stabilize my patient. Can you escort them out?" I couldn't afford another incident.

"Let's take you and your ma down to the office, where we can await the police. And Ma'am—you're gonna need a lawyer," Bert said.

"Mom!" cried Sloane. "Please—don't!"

Is one of them covering for the other?

Sloane's mom said, "It'll be fine—you just get better."

"Yes, Sloane—your mom's right—you are the priority," I quickly added in order to reduce her reaction.

"Doc—I'll need a statement from you too," he added.

God! Give me a minute! I huffed. "I'll be down soon. I need to make sure things are back in order for my patient here."

She and her aunt solemnly left the room with Bert as escort.

The peculiarity of this event felt like a strange chemical concoction blistering over like a test tube in a laboratory—explosive, yet likely with explanation. There was something more to this—something that defied my knowledge of science. One thing I did know after weeks of getting to know this family—the Gáspár women did not seem the homicidal type.

Tears streamed down Sloane's face, and she sobbed like I had never seen before. She was childlike—helpless—forlorn. I pitied her—felt for her. I did something I never do—broke one of my own rules. I hugged young Sloane until she cried it out.

Her body jerked with each passing moan—she sighed—wore herself out until she eventually fell asleep curled up in the fetal position. She no longer was fourteen but a tot. This—this small service—I could do for her.

So, this is what it's like to comfort a daughter, I thought. . . . I never allowed myself the luxury of entertaining such a notion. I always thought having kids was for the traditional female. I had never been accused of being traditional, that was for sure. But I wondered, *What if I made room for a child?* There were so many avenues—in vitro fertilization, adoption, even a surrogate. Did I even have time for motherhood? I had to admit—I felt a certain contentment after comforting this young lady. I'd give the idea time to ferment . . .

———————

I pressed the remote entry to my cashmere-colored Lexus RX in the hospital garage and saw Kelly Lamont get into the passenger side of an Aston Martin. Didn't her shift end a while ago? She leaned over to give the driver a hello kiss. Sometimes, I preferred to know less about my staff, but it seemed to me Lamont snagged a guy with a lot of money. I didn't need to know that—too much information. I preferred to keep my distance.

CHAPTER 13

PHOENIX RISING

I stroked my beard as I absorbed the storytelling of the incident that I had missed by minutes last night. *Click up, click down, click up*—I'm not sure she was aware of how frequently her habit controlled her. *Click down, click up, click down*—it must have been a method of self-soothing. I was always analyzing everything—I couldn't help it. Even as a child, I wondered what made people tick. I guess that was the psychiatrist in me.

There were some anomalies in the human condition that neuroscience was just beginning to uncover—really, we were in our infancy—just babes when it came to understanding the central nervous system. Sure, there have been strides forward—astronomical in some cases—but overall, we knew so little. The potential was exponential, and I wondered if Sloane Barzetti was the missing link. I picked up the framed black-and-white photo of my grandparents off my desk while I contemplated. I looked so much like my grandfather; it was uncanny.

Nora looked as if she hadn't slept a wink—she had bags under her bloodshot eyes—rare, really. She always managed to get just enough sleep to maintain her sharp mind. Problem was—she was always so damn serious. She lived for her work and couldn't see anything beyond the care of her patients. My protégé was married to her work. The very characteristic I cherished in her I condemned in my own self.

Neither one of us had surgeries scheduled today, but our schedules were known to change instantly. Bert, from security, was on his way up to my office so we could get an update. Too much was at stake—for Nora's career and for mine.

We sat in silence—trying to wrap our heads around the events that seemed to surround Sloane Barzetti.

"Nora—do you find it peculiar that Miss Barzetti burned her hand?" I took a sip of hot coffee.

Click up, click down, click up. "No, not really—burns happen all the time."

I'm not being specific enough. "Do you find it coincidental that Sloane landed in the burn unit and then, in her presence, plastic spontaneously melts?" I asked. "Why do you suppose that happened?"

She recrossed her legs—lots of nervous energy. "Coincidence—I hadn't thought of that. It was clear to me the burn wasn't child abuse—I see plenty of that—it was definitely an accident. Are you thinking that the two incidents are tied together? I'm not sure how." She yawned, likely out of pure exhaustion.

I leaned back further in my chair. There was something more to this. "What exactly was it that burned her hand?" I pondered.

She paused, trying to recall. "I know it was paper." She pondered more, and added, "I think one of the staff commented that it was something from court—yes—it had to do with the father."

I sat up in my chair and touched the tips of my fingers together, one opposing finger at a time. I liked the symmetry.

"This is the same man whose visit spurned last night's upheaval?"

She ran her fingers through her hair, reliving the incident. "Sloane's demeanor changed in the blink of an eye—Dr. Bruce Banner to the Incredible Hulk. What's even more perplexing is that her demeanor began changing prior to the entrance of the father." She sipped her coffee before continuing. "I know it makes no sense, but it was as if she knew."

I was intrigued beyond words, lost in Nora's story. This was one of the reasons I developed an interest in neurology and psychiatry. I nodded. "Yes—I see. The emotion turned to anger and appeared to be precognitive?"

"It did—but the key word is 'appeared,'" she clarified. Nora stirred her coffee, stopped mid-stir, and added, "Oh my God."

"What?"

Nora dropped the stirrer. "If Sloane Barzetti reacted that strongly to a visit in the hospital, how strongly did she react when she read the mail from the court?"

I leaned in more. Nora was on to something. "Is it possible her anger created a pyrokinetic response?"

"I don't know, Viggo." She took a sip of coffee. "Isn't that sci-fi nonsense?"

She was doing so well. "My dear Nora, isn't it nonsense that your patient resurrected from the dead without brain damage?"

"I'll give you that—it is rare. But it confounds me—it defies science."

Only science was the tip of the massive iceberg of that which we did not yet understand. I rocked in my chair and stroked my beard. Then I asked, "Who do you think stabbed the girlfriend?"

She wrung her hands and looked out the window. It was the biggest question of all—the one we wanted to avoid because no answer was the best answer. "I left that room for no more than ten seconds. Other than Bio-Dad, Bio-Mom was the closest in proximity. There was no way for Sloane to have done that—she was in bed—it would have taken too much time. And the aunt is not physically strong enough. She'd have to get past Bio-Dad, but . . ."

"But what?" I asked. Nora's logic was brilliant, and she was there last night, I wasn't.

"She doesn't strike me as a killer—none of them do." She stared longer out the window. "Is it possible Bio-Dad did it? He would have been close enough and strong enough."

I sipped more caffeine. "It depends—where did you leave the scissors?"

"Damn-it!" she said, slapping her hand on her leg. Rarely did I ever see an emotional reaction from my protégé.

"Nora—what?"

"I left them on the nightstand next to our patient, but it doesn't make sense. How could Bio-Mom move from where I left her, to the scissors, and then back to the girlfriend?"

Oh, how I regretted leaving the hospital when I did last night! "Where was the aunt standing?" I asked.

Nora paused. "She was standing closer to Sloane."

"Maybe she actually got some strength from the adrenaline and did it?" I wanted to address every angle of this puzzle.

"Hmm." Nora spaced out for a moment. "Only . . . only . . . there was no blood on any of their hands. There should have been blood."

I added, "The act of stabbing is a messy business. Do you know what else I think?"

"No—what?" She had a look of shock on her face.

"I think you've gotten too close to your patient, Dr. McDonald."

Her eyes flashed. "What makes you say that?"

I stroked my beard. I had too many years of experience to not notice the telltale signs. "You're trying to protect Sloane Barzetti." My God! Nora McDonald was human after all.

"Viggo, I just told you; Sloane Barzetti couldn't have done it," she said with a flare of temper.

"One moment, Nora," I said. "You mean, she couldn't have stabbed her through a traditional means."

Her eyes burned through me. "What are you saying?"

I really struck a nerve, but I must see this line of thinking through. "I'm suggesting that Miss Barzetti unintentionally stabbed her father's girlfriend telekinetically when she provoked her."

"That's ridiculous! I will *not* entertain that as an option," she said shortly. "And don't you dare suggest that to Bert either."

Americans! Sometimes they were short-sighted. I picked up my pen and flourished it. "Why—does it frighten you that I could be correct? What about the earthquake? Explain that one, Nora."

She shrugged. "What about it, Viggo? They're exceedingly rare in this part of the country, but still plausible."

I started typing on my computer. "Let's see if there was an earthquake last night." Let the science speak for itself.

Nora walked around my desk to see for herself. I pulled up the National Earthquake Information Center site that monitored the latest earthquakes. To no surprise of mine, there was no activity whatsoever anywhere near Pittsburgh. Most of the activity was in California.

"Are you suggesting that Sloane Barzetti made the room shake?" she asked in a feisty tone.

I lost Nora on this one. "That's exactly what I'm suggesting."

Click down, click up, click down. "Viggo—you may be illustrious, but you're over-the-top with this one."

I revolved the pen in my hand—thoughtfully. "Do you think

I require a psychiatrist?" I taunted.

She smiled for the first time in a long time. "You can be so pompous."

"Someone has to be," I said with a grin. I guess that was one of the aspects of our relationship that I liked—we could be honest with each other.

Just then, Bert, the security guard, knocked on my office door, which was already open. I waved him in. "Have a seat, Bert."

He lifted his belly with his belt. "Thanks, Doc—don't mind if I do—need to take a load off." He positioned himself just right to land in the chair between the armrests.

I continued spinning the pen, observing the dedicated and well-trained man sitting in front of me. "Bert—you look disheveled. Did you even go home last night?"

"Nope—I missed the entire game too. I had money on it with the boys at the station—lost my shirt. Still a diehard Steelers fan, though," he said, disappointed. "They'll take the ring next year," he said, assured.

I nodded, but I didn't follow sports. "Bert, you still have close ties to the police. Do you know what's happened?"

"They had no choice but to book Yekaterina Gáspár down at the station—with the ex-husband's accusation and her confession and all—it looks pretty bad for her. The prosecutor charged her with attempted second-degree murder." He looked down at the floor. "But here's the thing," he said, perplexed, "after the guys insisted the hospital move the girl to sweep the space for forensic evidence, they came up short."

Nora sat up a little straighter. "What do you mean, Bert?" she asked.

"I mean, there should be more to go on—there should be at least two sets of fingerprints on those scissors," he said with a blank look.

Nora said slowly, "There's only one set?"

Bert nodded. "That's right, Doc—only your prints."

I tapped my fingers together again. Yes—that made sense—I was not expecting Bert to find prints of anyone, other than that of a hospital staff member.

"But that can't be," she said, worried.

"Do you use gloves?" Bert asked.

She rubbed her hands on her Ann Taylor pants. This conversation was making her nervous, and understandably so. "I usually do, but those scissors are mine. They were a gift from my parents; I even have them sharpened by a professional every few months. No one touches those scissors but me."

We sat in silence for a while, contemplating all possible scenarios.

Bert could see Nora's discontent. He said, "Doc, if you're worried about being implicated, I got your back. You couldn't have done it."

She said dreamily, "No Bert, that's not what I'm worried about."

He awaited clarification, but she gave none.

He was holding back, so I asked, "What else, Bert?"

It was apparent he was deeply troubled. He said, "Look, before I retired, I'd been a cop for thirty-five years—I've seen my share of peculiar evidence—but there's something else that doesn't make sense, ya know?"

We waited on edge. This was beginning to look like one of those American soap operas.

He got up his nerve and said, "Whenever there's a stabbing, it's normally at an angle. Let me show you." He picked up my scissors from my desk dispenser and held it in his hand. "Ya' see—this is how you hold a pair of scissors if you're cutting—right?" The thumb and fingers go through the holes—it's a firm grip—strong enough to cut paper, but no more. Now—let's assume I'm the attacker, and Dr. McDonald is Ivy Fastidio. If I'm trying to stab you in the throat, would I hold a pair of scissors the same way? No—there'd be no leverage, would there? I'd have to have a firm grasp with my entire hand over both finger notches, like a wide fist."

We were with him.

"Stand up for a moment, Dr. McDonald," he said. "Now in order to penetrate flesh, I'd have to use a downward force when stabbing with scissors." Bert used a slow-motion technique to demonstrate. "There'd be no leverage if I stabbed upward—it's too awkward. So, here's the thing—the surgeon said there was no angle—the scissor penetrated the trachea at a perfect perpendicular angle, at ninety degrees."

Nora asked, "So you're saying that doesn't happen."

"I'm sayin' that someone, or something, had to have thrown those scissors to cause that deep of an insertion at that precise angle," Bert clarified.

She laughed sarcastically. "Wouldn't that take great skill? Like someone from the circus or an assassin?"

Bert said sheepishly, "Yeah—pretty much."

I rocked in my chair. "The only problem is that there were no fingerprints on the scissors other than Nora's."

"So, we're back to the drawing board," Nora said.

I remained quiet—Bert didn't need to know my theory. "Speaking of the girlfriend," I added, "how is she?"

Bert adjusted his girth and said, "Looks dicey for Ivy Fastidio. The good news is the surgery went well—the wound was clean—the scissors entered with force, but a chance for infection, with a dirty pen and all."

"But?" I added, sitting up straighter.

"But"—Bert raised his brows—"Ivy Fastidio has a collapsed

lung; it's pretty serious, and she won't be able to speak for a while, ya' know."

I glanced at Nora, who stared at the ceiling behind me. "Nora?" I asked.

"I don't know." She hesitated before she continued, "It's all running together—that day I mean—but I seem to recall Ivy Fastidio breathing heavily when she arrived."

I put my fingers in my pockets with the thumbs sticking out. "Pneumothorax happens, Nora. You don't know her history, do you? She could be a smoker, and that could have caused complications during the tracheostomy."

"Maybe," she said, lost in her thoughts.

"That reminds me—we found wilted flowers with melted wrapping near Ivy Fastidio—it didn't add to her injuries, but do you know how that happened?" he asked.

Nora and I both shrugged.

She asked Bert, "What happened with the husband? Bio-Dad?"

"Oh, Anthony Barzetti? I kinda expected him to be more upset about his girlfriend getting stabbed and all—seemed more pissed off at his ex-wife than anything."

Nora pushed her eyebrows upward. "I can see why Sloane Barzetti doesn't like either one of them."

I revolved the pen a few more times. "How is the stepdad doing?"

Nora responded, "I saw Dr. Rosen this morning—it seems that although John Mackenzie's surgery was successful, he isn't out of the woods yet."

"Be more specific, Nora," I added.

She sipped her coffee. "He's maintaining a high temperature. It's too early to tell if he's going to make it; sepsis is a strong possibility. I'd hate to be Rosen. He was in a tight spot—damned if he did the surgery and damned if he didn't. He had to take out a foot of diseased intestine—stirred up the infection."

"Sloane's stepdad is here?" Bert asked, thoroughly confused. Nora nodded.

"What's the chance, Doc?"

She said, "Don't ask," and rolled her eyes.

Miss Barzetti was vulnerable—no question. How might another loss affect her?

"When will you be discharging the Barzetti girl?" Bert asked Nora. He put his large hands on his knees to help support his girth.

"Soon—the burns are beautifully pink. But wait—to whom would I release her?" she asked Bert.

Bert stuck his thumbs in his belt loops. "That depends," he said, "Yekaterina Gáspár was denied bail on some legal technicality—I get the idea it has something to do with Anthony Barzetti's lawyer. They were both down at the station last night—made quite a scene—ranting and such." He shook his head. "I've seen social services intervene and give temporary custody to the father if the court sympathizes enough."

Nora's eyes met mine. Her eyes pooled with fear. She was attached to Sloane Barzetti—the boundary between doctor and patient breached—even though Nora couldn't admit it. Even worse, she knew subconsciously that Miss Barzetti was capable of manipulating matter when triggered. The potential result of such a union would be like the Capulets and Montagues at a dinner party—fatal.

"That cannot happen," said Nora. "Wouldn't they want to keep Sloane with her sister?"

"There's a sister?" I asked. "How old is she?" I tried to wrap my head around the possibilities.

"Yes," Nora replied. "Couldn't Sloane go with her aunt and grandpa? Plus, there's always a chance the stepdad will survive." She paused, recalling, and said, "She's younger than Sloane—that's all I know."

I nodded, tapping my fingers together.

Bert shrugged and said, "I dunno Doc—I'm not an expert."

Nora glanced at her watch and stood up. "I've got patients waiting—office hours start soon—don't want to get behind before the day even starts. Thanks, Bert, for the update. Can you let us know if anything else happens?"

"Will do," he said.

I added, "I'll check in with Miss Barzetti momentarily."

"We'll touch base later," she said to me and left.

"Bert, do you know when the hearing is scheduled?"

"I'm no lawyer, Dr. Nostrum, but I think the plea date is usually scheduled within ninety days."

I stood up to show him to the door. "Thanks for your help—keep me posted."

He adjusted his pants. "Sure thing, Doc."

Miss Barzetti was sitting in one of the all-purpose chairs next to her grandpa. He had her hands cupped in his and spoke to her in a deep, comforting tone. Her face was tear-stained, and her eyes swollen, but he appeared to appeal to her senses. I couldn't hear what he was saying, but the low pitch gave it an almost hypnotic feel. There was also an older female, the aunt I presumed; her wardrobe and her ample pieces of jewelry made it obvious that she was also Romani. With the two older family members, there was a little girl with reddish hair that must have been Sloane's sister. They seemed to wait their turn to comfort Sloane, although the sister's face was pink and blotchy. She had been crying too.

"Good morning, Miss Barzetti," I said while acknowledging the family. "Can you tell me how you're feeling, taking into consideration that last night was rough? Dr. McDonald told me all about it."

Grandpa said, "How do you think she feels? Her heart's broken—tiny pieces—you let me take *Nepáta* home." He shook his fist. "Nothing but bad happens here!"

For a split second, I thought I felt the floor move beneath my feet. I glanced at the little girl—her eyes had grown wide for an instant—she must have felt it too. I wondered if she could bring the building down—I was beginning to think anything might happen with this family around.

This grandpa wasn't as unpretentious as he looked. Now I was beginning to understand where Miss Barzetti inherited this passion I'd heard about—especially through the staff that loved to talk when "the McDonald" wasn't around. Nora had earned an ironclad reputation as a physician, but she wasn't a favorite when it came to her people skills, especially with subordinates.

The elderly man's point was well taken. "I understand—but first we need to make sure she is well enough to go home." I perused through her monitor history and saw the massive spike in her heart rate at the time of the incident last night. "Your burns are healing, and I no longer see you as a cardiac risk—all good news."

The aunt, with the little girl on her knee, said, "We'll take Sloane home soon—yes?"

I adjusted my tie. "Ultimately, it's up to Dr. McDonald, but I think she will discharge her tomorrow."

"But we take her home?"

"Madame—I would like to say 'yes' to that request, but I

regret that decision lies with the court," I said sympathetically.

"The court boss—he won't let Katya come home," the grand-father said, choked up. "What happens if the *gazhi* die?"

"I'm sorry, Sir—*gazhi*?"

Sloane sighed heavily. "He's speaking about Ivy—the one who got stabbed."

I added, "I see—you are concerned. If she dies, it could become a murder charge. She is stable but with complications; luckily, Dr. McDonald saved her life."

The grandfather said, "You call us Django and Jeta Gáspár—and the little one is Noelle MacKenzie."

It was necessary to gain his respect before he let me into his world. I nodded and paused to gather my thoughts. "If I may be so bold to ask—do you believe your family is misunderstood?" I slipped my hands in my pockets.

He wiped his tears. "Misunderstood? We have been misunderstood for a thousand years—that's all we know—misunderstood!" he said with zeal.

I cleared my throat. "You're Romani?"

He nodded. Mr. Gáspár must have been in the States long enough to know it was safe to speak to medical professionals about a racial identity that was best kept secret overseas, out of pure survival.

"Is it fair to say that Miss Barzetti's astonishing recovery, in part, is due to her Romani family?"

He thought about it. "Yes—the Gáspárs known for—what *gazhe* call magic. But some things are a mystery; this"—he showed me the magnitude with his hands—"this is beyond Django's *chelyédo*."

I agreed. The untapped phenomena could be groundbreaking.

Mr. Gáspár wrinkled up his brows. "How do you know so much about Romanies? You think we're crazy?"

I put Miss Barzetti's chart down. "The talents of the Romani are no surprise to me; I have been captivated by your people and their plight for some time."

Miss Barzetti seemed to have forgotten her sorrow for a while and said, "Where from?"

"Most recently, England, but I have never settled in one place for very long," I said. "My work determines my residence."

Mrs. Gáspár had a faraway look in her eyes. "I know you know," she said, as if she was a radio receiver. "Sloane cannot be near Tony or Ivy—we're afraid of what might happen—it could be deadly," she warned.

I hesitated to respond.

Miss MacKenzie stood up from her aunt's lap and stepped toward me. "You are my sister's doctor—you want to help her—I know you do," she said bravely. "The lady doctor wants to help too." I found the little girl endearing.

"My mom's lawyer said the situation is looking bad," said Miss Barzetti. She had to put aside her grief in order to convey, due to the language barrier her older relatives endured. "Tony, my father, wants to put me with foster parents," she said, blinking back tears.

"He doesn't want your stepdad to take care of you and your sister? They usually try to keep siblings together," I said.

She shook her head. "No—her lawyer said my stepdad doesn't have a right to me, and she seems to think Tony, my father, is making a case against *Pápa* and *Bibíyo* Jeta." She gestured to her grandpa when she used the term "*Pápa*," so I could understand.

"But to put you in foster care when you have family—a sister," I said, looking at Miss MacKenzie. "That's senseless."

"Yeah, that's Tony; it's his way of punishing my mom—and me for existing. And his lawyer—Beef—he's a scumbag. Nasal,

I mean my mom's attorney, thinks Beef did something to make sure my mom couldn't get out on bail," Miss Barzetti said.

"Wouldn't your father want to at least visit with you?" I asked. She said, "We don't know yet."

Her emotions must have been mixed because the floor shifted yet again with a low *rumble*. Miss Barzetti's eyes fixated on mine for what seemed an eternity. She was surely responsible.

If there was any certainty in life, this much I knew, Sloane Barzetti was broken—wounded—but the telekinetic abilities that had been dormant for most of her life had been awakened through her Lazarus Experience. She was a phoenix rising but untamed; she had the innate ability to destroy lesser mortals. If Sloane Barzetti fell into the wrong hands, she could be weaponized. Destiny had put Miss Barzetti into my path for a reason—I'd have to be a fool not to recognize it.

———

Back in my office, I contemplated the unusual events of the past several days. I picked up the black-and-white photo of my grandparents, which dated back to the early 1940s, and rubbed the frame with my thumb. Were they with me? After a few phone calls, I connected to the person that was in a position to assist. He was the ultimate decision-maker. "Magistrate Ian Schluser," I said to the clerk on the other side of the phone.

CHAPTER 14

STRIPPED

T sat in the back seat of the Ford Focus, numb from the experiences of the past month. I felt unimportant—a possession to be handed off like some sort of hand-me-down dusted off from *Bibíyo*'s closet. I listened intently to the car tires rhythmically rotating against the concrete panels of the road. The woman who was driving me kept looking in the rearview mirror, hoping to get a response from me, but I heard nothing that she said. She droned on about how lucky I was to be placed in a home with money. *Lucky! What the hell?* It was all meaningless, anyway. She was a social worker assigned to me—I don't even recall her name—it wasn't relevant, anyway.

I wondered what my life would be like if Tony Barzetti never married my mom. Would I have been born? If I hadn't been, I'd be fine with that. How many other lives has he hurt that I don't know about? The obvious was my mom's and mine, but he certainly impacted my dad, Noelle, *Pápa*, *Bibíyo*, and even Aunt Bianka. He probably did this—made sure I was stripped of my loved ones—sent me to some foster family who could never understand me.

Why did I come back to life? I can find no purpose—not yet anyway. It would have been easier to slip away, undetected, without the whole Lazarus thing. Why can't I be normal? Die like a normal person? My death would have saved Mom—and possibly Dad. Mom would've been able to focus her attention on Dad—not me. Maybe—maybe Dad wouldn't be clinging to life right now—he'd be better. It would've even saved my sister, who's now at risk of losing both parents—just like me. Little Strawberry—who will take care of her? Will it be Pápa and Bibíyo, or will Aunt Bianka take care of Noelle? Darby and Elijah would be like siblings to her, but still, it wasn't fair! Damn it! It's bad enough I've been cheated, but Noelle? It makes me so angry!

Kaff, kaff, kaff . . . The social worker—Miss-Whatever-Her-Name started hacking—just like Ivy. I know now that I'm the one responsible for Ivy's choking—I own it. I glanced up at myself in the rearview mirror. My face was so red! I could end this, right now; if I kill her, I kill me, but what will that accomplish? *Kaff, kaff, kaff*—she's starting to struggle. Or how about this? *I can use my anger to make these tires explode right now, so I can escape, but then what? I can't conjure up food or a bed to sleep in. At least, I don't think I can.*

Just then, I got a whiff of that cigar smoke again. In my peripheral vision, sitting in the back seat next to me, was the woman with the *diklo*. Determined to not let her get away, I said telepathically, "Who are you?" It was more of a demand.

After she adjusted her scarf around her head, she raised her eyebrows, and said, "I'm Speechless."

Miss-Whatever's eyes welled up with tears from the hacking and was oblivious to both Speechless's presence and our discussion in the back seat.

"Sloane, I suggest you get a handle on the consequences of your anger. You're making our job more difficult than it needs to be." Speechless eyed the ancient social worker.

"What are you talking about?" I said, frustrated. "What job?"

Speechless focused her eyes back on me. "Remember Madame Sinfi's prophecies? Even though you are entangled in something much larger than yourself, you must use your leadership capabilities and focus on the war, not the battles." She then gestured toward the driver with her hand donned with many rings.

"Oh, right." *If I keep this up, I'll crush Miss-Whatever's throat. What am I doing? I've got to stop! I'm not a killer.*

I pulled back my energy from Miss-Whatever. The tension in my body loosened—the tight spot in the middle of my forehead slowly released. I stole a look at myself in the mirror—the redness started to fade. Miss-Whatever stopped struggling, but she was still freaked out.

There were so many questions that I wasn't sure where to start. I formulated the first of many but then realized Speechless was gone before I could open my mouth. *Who the hell was that anyway?*

Kaff . . . "I don't know what came over me—to cough like that—right out of the blue! Oh my stars," said Miss-Whatever, who clearly hadn't seen or heard Speechless. She worked on composing herself, but I said nothing.

I've gotten off track. No—sit tight—devise a plan. You're smart, Sloane. Don't let them beat you at this risky little game. There's still hope—it's dim—just like the Tarot's Eight of Swords card. She is entangled, blindfolded, and basically imprisoned. She must move slow and steady to maneuver through the prison bars made of swords. It's treacherous, but doable. I must not lose sight that the Emperor card was in the spread. He is a leader, but I'm not sure what to do with that right now.

How coincidental! The sun was peering out through the clouds—just a little. *Is God there, looking out for me? I don't know what to believe right now. No—I'm pretty sure God hates me. Don't get stupid.*

We traveled for a bit when Miss-Whatever said we were close—I think the sign said Mt. Lebanon, "A Community with Character." They weren't kidding. Even though snow covered the ground, it was obvious the landscaping was kept up in this suburb. Shrubs and trees were trimmed; the roads were snow-free; park benches were scattered, and recycle bins were available. Even the businesses were appealing—cute, even, with their perfect custom-made signs. Eventually, we left the main street and traveled down a winding road that seemed less traveled since I saw no cars on it. We pulled up a long, gated driveway with a roundabout that was surrounded by evergreens providing color to what otherwise would have been latent, considering it was still winter.

From the road, I never would've seen the house; it was so well hidden. I was sure the foster family wanted it that way. You know—privacy. It really was more of a mansion anyway. It was enormous and made of light gray brick with a black roof. The house had three floors, many tall, narrow windows, and several garages, where the owner must have kept several cars, none of which were out. I wondered what kinds of cars were behind those doors. Chimneys popped up throughout the roof landscape. How many fireplaces could there be? More importantly, how many people lived here?

I knew nothing about the foster family. Would they treat me like their slave, like Cinderella? I hadn't thought of that. This could go badly, especially for them, if they treated me poorly. I didn't want to hurt anyone, not even Ivy, but it still happened. *There's got to be lots of rooms in this house—I might have to get lost—keep myself away from them. I must check it out, privately, as soon as I get the chance. Who knows? This could be decent, in the short-term, if I make the right use of the situation.*

The social worker hadn't shut up for a single second, but she also hadn't provided me with any information—it was intentional. *What is this—surprise foster family? One Fruit Loop shy of a full bowl.*

I got out of the car, felt the chill of January air, and walked to the trunk to pull out my suitcases; Miss-Whatever helped. She walked me to the front of the mansion, where we climbed a few stone steps that led to a double set of huge black doors with knockers. Miss-Whatever lifted the heavy metal twice against the door. I nearly fell over when a uniform-wearing servant opened it. *A servant! Maybe they have no need for a Cinderella.* His head was full of white hair, and he wore black-framed glasses, but had a slight stoop to his posture. His uniform included a bluish-gray tie with a matching button-down sweater, trousers, and a white dress shirt. He greeted me with genuine respect, "Welcome, Miss Barzetti, my employer has been expecting you." He had a British accent. *Interesting.*

I smiled from ear to ear. *This is just like the movies.* Makes sense—I figured the dude had money. *Okay—play it cool—so what if he has a butler?* The social worker disappeared out the front door—it would have been decent if she could've introduced me to the family. *Whatever. I've never had high expectations before. Why start now?*

"Right this way, Miss," Brit said, and he showed me to one of the many rooms. My eyes took in the beautiful dark wood, the books that lined the shelves—oh—it was a library. *A library—seriously?* The drapes were a rich green with taupe-colored walls; a large globe sat on a wooden stand. I wondered if the owner actually read the books or was it more of a place to put fosters?

"How do you like your tea, Miss?" asked Brit.

I was surprised. "My tea? I don't drink tea. Well, unless it's sweet iced tea," I said, looking around the library. *You can wait on me all you'd like, Brit!*

"Would the young lady prefer coffee?"

He was so proper! Brit was killing me. "I would, thanks," I said, wondering how many others worked for this dude.

Hmmm. "Where are all the other kids who live in this massive place?" I asked.

Brit cleared his throat. "Oh, there are no children, Miss."

I wasn't expecting that.

"How does the young lady take her coffee?"

How do I take my coffee? "Lots of creamer and sugar, please." I could get used to this. Brit walked away, toward the kitchen, I assumed, to fill my "order." It might take a while—Brit had seen a lot of mileage, but he seemed like a nice guy. I moved near the books, gazing at the spines. Lots of classics—looked like most of the books were read since the spines were creased. Hopefully, that meant I wasn't going to have to live with a dumbass.

Just then, I heard footsteps coming toward the library, but the gait was different than Brit's gait. These were long strides. I waited to see who would round the corner when my heart skipped a beat.

"Hello Miss Barzetti, welcome to my home; I mean, *our* home," said Dr. Viggo Nostrum.

THE END

GLOSSARY

The terms listed below are from the *Kalderash Vlax* dialect. *Romani Dictionary: Kalderash-English*. Compiled by Ronald Lee. 1st ed. Toronto: Magoria Books, 2010.

baxt (luck)
baxtalo (lucky)
bi-baxt (bad luck)
Bibíyo (Auntie)
chelyédo (family)
diklo (woman's headscarf)
drabarni (counselor, psychic, reader-advisor, fortune-teller, herbalist, healer)
fármichi (sorcery)
gazhe (non-Romani people, mixed group)
gazhi (non-Romani woman)
gazho (non-Romani male)
gazhya (plural for non-Romani females)
marime (polluted/defiled)
nepáta (granddaughter)
Pápa (Granddad)
Rrómani-ship (Romani language/dialect)
vrêzhitórka (sorceress)
vrezhitóri (sorcerer)

The phrases below are from Ian Hancock, who has represented the Romani people at the United Nations.

Hancock, Ian. *We are the Romani people*. Reprinted 2017. Great Britain: University of Hertfordshire Press, 2002.

Rúgjon meg a ló! (May the horse kick you!)
A ménkű csapjon beléd! (May the lightning hit you!)

ACKNOWLEDGMENTS

Much love to my parents who always pull for me no matter the circumstances.

For my girls, who have been a source of inspiration and encouragement.

My husband, Rocky, who balances out my serious side with his fun-loving humor.

Many thanks to Amy Smialek, who not only believed in the project, but gave much needed feedback on the earliest versions of the manuscript.

For the talents of Doug Isom of Digital Creative Services who, as always, did an amazing job on my website.

Respect for Dr. Ian Hancock, who may be the world's most renowned expert on the Romani people. Even though the *Romani Redd* series falls into the genre of young adult fantasy, my hope is that I have peppered in enough material to spark the interest of readers to advocate for an accurate representation of the Romani in history books. The Romani and their legacy are important! Please see the works of Dr. Hancock for an accurate representation. He has represented the Romani people at the United Nations and served as a member of the U.S. Holocaust Memorial Council.

During my research, I was shocked to find that over sixty dialects of Romani exist, in part, due to extenuating circumstances. Gratitude to Ronald Lee, a native Romani speaker, who compiled a comprehensive *Kalderash Romani* dictionary, using the Vlax dialect.

And, much appreciation to the team at Mascot Books for taking a chance on a new author. You've been so responsive and helpful in more ways than I can count.

ABOUT THE AUTHOR

Cindy Summer, a practicing psychic medium, knew there was truth to the rumor that her family had Romani blood. Captivated by their plight, Cindy was called to shine a spotlight on those who have been dismissed throughout history as being irrelevant. Her mission, as an author, is to empower young adults to stand in their truth and be heard. Cindy wants

her readers to know that they matter. Her spiritual practice is in Cleveland, Ohio, where she resides with her husband, Rocky. You can visit her online at cindysummerbooks.com.